# KILLERWATT

*Best Wishes!*

# KILLERWATT

## SHARON WOODS HOPKINS

*Sharon Woods Hopkins*

Cover photos by Bill Hopkins, Sharon Hopkins, and Jeff Snowden
Book and cover design by Ellie Searl, Publishista.com

ISBN-13: 978-0615537238
ISBN-10: 0615537235

LCCN: 2011938258

This is a work of fiction, and a product of the author's imagination. Any similarity to actual persons is purely coincidental. Persons, events and places mentioned in this novel are used in a fictional manner.

Deadly Writes and the Deadly Writes image and colophon are trademarks of Deadly Writes Publishing, LLC

Email: deadlywritespublishing@yahoo.com

Deadly Writes Publishing, LLC
Marble Hill, MO

# ACKNOWLEDGEMENTS

I have so many people to thank, especially my family and friends who inspired and encouraged me. At the top of this list is the love of my life, my husband, Bill, who is always there for me, who prods me, helps me, puts up with me and who loves me. I couldn't have written this without him. He is my rock.

To my wonderful son, Jeff Snowden, mechanic *par excellence*, who takes care of the real Cami, and to my delightful daughter-in-law, Wendy, and my terrific grandson, Dylan—Love you guys!

To Hank Philippi Ryan, thanks for your wonderful enthusiasm and ongoing support and encouragement.

To Sharon Potts, thanks for your critical eye, your kindness and help.

To Sue Ann Jaffarian, thanks for your friendship and inspiration.

And a huge thanks to those folks who allowed me to pick their brains and gave unhesitatingly when I asked my many questions: Joe Russell, Dr. David Schnur, Ken Steinhoff, and Van Riehl.

I took liberties with the geography of Southeast Missouri to fit the story. As my dad would have said to anyone taking issue with that, "What do you want, an argument, or a story?"

# DEDICATION

To my mother, Agnes Vienneau Woods (1920-1973), who introduced me to the entire collection of Nancy Drew mysteries as soon as I could read.

To my father, John (Harry) Woods (1915-1984), a newspaper typesetter who taught me to read before I started school. He also taught me to read upside down and backwards.

# CHAPTER 1

**Thursday morning, June 25**

"Al-Serafi is dead!"

Rhetta McCarter heard Woody shout to her as she tugged open the door of Missouri Community Bank Mortgage and Insurance Group, but it took a minute for what he said to register. Arms loaded, she peered at her loan officer over her reading glasses, while balancing her diminutive frame on one foot and shoving the door shut with the other.

Today was her first day back from a branch managers' seminar on federal lending changes. She was thinking about all the work that piled up in her absence. Woody Zelinski, her sole loan officer and agent, swiveled his oversized chair to wave the newspaper at her even before the door closed.

She snapped her head around to stare at Woody, whose forehead glistened with sweat droplets. "What did you say?"

She continued to her desk without dropping anything, especially the grande light cappuccino. After plopping her overstuffed leather briefcase, legal pads, and a tote bag of overdue mystery novels on her desk, she hunted for her glasses. When she bent to search the desktop, they fell from her nose.

Woody thrust the turned over page at her as proof. She snatched the newspaper from him and scanned the photo of a vehicle nose down in the water, then read the accompanying article.

*Forty-three year old Doctor Hakim Al-Serafi, a staff physician at St. Mark's hospital, was found dead early yesterday morning in his car in the Diversion Channel, just south of Cape Girardeau. Marvin Englebrod, a Scott City farmer, was heading south on Interstate 55, when he noticed the partially submerged Lexus in the channel, especially full this year due to the recent flooding. "I spotted something as I crossed the bridge. I pulled over to investigate, and when I seen it was a car nose down in the water, I dialed 9-1-1," Englebrod recounted. Police identified Al-Serafi from a driver's license found on the victim's body. Cause of death was not immediately known. Cape Girardeau County Coroner, Doctor Julian Sickfield, said the autopsy results would be available in about ten days.*

*Al-Serafi was a staff physician at St. Mark's hospital since coming to Cape Girardeau a year and a half ago. His wife, Mahata Al-Serafi, could not be reached. They have no children. Co-workers at St. Mark's remember him as a very private person and an excellent doctor. Information about funeral services for Al-Serafi is unknown at this time.*

*Members of the Muslim community in Cape Girardeau expressed sorrow at the loss and grief of being unable to bury him immediately as is customary in the Muslim faith.*

*(See sidebar on Muslims in Our Community)*

Goosebumps stood at attention on Rhetta's arm. She started to hand the paper back to Woody, who dabbed his forehead and his glistening head with a spotless white handkerchief.

She snatched the paper back. Shaking her head, she reread the article.

"Didn't you read the paper this morning?" he asked. Even though Rhetta couldn't remember her own father, Woody sometimes sounded like a father and towered over his manager like one, too. Although he outweighed her by over a hundred pounds, he swiveled with the ease of a dancer, and returned to his desk.

Rhetta reached for her coffee and inhaled deeply, the fragrance making her mouth water. Then she began arranging the items on her desk. "No, Mr. Newsaholic, I didn't. I had a few errands to run on my way to work this morning, so I picked up the St. Louis paper to read later." She sipped, savoring the burst of flavor.

Rhetta pointed to a *St. Louis Post-Dispatch* among the items piled on her desk. It annoyed her that Woody didn't remember how much she disliked the local paper. "You know I don't buy the Cape paper. It's all advertising. The last time I read the thing there was a headline proclaiming that a Butler County cow gave birth to triplets. I can't stand that much excitement." Anticipating his next question, she added, "And, no, I didn't watch much of *First News* this morning either."

She propped her elbows on her now-organized desk. "The TV reporter is much too chirpy. I turned the news off after hearing about the upcoming music festival." Then, thinking about how many visitors would converge for the annual event, she muttered, "Traffic will be worse than snails racing turtles while that's going on. Remind me not to go downtown."

Woody paced, tugging at his neatly trimmed grey beard, apparently ignoring her assessment of the local news media and the popular annual music event. "What should we do? Do you think we should call the FBI?" The sunburn he'd acquired on a recent fishing trip couldn't hide the paleness of his face, drained of blood.

After running her hands through her cropped hairdo, Rhetta reached for the phone, but changed her mind. Instead, she rested her hand on the receiver.

"What's the point? The FBI ignored you when you called them before. What good is it to call again? Besides, what, exactly, do we tell them?" Rhetta craned her neck to gaze up at Woody.

Woody snatched a handful of tissues from a box on Rhetta's desk and resumed pacing. Picking up a pen, Rhetta stuck it into her mouth, and gnawed. She returned the box of tissues to its previous location. "It's useless to call them again."

"We have to tell somebody what happened." Woody stopped pacing and dropped into the guest chair in front of Rhetta's desk.

The swoosh of air that followed him knocked off a stack of while-you-were-out messages that he'd earlier placed on the corner of her desk. A pink blizzard covered the floor near Woody's chair. He bent and retrieved each sheet, stacking them neatly into piles according to how she always classified them—Hopeless, Maybe, and Good. There was barely enough room on her desk to make three stacks. Woody's desk was always arranged with the precision of a Japanese garden while her work area generally looked like the aftermath of a tornado.

He leaned forward. "What about calling the local police or the FBI again? Do you think they'd be interested now?"

Rhetta removed the chewed-up pen from her mouth. "They should be. I don't believe this"—she tapped the newspaper article—"was an accident. Aren't those cable thingies the state put up last year supposed to stop such a thing from happening?"

Woody picked up the paper as she continued, "After everything that happened when we did his loan? He got a ton of money from his refinance, and now he's dead. It's too coincidental." She eyed the tissues, wondering if blue ink had leaked on her face.

Woody rubbed his head with both hands. "Why did I have to get that stupid phone message in the first place?" She recognized Woody's head rubbing as a familiar gesture that he repeated whenever he was under stress. Two-handed meant he was doubly stressed. Apparently, being a star linebacker for Mizzou and a former Marine who served in Iraq and Afghanistan hadn't prepared him for coping with the stress of the mortgage and insurance business.

Although Woody, at forty-four, was a year older than Rhetta, she had to check herself from treating him like a younger brother. She dug to the bottom of her oversized purse, grumbling, "This thing is a freakin' black hole." Eventually, she surfaced with her billfold. After riffling through several of its pockets, Rhetta found a business card, snatched the phone, and punched a number into it.

"Who're you calling? The FBI could care less, remember?" Woody said.

"It's *couldn't care less*, and to heck with the FBI. I want to see that car for myself. I know we don't have to inspect our customers' wrecked vehicles, but let's just say I'm suspicious. I just don't think he could have simply driven off into the Diversion Channel."

Eddie Wellston, owner and manager of the impound lot, answered on the third ring.

### # # #

"Great. Thanks, Eddie," Rhetta said and hung up. Eddie said he would still be at the lot if she came over to view the car. She returned the phone to the cradle, spun her chair around, grabbed the rest of the contents of her purse, and said, "I was right. Eddie said that he towed Al-Serafi's car there yesterday, and it's still there. He also told me our adjuster called him, and will be over to look at the car sometime today. I want to get there first."

Considering what happened six weeks ago during Al-Serafi's loan transaction, she was determined to see Al-Serafi's car before anyone else did.

# CHAPTER 2

**Six Weeks Earlier, Tuesday, May 19**

In the frantic week before the Memorial Day weekend, Rhetta was helping Woody with the paperwork to refinance Doctor Hakim Al-Serafi's home. The doctor's mansion sat nestled in Woodland Crossing, a prestigious new subdivision west of Cape Girardeau, Missouri.

A little over a year ago, Al-Serafi bought the foreclosed house for cash when he arrived to start working as an emergency room physician at St. Mark's Hospital. The house had belonged to the developer who went broke when the recession punched a hole in the housing market balloon. Even with the depressed market, the house was worth $100,000 more than when Al-Serafi bought it. Property values had mushroomed in that area since his purchase.

Although the photocopy of Al-Serafi's alien registration card, also known as a green card, proclaimed him a German citizen, Rhetta noted that the dark skinned, black haired doctor didn't speak with a German accent.

Woody studied Al-Serafi's picture intently. "I was stationed in Germany for over two years," Woody said. "I can tell you, he doesn't sound German to me. Al-Serafi speaks English with a British accent." Woody withdrew a copy of the doctor's permanent visa from the file and examined it. "We worked with a lot of Arabs who spoke English with a British accent." He slid both back into the file and closed it. "He sounds a lot like they did."

Looking up from her computer, Rhetta turned to Woody. "Why did Arabs speak English with a British accent?" She remembered that Woody had also spent two years in Kuwait, and was doubtless familiar with all the accents in that area.

"Most of the Arabs we worked with had wealthy parents who sent them to school in England. When I asked Doctor Al-Serafi if he had also gone to school in England, he got huffy with me. I took that for a no."

Because Rhetta's desk was close to Woody's, she was able to overhear all of their conversation. The entire main office area was barely sixteen feet square. Rhetta and Woody routinely heard conversation from customers at each other's desk. If more privacy was required, either of them could move to an office in the back. Both she and Woody preferred to sit out front near the windows.

Al-Serafi told Woody he graduated from the American school in Munich before going abroad to medical school. He also explained his affinity to a Western lifestyle. "I am a Muslim. But I am not Sharia."

Sharia, Rhetta knew, was the strictest form of the Muslim religion. In fact, if she remembered correctly, a Sharia Muslim wasn't permitted to borrow money and pay interest to a non-Muslim bank. His not being Sharia explained why he'd come to Missouri Community Bank Mortgage and Insurance. Besides that, there were no Muslim banks in Southeast Missouri.

Al-Serafi continued, "I do not approve of those who say they are Muslims, but are bent on waging war against the West. I have always lived in the West. Allah," Al-Serafi then bowed in reverence, "is called AS-SALĀM, the Bestower of Peace."

Woody withheld comment.

Seeing him turned out in crisp Dockers, tasseled loafers—no socks—and a starched blue Oxford shirt, Rhetta conceded that Al-Serafi dressed like many other western doctors she knew. She wondered what his wife looked like.

Rhetta heard Woody reviewing the closing figures with his client. "Everything's ready," Woody said. "Your closing is set for next Thursday. Make sure your wife brings photo identification."

Al-Serafi's voice changed its tone, growing louder. Rhetta glanced at Woody. She saw only the back of Al-Serafi's head and couldn't read his expression.

"My wife does not have anything to do with the finances of our household," Al-Serafi said. He sounded like a man accustomed to being in charge. She swore she heard his neck hairs bristle. *Yeah, that sounds real American. Right.*

Woody answered in a calm voice. "You're the only one on the promissory note. That means you're the only one responsible for paying back the money." Woody stared unwaveringly at his client. "Under Missouri law, a spouse must sign the mortgage. She must agree to your home providing collateral. That's why she has to sign."

Rhetta observed Al-Serafi as he turned sideways, breaking eye contact with Woody and glancing down to the table at the paperwork. "Very well," Al-Serafi said. "I will have my wife here to sign the papers at three o'clock on Thursday." The doctor gathered up his own copies, arranged them in a slim burgundy leather folio and left.

Rhetta separated the vertical blinds at the nearby window to observe the doctor striding toward his tan Lexus ES 330. "That guy sure doesn't look German to me. I wonder what his real story is." She sauntered over to Woody's desk, picked up the file and thumbed through it. "I can't wait to see his wife. What's her name?"

"Mahata," said Woody.

From the copy of the green card, Rhetta learned that Al-Serafi had entered the U.S. at O'Hare International Airport in Chicago eighteen months earlier. She flipped through the pages of his application. Rhetta whistled when she saw the amount of cash he'd get. One eyebrow shot up. She snapped the file closed. "Holy crap, what's he going to do with $500,000?" Her suspicions flared. She claimed her wariness intensified from being married to a cynical judge for over ten years. Judge Randolph McCarter, who retired two years ago after he turned fifty, claimed that his mistrustful nature was due to the preposterous stories he'd heard from criminal defendants and their lawyers.

Rhetta had met her share of liars and frauds over the years in her line of work, too.

"Claims he's going to buy a second home at Lake of the Ozarks," Woody said.

"Right," Rhetta said. "Al-Serafi can go fishing while Mahata sunbathes in a teensy-weensy bikini."

Woody's lips twitched in the tiniest of smiles.

# # #

At precisely three o'clock on Thursday, the twenty-first, Al-Serafi pushed open the office door and strode in. The warm humid outside air followed him in, along with the smell of impending rain. Rhetta swiveled in her chair to watch, curious to see Al-Serafi's wife. Mahata followed several steps behind the doctor.

After Woody greeted his customers, the men turned to walk to the conference table. Although a shawl-like, gauzy garment covered Mahata's head, her face was exposed. She wore no burqa, the traditional garment that Rhetta thought Muslim females usually wore. Black hair peeked out of the head covering. Rhetta assumed her eyes were dark, although she'd yet to see them.

Al-Serafi pulled out a chair and sat, then motioned for his wife to sit. He did not hold out a chair for her. Mahata gazed downward, avoiding any eye contact with Woody. It disturbed Rhetta that Al-Serafi didn't extend any courtesy to his wife. Woody slid a chair out for her. Mahata took her seat in silence.

While everyone took their places, Mahata kept her head down and fingered a fold in her black robe. Al-Serafi made no move to introduce his wife. They sat without speaking until Woody turned to Mahata. "May I please—"

Throwing his right hand, palm-up in a stop gesture, Al-Serafi interrupted. "You must not speak directly to my wife, sir. It isn't proper. You must speak only to me. Also, you must not look directly at my wife."

Woody faced Al-Serafi, blinking rapidly, as though trying to determine where to look. He inhaled, and let out a deep breath before speaking. "May I please see your wife's driver's license? I need a photo ID." He extended his hand but didn't look at Mahata, keeping his eyes instead, on Al-Serafi.

Al-Serafi glared at Woody. "Mahata does not drive. I will provide you with her green card. It has her picture. Will that not do?"

"Yes, of course. That'll be fine." Woody continued holding out his hand, waiting for the doctor to produce the card.

Al-Serafi turned and offered his open palm to his wife. Mahata reached into a small dark cloth bag trimmed with colorful beads. After a moment of searching, she withdrew a laminated card and dropped it into her husband's hand. Al-Serafi glanced at it before presenting it along with his own ID.

Woody's chair scraped noisily as he pushed it away from the table and stood. "I'll be right back. I, uh, just need to copy them." He disappeared around the corner, paperwork in one hand while his free hand rubbed his head.

It was time to step in. Rhetta sauntered over to the conference table and thrust her right hand at Al-Serafi. "How do you do? My name is Rhetta McCarter. I'm the manager here. Is everything all right?"

Al-Serafi stared at her proffered hand then slowly shifted his gaze to her face. Rhetta felt self-conscious about wearing her two expensive rings. The facets on the princess cut diamond cluster ring that Randolph had given her as a first year anniversary gift sparkled in the bright lighting. The glittering ruby she wore on her middle finger had been a fortieth birthday present to herself. Moreover, she wondered if the man had an aversion to shaking her hand, a mere woman in his eyes, since he took so long to respond. She presumed from his hard stare that began at her head and ended at her hand, that he wasn't impressed with her spiky, blond-streaked hair either.

Eventually, Al-Serafi offered his hand and brushed hers in the briefest of handshakes. Then he snaked his right hand across the table and snatched a pen. He began rolling it between his right thumb and forefinger, avoiding any further physical contact. He stared straight ahead. Al-Serafi wore no rings. Rhetta wondered if that was a Muslim tradition.

Rhetta smiled. For all his western talk, Al-Serafi's manners wouldn't qualify under her definition of good manners. She offered her hand to Mahata. The woman's eyes darted to her husband, who nodded his assent. Mahata slowly held out her hand. Rhetta grasped it, feeling the woman's reluctance through her limp response. Then Mahata quickly withdrew her hand, folded it into her other hand on top of the bag in her lap, and resumed studying the tabletop.

Rhetta pulled out a chair for herself and joined them. Woody returned copies in one hand, their ID in the other. Handing the doctor the cards, Woody assembled the documents for the closing.

When Woody began explaining the first of the many pages, Al-Serafi waved him on. "We are in a hurry. I must return to the hospital. Just show me where I must sign." They completed the rest of the transaction in silence. Al-Serafi didn't ask any questions. Mahata never uttered another word while she signed.

Wasting no time after they finished, Al-Serafi immediately stood to leave. His wife followed his lead. Rhetta also stood, turned to the doctor, and smiled broadly. Again, she brazenly extended her sinful hand. "Thank you, sir. We appreciate the confidence you've placed in Missouri Community Bank Mortgage and Insurance."

Al-Serafi repeated his earlier reaction and stared at her hand. He tilted his head sideways and afforded her the briefest of smiles. He returned her handshake, then abruptly turned toward the door. Mahata trailed him, silent, head still bent. Woody hurried to reach the door first, where he held it open. Al-Serafi tugged his wife past Woody.

After they'd left, Woody closed the door and leaned back against it.

"That sure was different."

"He brags about being so westernized," Rhetta said, scoffing, pushing her chair back to the table. "Yet he subscribes to the subservient wife channel. How western is that? Poor woman. I'd hate living with a man like him. He stared at my hand like he was going to catch cancer." She eased behind her desk to the window and peered through the steel blinds to observe the strange couple making their way to their car. The woman lagged several steps behind her husband. They didn't speak to each other. Al-Serafi didn't open the car door for his wife.

"What a jerk," Rhetta commented, turning away, letting the metal slats of the blinds snap back together.

"Whew, I'm glad that's over." Woody exhaled loudly.

Rhetta removed her glasses and chewed on the tip of one of the arms. "What was it about him that rattled your cage?"

"I'm not rattled." His hand shot to his head.

*On the contrary, you're rattled worse than a timber rattler coiled to strike.*

# CHAPTER 3

**Tuesday Morning Following Memorial Day, May 26**

Returning to work after the long weekend, Rhetta cruised through McDonald's, seeking a large coffee for a badly needed caffeine jolt. She and Randolph had spent Memorial Day weekend at their cabin at Land Between the Lakes, Kentucky, fishing and relaxing. Exhausted from all the relaxing, she'd overslept and hadn't had time to make coffee at home.

The ride in had been spectacular. Well, to her it was. The first working day after Memorial weekend was always the day she brought out Cami, her beloved two-toned blue '79 Camaro Rally Sport she drove only in summer. She parked the Chevy Trailblazer she drove in winter, its summer duties relegated to grocery shopping. Feeling the power of the restored muscle car always made her happy. Cruising along with the sunroof open and the oldies blasting was as near to heaven as Rhetta could imagine getting.

She arrived at her office before Woody and stole his favorite parking spot—the one closest to the building.

After setting her briefcase by the door, Rhetta transferred the coffee to her left hand and inserted the key into the lock. The door, however, was already unlocked. Through the window, she noticed the lights were on. She hesitated, glancing around. Cami was the sole car in the parking lot. That reinforced her first impression that Woody wasn't here. Who was inside? Her heart felt like a bird's wing caught in the bars of a cage. Just as she put her hand on the doorknob, someone yanked open the door, causing her to spill coffee all over her linen pants suit.

"Damn, Woody, you scared the living snot out of me," Rhetta grumbled while she edged past him, balancing the dripping cup out ahead of her. "I'm sending you the cleaning bill."

Woody ignored her comment. "Jenn dropped me off this morning on her way to work." He closed the door and followed Rhetta.

"Why did she have to get to work so early?" Jenn managed the jewelry department at Macy's, which didn't open until ten.

"They're doing inventory this morning. Besides, we took the Jeep in to the repair shop. The tranny's making a weird noise again."

In spite of the air conditioning blasting from the vents, Woody was dabbing sweat off his slick head. His complexion paled.

Still clutching the cup, Rhetta plopped her briefcase on the floor, and bent over, allowing her purse to slide off her shoulder. It landed upside down on her chair. She glared at it, cussed to herself, then went to the kitchenette in search of paper towels.

Woody followed her into the small area. He pulled a bottle of water from the compact refrigerator and gulped most of it in a single swallow.

"Are you all right?" Rhetta asked, as she ripped a handful of paper towels from a nearby roll, and began working at the splotches of coffee on her pants. She wrapped her cup in another paper towel, muttering the whole time. Woody tossed the empty water bottle into the trash and shook his head. He followed Rhetta back to her desk.

"What's wrong with you?" She slid her cup to rest on a calendar blotter and wiped the coffee ring from her desk. "Are you sick?"

"I'm not sick. You need to look at this." He thrust out his iPhone.

She stared at it blankly. "What am I looking at?" She glanced from the phone up to his face as she reached down with one hand to adjust the height of her chair, which, due to a weak hydraulic, gradually sank. She yanked the handle upward. With the other hand, she clutched her coffee.

"It's a voice mail from Al-Serafi."

"Did he rescind? Damn!" She blew across what was left of the steaming liquid and sipped carefully.

If the strange Muslim doctor had cancelled his loan during the three-day rescission period, she'd be thoroughly ticked off.

"No, no, that's not it." Woody shook his head and waved his phone, as though chasing flies away. He scrolled through his screen until he found the speaker icon. "Listen to this." He held the phone up.

She sat forward and listened to a familiar voice. "Lawrence, this is Hakim. I was there yesterday for the flying lesson, and I waited for over an hour. You know we are on a tight schedule." He pronounced it *shed-yule,* like the British did. After he said, "Please call me right away," the message ended abruptly without him leaving a call back number.

*Who's Lawrence? Whoever he is, he must know how to reach Al-Serafi.*

They both stared at the phone in Woody's large hand.

"What was—" Rhetta began.

Before she could finish, Woody blurted, "I got the call yesterday but when I saw Al-Serafi's number, I didn't feel like answering. I figured it could wait 'til I got back to work. The call went to voicemail." Woody began pacing. "I guess he didn't realize he'd called me instead of whoever this Lawrence guy is." He waved his phone around as he paced.

"Flying lesson? Why is Al-Serafi taking flying lessons?"

"Good question." Woody returned the cell phone to his belt holster. "I got a weird feeling and figured I was overreacting. Then, I played the message for Jenn. She said to call the cops, since we had just watched a television news story on Muslim cells in the US, which said that one of the things to watch for, along with the cell members usually being here on German visas, is when they take flying lessons. I reminded her that the report said to call the FBI. Local cops wouldn't care who's taking flying lessons." He grabbed for a tissue. His head glistened.

"What did they say?"

"I didn't call them. I wanted to let you hear the message first. Besides, it was a Sunday."

"What does Sunday have to do with it?"

"They're closed on Sunday, aren't they?"

"No, they're not. Do you think bad guys don't commit crimes on Sundays?"

Woody, she felt, believed the misdialed message meant that Al-Serafi was participating in something suspicious. Now he wanted her to believe it, too.

She eyed Woody. Although he was impeccably turned out in tan slacks and white shirt, his head was wet with perspiration. He once told her he suffered from Post Traumatic Stress Disorder. Was it kicking up? Woody had related how sometimes stress caused an onset. He'd suffered shrapnel wounds in his legs when an IED exploded in front of his Humvee in Afghanistan. She'd never seen him in a full-blown episode of PTSD, but from the way he was acting, she wondered if she was about to.

"Maybe you should've called the FBI," Rhetta said. "Who gives flying lessons on a Sunday? Besides, didn't Al-Serafi know this was a holiday weekend?" She could hear her own voice rising as she fired off the rhetorical questions.

Woody didn't answer. She went on. "I saw that news report too. They said that those terrorists who bombed the Twin Towers took flying lessons, and many of them were here on German visas. The talking heads all say that's a red flag." The moment she said the words, she realized how paranoid she sounded, but she felt herself on a roll. She wondered if paranoia was contagious.

"Could there be a terrorist cell operating here? I know Al-Serafi is Muslim, has a German visa, and is definitely strange, but...." She stared at Woody, letting her voice trail off.

Neither of them spoke. The air conditioner rumbled on. In spite of the frigid air blasting out of the vents, the office felt warm and stuffy.

Almost to herself, Rhetta said, "Could Al-Serafi really be a terrorist?" She could barely say the word *terrorist* aloud.

Woody paled. "Here? In Cape? Terrorist? What's to terrorize? That only happens on TV or in New York, right?" His voice cracked.

Rhetta marched to her desk, opened a drawer, and rummaged through the contents. Snatching a phone book, she flipped a few pages, then scribbled a number on a sticky note.

"Here's the number for the local FBI office." She thrust the note at him. "Call them. The news report said to call the FBI."

Woody wavered. "How dumb are we going to look if we report this, and it turns out to be nothing?" He tugged his chin whiskers.

Rhetta narrowed her eyes and pointed to the phone. "How are we going to feel if he turns out to be a real terrorist? Call them." She felt her stomach quiver. Could Doctor Al-Serafi really be part of a terrorist cell? True, she didn't like the man, but a terrorist?

Still. . . .

Woody tapped the keyboard on his cell phone.

Rhetta pointed to the desk phone. "Use the office phone. I'm sure the agent will want you to play the recorded message."

"Right." He set his phone down and snatched the phone.

Once connected, he waited for over five minutes for someone to pick up. Woody drummed his fingers, and twirled the phone cord. Once whoever finally answered, he repeated the story. Then he shook his head. When he finally had a chance to speak, his voice was clipped. "Don't you even want to hear it?" A moment passed while whoever answered. Then, he said, "What was your name, Agent, in case we need to refer to this incident later?"

Woody slammed the phone down, a little firmer than was necessary. The receiver bounced to the desktop. He retrieved it and set it down again. "I guess that's our stupid maneuver for the day." Then he mumbled something Rhetta didn't quite catch, but she thought it sounded suspiciously like, "Freakin' G-man."

He pulled the curly phone cord taut several times before Rhetta finally objected. "For goodness sake, stop doing that, Woody. You know that cord isn't rubber. When it breaks, you'll be without a phone until I can buy a new cord."

Woody let the cord spring out of his hands. "The agent told me I was an idiot. He acted like the FBI gets phone calls about terrorists every day."

"An idiot? He used the word idiot?"

"Not exactly. The guy yawned. A yawning FBI agent tells me he must get calls about terrorists every day and that I must be an idiot for bothering him."

Rhetta steamed. "Did you get his name?" She stomped through the office toward the kitchen.

"Cooper. He said he didn't need to hear the recording," Woody called after her. "I can't believe we're the only ones who think this is suspicious. After his attitude, now I'm not so sure, either."

"What did you say?" Rhetta said, reappearing with a bottle of water. "You're giving up that easily?" Twisting off the cap, she tilted the bottle and drained half of it. She tossed the half-full bottle to the wastebasket. She missed. It landed a foot away and rolled into the corner. Snatching her shoulder bag and car keys, Rhetta strode to the door.

Changing her mind, Rhetta stopped, whirled around, and returned to her chair with keys in one hand and purse in the other. "I've got it. Maybe the FBI is already on to him." Rhetta nodded, "Sure, that's it. They don't want us to get too excited and maybe say or do something we shouldn't." She sighed, retrieved the water bottle from the floor, and dropped it in the trash.

She'd intended driving straight to the agent's office in Westerfield Center to confront Agent Cooper in person. She changed her mind, reasoning that the authorities probably had everything under control. What "everything" consisted of, she wasn't sure. Whatever it was, there was nothing more she and Woody could do. They'd done their duty. They'd reported a suspicious call.

Woody shook his head. "If that's the case, why didn't Cooper say he already knew about it?"

Rhetta pondered that. "You know, this is a damned-if-you-do, damned-if-you-don't situation."

Woody furrowed his eyebrows. "What do you mean?"

"That agent can't confirm or deny anything. By brushing us off, I'm sure he hopes to discourage us from getting panicky."

"Us? Panicky? What do you mean?"

Rhetta yanked open a bottom desk drawer and stuffed her purse into it. "You know how closemouthed the FBI is. They don't want us civilians knowing anything. Especially, they don't want us knowing anything important. I bet they're all over this. We did our civic duty. Let them take care of finding out about this." Rhetta almost had herself convinced.

"Yeah, we don't need to get involved in—"

The phone rang, interrupting Woody. He answered and kicked into full professional mode. "MCB Mortgage and Insurance. Yes, ma'am, let me just get some information from you." He opened a drawer and withdrew an application form.

Rhetta was relieved that the call was from a customer and not Wilfred Graham, III, who hated it when Woody abbreviated his family-owned bank's sacred name.

The phone rang again, and the business day shifted into gear. Neither of them mentioned the unusual voice message the rest of the day.

Rhetta had all the confidence in the world in the FBI.

Sure, she did.

# CHAPTER 4

## Thursday, June 25, late morning

It was time for action. "Come on," she said, heading to the door. Woody remained at his desk.

"Aren't you coming with me?"

"Where are you going? What do you want to look at?" Woody hesitated. "What're you thinking?"

She faced him. "There's something too peculiar about Al-Serafi's accident. I can't imagine where the heck he was going on I-55 south, obviously alone, so early in the morning. He didn't live anywhere near the Diversion Channel." She snorted. "Al-Serafi lived on the west side of Cape. I'm sure he wasn't making a house call." Another safari through her bag produced the door key. "He doesn't have any other family around here, and I remember him saying how he doesn't like to drive too much because we drive on the wrong side of the road. Or at least compared to how he drove in England."

Woody didn't budge from his chair. "Aren't you just being nosy? Anyhow, the car is in impound. That means we can't see it."

Rhetta rolled her eyes. "Woody, honestly, this isn't New York. I've known Eddie Wellston forever. Did you forget how small a town Cape is? Besides, we're the insurance agents. We can look at the car."

"I'm his agent," Woody corrected Rhetta.

"Right. Whatever. Let's go."

Woody still didn't move.

She gathered up her purse and keys. "I'm no expert in looking at wrecked cars, but Eddie is. I don't believe how the paper says this happened. I have a gut feeling that Al-Serafi's accident was no

accident. I'm sure somebody will investigate, if they haven't already."
Rhetta headed for the door. "I want to see the car for myself." She
veered to Woody, still seated at his desk. "Besides, we need to prepare
in case we have to clear ourselves."

"What does that mean? What did we do?"

"You and I know we didn't do anything, but the paper may see
it differently." Rhetta fanned out her palms, mimicking a banner.
"Would you like to read a headline that says, 'Doctor Dies in Crash
after Missouri Community Bank Lends Him a Huge Sum of Money'?"

"Are you saying it's our fault?"

"It's not the bank's fault, but the article might start with,
'James Woodhouse Zelinski, the loan officer who handled the loan....'"
She glared at him. "You want that kind of free advertising?"

Woody rose. "We'll have to lock up the office and leave a note,
since LuEllen won't be in." Ever practical, he grabbed a note pad and
stood. He picked up the desk phone. "I'll forward the incoming calls to
my cell phone." After he entered in the proper code, he began writing.
LuEllen, their part time receptionist, had taken three weeks off to visit
family in Idaho, so they would have to lock the office.

Rhetta watched him write in his painstakingly neat hand.
"What are you going to say? 'Gone to look at terrorist's wrecked car.
Be back soon'?"

He ignored her until he finished. "How about, 'Sorry we
missed you. Be back by 1:00 PM'?" After taping the note to the door,
he locked it behind them.

Rhetta knew how Woody fretted about the bank president
calling the branch and having the call drop into voice mail or having
LuEllen take a message. Rhetta, however, never worried about that.
There were times they needed to be away from the office, meeting with
real estate agents or going to a customer's home to take an application.

Rhetta was already behind the wheel when Woody folded
himself into Cami's spotless white passenger seat. After he buckled in,
she pressed the Camaro into the southbound Kingshighway traffic. She
made a mental note to check the Missouri State Highway Patrol
website, appropriately called *The Crash Website* that posted
information on all wrecks. Accidents were usually updated within
hours.

He shouted above the oldies pouring through her speakers.
"Should we really be checking out Al-Serafi's car?"

After she reassured him one more time they should, they sped across town to the Tri-County Impound Yard, located on a bluff off State Route 177 near the Mississippi River. The city of Cape Girardeau, settled by French-Canadian settlers, sits in a large bend in the Mississippi River, framed by massive limestone bluffs overlooking the river.

Eddie Wellston owned the impound lot which served not just Cape Girardeau County but two surrounding counties, Bollinger and Perry. The three counties contracted services with Eddie, thus saving them from the expense of having to maintain lots of their own. When they topped the hill, Rhetta, not for the first time, marveled at the awesome sight of the broad river. Its surface sparkled like golden fireflies in the afternoon sun. The riverside trails were full of joggers and cyclists taking advantage of the perfect day.

The impound lot was completely enclosed by an eight-foot tall chain link fence topped by razor wire. A large rectangular metal shop building-cum-garage had a small wood-sided addition on the front, which served as an office. Behind the lot, Eddie owned a large junk yard that was enclosed like the impound lot.

Woody extended his long legs and scrambled awkwardly out of the car, putting him three steps behind Rhetta, who aimed for the screened front door. Over the doorway, a faded metal sign read, *Tri-County Impound.*

"And if it's an *or what*, what do you suggest we do? And what, exactly, is an *or what*?" Woody picked up the conversation while he tugged the squeaky screen door open, allowing Rhetta to step through ahead of him.

"*Or what* means sabotaged. If it wasn't sabotaged, that means that Al-Serafi went into the channel for some other reason. Maybe he had a heart attack, or somebody forced him off the road, or something."

"I don't like the sound of an 'or something' either," Woody complained, as the door slammed shut.

Eddie Wellston obviously didn't feel the need for fancy surroundings. There was neither a desk nor a customer chair anywhere in sight. Four mismatched metal filing cabinets stood lined up against one wall, like worn-out soldiers who'd lost the war. A folding table covered with papers and scattered file folders sat under the room's only window on the opposite wall.

Tall and lean in well-worn jeans and a white T-shirt, Eddie sauntered in through a doorway that connected the office to the secure back area of the building. He wiped his brow with a red paisley handkerchief, which he folded before returning it to a back pocket.

"Don't you have AC in here?" Rhetta braced against the tornado blowing from an oversized floor fan. She was grateful she hadn't worn the peasant skirt she'd originally planned for this morning. It would've been wrapped around her head by now.

"It's broken." Eddie reached for a rag to wipe his hands. "Went to turn it on last Thursday, and it wouldn't cool. The technician from Allied Service said it needs its regular spring shot of coolant."

"Eddie, this is my associate, Woody Zelinski," Rhetta said, motioning toward Woody.

"Good to meet you," Eddie said as he grasped Woody's outstretched hand. "The car you want to see is back there." He pointed toward the rear of the lot. They trooped outside.

"That's Al-Serafi's car, over there." Eddie motioned to a four-door tan Lexus resting on the flatbed trailer he'd used to haul it. Rhetta recognized the car. The last time she saw it was when she watched Al-Serafi and his wife leave the office after their loan closing.

"There's no yellow crime scene tape surrounding the car," Rhetta said. "Means the police deemed the event an accident."

"I looked the car over but I sure can't tell what happened," Eddie said, accompanying Rhetta on her tour of the trailer. "Maybe the driver fell asleep at the wheel."

"I don't know." Rhetta shook her head. "That seems doubtful. Woody and I both knew Al-Serafi, and we can't believe he'd do that. He had a regular schedule at the hospital. There was no reason for him to have been out at that early hour. He hadn't worked the night before." Rhetta had called her friend Dr. Phillip Islip, another emergency room physician, and found out what Al-Serafi's hours had been. Phillip later called her back and told her that hospital administration had sent a memo to its employees not to discuss Al-Serafi's death with anyone. She promised she wouldn't. This didn't count, did it?

Other than a badly smashed front grille, probably from landing nose-down, a thick layer of sludge coating the front two-thirds of it, and a deep green scrape mark along the front driver's side fender, Rhetta found little evidence of what may have caused the accident.

The Diversion Channel emptied water and mud into the Mississippi River; she wasn't surprised to find the vehicle caked with foul-smelling muck.

"I want to look inside." Rhetta searched the trailer for a ramp or a step.

"The car's pretty dirty," Eddie cautioned, producing the wobbly wooden chair she'd spotted outside the front door. He steadied the chair while she clambered on to the trailer. *High-heeled sandals aren't meant for field investigating.*

Woody didn't follow her.

*Probably doesn't want to get his spiffy slacks dirty or get mud on his shoes.* She shouted down to him, "Aren't you coming?"

He shook his head. "I'll just wait here."

Eddie, however, vaulted on to the trailer.

"That's funny," Eddie said.

"What?" asked Rhetta, glancing around.

"I could've sworn that window wasn't broken out yesterday." Eddie pointed a skinny index finger at the driver's window that bore a baseball-sized hole, while shards of glass littered the trailer. "A guy from the insurance company was just here looking it over, too." Eddie looked around as though the man might still be close by. "Guess he left. No, that's his Explorer over there." He pointed toward the back of the lot. Rhetta followed his gaze. A man opened the driver's door and slipped inside.

Rhetta said, "I don't know who that might be. I thought I knew all of our adjusters." She turned her attention back to Al-Serafi's car.

Eddie worked on the driver's side door, which was closest to them. It took a few minutes before he successfully tugged it open. "I'll leave you to it." He leapt off the trailer and rejoined Woody, leaving Rhetta to snoop alone. She kicked aside the glass pieces since she didn't want to wind up wearing one inside her sandal. She turned her attention to the inside of the car.

A grey, putrid-smelling slime covered the interior dash, steering wheel, and all of the front floor carpeting. Rhetta wrinkled her nose. She noticed a similar coating along the outer edge of the front seat. Tilting her head sideways, she estimated that if the car was nose down, how high the water must have been. There was nothing, not even mud, in the back seat. Even after surviving a dunking in the channel, the back seat was cleaner than in most cars. Not a scrap of anything lay on the seat or on the floor.

Rhetta's eyes swept the interior once more. Beside the broken window, there was nothing significant in or about the car. She didn't know what she thought she'd find, but she was disappointed that her search produced nothing.

Glancing back at Woody and Eddie, who were engrossed in deep conversation, Rhetta closed the door, stepped carefully through the broken glass to cross the front of the car to the passenger side front door. Her destination was the glove box.

The door refused to budge due to mud as hard as concrete clogging the hinges. Rather than call for Eddie to help, she returned to the driver's side. This time she was able to tug the door open herself. Then she stretched across the interior to pop open the glove box. The soft click went unnoticed by the two men engrossed in conversation. She glanced down at the swipe of dirt that had leapt on to her blouse from the steering wheel.

The smell from the dried slime in the glove box made Rhetta turn her head aside. She wiped the back of her hand across her nostrils in an attempt to dislodge the foul odor. When she looked back inside, she found a small stack of mud-soaked papers. Under the stack was a sealed plastic bag, containing the owner's manual. *Why would the owner's manual be sealed in a bag?* She removed the bag and pried open the plastic zipper.

Using her thumb, she fanned the pages of the owner's manual. Deciding there was nothing interesting or unusual about the booklet, she began to reinsert it into the plastic bag. A sheet of loose paper the same size as the book's pages escaped from the owner's manual and floated to the seat. Covered with undecipherable scrawls, the sheet was decidedly different from the handbook pages. She snatched the sheet and then folded it while glancing surreptitiously at the men. Seeing that they weren't paying any attention to her, she quickly pocketed her prize.

After coaxing the glove box closed, she slammed the driver door shut. The only way down was the way she'd come up. She stepped gingerly onto the chair, and then hopped to the ground, hoping to keep her shoes out of the dust. She turned her ankle and nearly fell. Did anyone see her? There went her pedicure. Along with having messed-up toenail polish, mud had splattered the back of her pants leg.

Eddie and Woody were discussing the merits of refinancing Eddie's house when Rhetta, acting as if nothing had happened, strolled up to them. She was still brushing smudges off her pants.

"Sounds good, Woody." Eddie shook Woody's hand. "I'll stop by after work tomorrow to get started."

"Are you ready to go now?" Woody asked. He looked pointedly at her shirt then at her splotched pants leg, raising an eyebrow. Following his gaze to her shirttail, she rubbed the dots of mud spatter that decorated it.

"Yep, let's hit it." She veered toward Cami. Eddie had already disappeared inside the office. "Let's go, nothing left to see," said Rhetta, swiping at the mud on her shirt one last time before scrambling in and closing the door. Woody climbed in and reached for his seat belt.

"You look like the dog that swallowed the canary," Woody commented while Rhetta shifted into second, pulled out onto Highway 177, then shifted twice more. The speedometer tattled on her, the needle pointing to 65. She eased back to the speed limit of 55.

"Cat," she said, peering in the rear-view mirror, grateful that there were no blue lights flashing on top of the police car that had pulled up right behind her.

"What?"

"It was a cat, not a dog that swallowed the canary." Rhetta favored him with a fleeting sideways glance.

"Whatever. What did you find?"

"What do you mean?"

"I know that look all too well. Tell me what you found."

She stretched out her left leg to withdraw the folded paper from her pants pocket and handed it to him.

He whistled. "Should you have taken that?" He reached for the paper, shaking his head in mock disapproval.

"Hey, you heard Eddie. The adjuster will probably have the car hauled away at any time. Why shouldn't we take this one lone piece of paper?"

"We? I didn't take anything." Woody arched an eyebrow. "Where did you find this?"

"It fell out of the owner's manual."

"Fell out?"

"Sure."

"Where was the owner's manual?"

"In the glove box. I found it."

He raised both eyebrows. "Just happened to find it?"

"The whole front seat area was full of mud, but the back seat was spotless. There wasn't a scrap of anything personal lying around either in the front or the back. All I found was the owner's manual in the glove box, and this strange paper fell out. I didn't even find the insurance or registration papers. Isn't that odd?"

Before he could answer, Rhetta, who had slowed down to approach the one lane bridge on 177, slammed on the brakes. A green SUV sped around them. "Holy crap," Rhetta shouted as she hit the accelerator and swerved hard to the right. "That guy nearly hit us!" A glance in her rearview mirror told her that, of course, the police car was no longer behind her. "Where are cops when you need them?"

The Camaro rested precariously on the remnants of the shoulder of the bridge approach.

"A few seconds later and we would've been on the bridge! We could have been forced to hit the side of the bridge."

She jumped out to inspect her car and shake her fist at the departing SUV as it disappeared down 177.

# CHAPTER 5

Ten minutes later, after her tirade at the offending driver had subsided and they were downtown, Rhetta remembered the piece of paper. She slid Cami into a quick left on to Spanish Street. "Let's stop at Dockside and get lunch. I can't wait to look at this."

After making two tours around the block, Rhetta settled for a parking place in the courthouse parking lot two blocks away from The Dockside Diner. She jogged down the hill to the restaurant, while Woody ambled alongside her. By the time Woody pushed open the heavy wooden door, he was pulling out a clean handkerchief from a back pocket to mop his brow.

Hungry patrons, eager for a speedy lunch, packed the popular eatery. The din of clattering dishes along with numerous conversations made the prospect of quiet conversation bleak. Most of the customers were courthouse employees on their lunch break. Rhetta and Woody lucked into a table for two in a quieter area near the back door.

Woody ordered a half-pound Dockside Burger and double fries. The service was fast. Within minutes, the server arrived balancing their steaming plates, along with several others, down the length of her left arm.

The thick burger looked delicious and smelled even better. Rhetta's stomach growled. The breakfast shake that she'd gulped after her morning run had dissolved by ten o'clock. Her passion for running increased after she turned forty, as did her determination to stay in shape. Although her weight hadn't varied much from when she'd graduated from Southeast Missouri State University, she was convinced that certain parts of her anatomy were beginning to shift and relocate, mostly south, to her butt.

She dipped her fork into the ranch dressing that, at her request, the server had poured into a small bowl alongside her plate of grilled chicken salad, then stabbed at a chunk of lettuce. After each bite, she repeated the dunking procedure.

"Why don't you pour the dressing over your salad?" Woody wiped at his beard, which had trapped a generous dollop of burger juice.

Rhetta glanced up, interrupting a forkful of salad on its way to her mouth. "By dipping your fork into the dressing, you don't actually consume much dressing. You still get the taste with half the calories." Her mouth closed over a chunk of iceberg lettuce.

Woody cut a glance her way. "Want some fries?" He slid the plate across the table, tormenting her with the delicious smelling, thick-sliced fries. She glared at him.

Rhetta dabbed her lips with a napkin after her last bite of salad, then pushed the empty bowl aside. She unfolded the mysterious paper and flattened it on the table where the bowl had been. She twisted her neck first one way, then the other, and turned the paper around several times. Each turn of the paper generated another neck twist.

She finally gave up guessing. "I wonder what this is supposed to be?"

"Let me see it." Woody pushed his own empty plate aside and stirred a second heaping teaspoon of sugar into his sweet tea. He swiped a napkin across his beard again.

"That's already sweetened." Rhetta jutted her chin toward his tea. Woody ignored her, and continued stirring. "Here, look at it. I give up. I can't tell what it is." Rhetta slid the wrinkled paper across the table for his inspection.

Woody drained half of his beverage then reached for the paper.

He took his time examining it, likewise turning the paper several different ways. He finally settled on a direction and bent over to scrutinize the seemingly meaningless lines and squiggles pictured there. Rhetta waited, scraping her fork around the bottom of her empty salad bowl.

"There's something familiar about this." Woody pointed to the paper. "But I'm not sure."

"How do you mean, familiar? Have you seen this before?" She craned her neck to look at the paper again.

"Not this particular paper, no. But I remember something like this from the military."

She looked up at him. "Military? Like what? What is it?"

Woody held up the document. "I think it's a schematic."

"What's a schematic?" Rhetta grabbed the paper and turned it around for a better view.

Woody pulled a handful of napkins from the dispenser and resumed working on his beard. "A schematic is an electrical map, a blueprint for an electrical appliance or motor. Anything wired has a schematic, from a heating thermostat to a nuclear power plant. It identifies everything about the unit's circuitry and wiring."

"What was our good doctor doing with something like this?" She handed the document back to Woody.

Before Woody could answer, the server appeared with an icy pitcher of tea and refilled his glass. He waited until she'd refilled both their glasses before answering.

"Maybe it's for something he wanted to get fixed." Woody studied the paper again, and pointed to the lines and boxes on the diagram. "The writing is so small that I can't make out any dimensions. I need a magnifying glass."

"Okay, then let's get out of here." Rhetta picked up the sheet, refolded it carefully, and crammed it in her purse. Snatching the check, she left a tip and headed to the cashier near the front door.

Woody scooted his chair back and gulped the rest of his sweet tea.

Rhetta handed the cashier her credit card. "We'll use our copier to enlarge it. Maybe when it's bigger, you'll be able to distinguish what it says."

# # #

After enlarging different areas of the drawing by two hundred percent, as large as the copier could accommodate on a legal sized page and still have a decent image, Rhetta helped Woody tape several sections together, finally producing one larger, but fuzzier version of the original wrinkled sheet. They spread the photocopy out on the conference table.

They re-examined the schematic. "I can't quite identify what all this represents, Woody said. "Some of the characters are numerals, but...." He stopped then, and looked at her. "I think this writing is in Arabic. I can't read it, but I saw a lot of it while I was in Kuwait."

"Arabic? I guess that makes sense. Al-Serafi was Arabic." She squinted at the image, having left her glasses in her purse. "Do you know anybody who can read Arabic?"

"Sure don't," Woody said, glancing up.

Rhetta left the table and went to her desk where she rummaged through her purse in search of her iPhone. Not locating it quickly enough to satisfy her impatience, she dumped the entire contents on the desk. She snatched the packet of plastic gloves that also tumbled out and tossed them back into her purse before Woody could see them. She'd meant to put them in Cami's console with her hidden emergency stash.

She plucked the phone from the pile and began tapping. "Randolph knows everybody. I bet he knows someone who can read Arabic."

After several rings, her call went to his voice mail. She slid her thumb across the END bar without leaving a message. He'd see the number and return her call. She'd barely rejoined Woody at the table when her phone buzzed.

She greeted him before he could speak. "Hi, Sweets. Do you know anyone who can read Arabic?"

# CHAPTER 6

Randolph sipped his drink. He smiled at how Rhetta always got right to the point, especially when she thought something was boiling over with importance.

"Possibly," he said. "Why do you need someone who can read Arabic?"

Most of Randolph Scott McCarter's family suspected his mother had named her son after her favorite actor, screen cowboy Randolph Scott. No one could ever get her to admit it. The only person who ever dared abbreviating his name to Randy was his grandmother, whom he'd feared and revered. Rhetta always called him Sweets—unless he forgot to lower the toilet seat.

She told him about her trip to the impound yard, and her discovery in the owner's manual. His stomach boiled like he'd swallowed bleach at hearing she removed the paper from the car. "You took it? That may be evidence. You need to call the authorities and give it to them." He massaged his tightening stomach.

"What authorities? I told you about the time Woody called the FBI. They weren't interested in hearing about Al-Serafi then. Why should I give this to them now?"

Randolph groaned. He knew better than to attempt to persuade her, especially when she took a stand, but he tried anyway. At least this argument wasn't about politics. On one of their first dates, their talk had turned to politics. That discussion became their first and last political discussion. He was a staunch conservative while Rhetta was as strong a liberal. He had to admit he admired her courage in standing up for her beliefs while living in a tight-knit, politically conservative region.

"Perhaps you should call the FBI again." Randolph waited for her to answer. She didn't. He clicked his tongue in disapproval. Finally, he caved. "All right, you win. Doctor Peter LaRose at the university probably can. He's my anthropology professor friend who's made several trips to Saudi Arabia. I'll call him, and then call you back."

"Was he that really nice professor I met one afternoon when you first started the gallery?"

"Yep, that's him. I'll let you know what he says."

After disconnecting, Randolph pondered what he should tell Peter, whom he'd known for several decades. They hadn't seen each other in over a year. The last time he saw the eccentric professor, the already rail-thin Peter had lost even more weight; something Randolph couldn't believe possible. The gaunt teacher had never married. He told Randolph he still lived in the same second floor walk-up apartment in the downtown area that he'd lived in for thirty years.

Randolph's gut told him the scrap of paper that Rhetta had removed from the car was significant, even though he hadn't seen it and didn't know what it was. When Woody received the weird phone message from Doctor Al-Serafi, Rhetta was sure the doctor was a terrorist. He told her that she was overreacting. He couldn't imagine what, if any connection this paper had to the phone message. The doctor did end up dead, though. That was more likely a coincidence. Still, he knew he'd never convince his wife of that.

When Rhetta called, he'd been in his studio painting. While still on the bench, Randolph planned on retiring and becoming a law scholar. Instead, his life had forged a new direction. Although he'd never taken any formal art training, he was a naturally skilled sketch artist. He'd loved drawing the characters that appeared before him in court. One day, on an impulse, he sat in on an outdoor painting class and became hooked on painting landscapes.

After retiring, he'd thrown himself into his art. His landscapes were selling briskly on the Internet. He and three fellow artists had organized Rivers West Creative Group, a local co-operative art gallery on Main Street in Old Town, on the banks of the Mississippi River.

He set his drink down, wiped his hands with a turpentine soaked rag, and picked up the phone book.

Peter answered on the third ring. Even though university classes had been out for several weeks, Randolph figured that Peter, like most of the professors, would still be working in his campus office. Not having Peter's cell phone number, Randolph had called the office number listed in the phone book.

After initial pleasantries, Randolph dove in. "Rhetta has a document that she thinks is in Arabic. Could you translate it for her?"

Peter chuckled. "My written Arabic isn't the greatest. But for you, I'll be happy to take a stab."

After agreeing to meet at Rhetta's office in an hour, Randolph called his wife to give her the good news.

Rhetta cheered. "That's why I love you, Sweets. You know everybody." He heard her put her hand over the mouthpiece to shout to Woody, "Randolph found somebody."

"I told Peter I'd meet him at your office. I've been working in the studio. I'll clean up and come over." After he disconnected, Randolph headed upstairs to shower. He could imagine her high-fiving Woody. Peeling off his painting shirt and jeans, he emptied the rest of the whiskey sour down the toilet. Before showering, he brushed his teeth vigorously and gargled. He counted on the medicinal tasting mouthwash to cover up the two drinks he'd had since lunch.

### # #

Ten minutes later, Randolph slipped a T-shirt over his damp, silver-streaked black hair, pulled on a clean pair of faded jeans, and slipped into canvas deck shoes. Glancing at the full-length mirror, he reflexively sucked in his stomach. Although still trim, the six-foot tall Randolph knew he should be exercising to keep fit, but always procrastinated. He was grateful for the great genes he'd inherited from a family of thin people.

The good genes, however, didn't extend to eyesight. He had to remember to grab his reading glasses. He found he needed his cheaters more and more to read or paint with each passing year. He tucked them into his shirt pocket and went off to find his keys.

After searching the bedroom, kitchen, and bathroom, Randolph finally located the keys to his pickup truck where they were supposed to be—on a hook by the back door. With the keys jiggling in his hand, he jogged to the three-car detached garage that Rhetta christened the

Garage Mahal, because it was built and finished out as nicely as the house.

The 1999 Ford F-100 pickup fired right up. Normally, it stayed hooked to an enclosed utility trailer filled with his paintings. The truck had needed gas when they came home from the last art show. He'd unhooked the truck from the trailer as a reminder to fill the tank the next time he went to town.

Thankfully, none of the three cats was asleep under the truck. Rhetta's cats were supposed to be barn cats, inhabit the Garage Mahal, and catch mice. "Barn cats, indeed," Randolph said, shaking his head. Of course, since Rhetta regularly fed them canned cat food on the deck, he needn't have worried about them being anywhere near the truck.

He smiled and waved at Mrs. Koblyk, their senior citizen neighbor, as he pulled out of his driveway and turned on to the gravel road. Mrs. Koblyk and her husband, a retired railroad engineer, watched all their comings and goings, and were the epitome of nosy neighbors. However, Mrs. Koblyk often redeemed herself by bringing him home-baked Hungarian poppy seed bread.

Life was idyllic for Randolph McCarter these days. He was thankful for the blessed change from the chaos his life had become when he found himself widowed ten years ago. His wife, a dedicated oncologist, died in a plane crash coming home from an overseas conference. They had no children. Anger and loneliness carried him directly to a whiskey bottle.

Arrowing down their lane and on to the gravel county road, he wondered how differently his life would have turned out had he not met Rhetta. Judge Rosswell Carew, a fellow bachelor and drinking buddy, introduced them at a Humane Society fundraising dinner auction six years ago. Rhetta, a sworn single, promptly informed Randolph she wasn't interested in marrying anyone. That suited Randolph just fine. Rhetta and Randolph struck a major chord together, marrying two years later.

Randolph's wedding gift to her was his promise to quit drinking. Her gift to him in return was a promise to quit smoking.

Although he did quit bingeing and meeting friends for drink fests, he hadn't quite managed to stop drinking completely. He didn't always tell Rhetta when he had a drink or two, although he suspected she always knew. Privately, he feared being lulled into his former pattern of excessive drink.

Alcohol had nearly killed Carew last year. After a night of heavy drinking, he fell asleep at the wheel. Fortunately, Carew had had sense enough to fasten his seat belt. That saved him from flying headlong into the windshield when he missed a curve and plowed into an oak tree.

### # # #

Randolph edged the pickup into a slot outside Rhetta's office a half hour later. Rhetta had christened his truck The Artmobile. She had a nickname for everything.

He spotted Peter LaRose bent over the conference table alongside Rhetta and Woody. They were all absorbed in studying several sheets of paper and hadn't noticed him entering. Randolph ambled over to join them.

"We've introduced ourselves," Rhetta said after brushing her lips against her husband's cheek. She gestured toward the angular professor who was still examining a document.

"Thanks for meeting us on such short notice," Randolph said, shaking hands with Peter.

"I'm not sure what you have here," Peter said without preamble. He motioned to a paper spread out on the table. "This is definitely written in Arabic." He furrowed his brow. A strand of thinning grey sandy hair fell across his wide forehead. "I translated the best I could. It appears that the writing is identifying different components in the drawing. As I said, my written Arabic isn't that great."

Randolph glanced down at the document. He couldn't decipher it. He pointed to the sheet. "What's your best guess?"

Peter scratched his chin, taking a moment to answer. "Looks like it could be some kind of schematic. Maybe a transformer of some kind. It's pretty large, bigger than what's in the short wave radios I work on in my spare time."

# CHAPTER 7

Rhetta felt her stomach knot. "Why on earth would Al-Serafi have a schematic for something like that?" She had no idea what she expected Peter to say.

Peter's thin shoulders raised and dropped. "I'm sorry I wasn't more help."

"Actually, Peter, you've been a great help," Randolph said, glancing at Rhetta.

"Yes, Peter. Thanks so much," Rhetta said.

Woody remained silent. He continued examining the schematic.

"I've got to run." Peter squinted at his wristwatch and frowned. "I have an appointment with a graduate student in fifteen minutes."

Randolph thanked his friend, and the two men shook hands. "I owe you lunch for this, Peter. I'll call you soon and we'll catch up."

After Peter left, no one spoke. Randolph finally broke the silence.

"A transformer?" Randolph said, sidling back over to the table. He peered at the drawings. "Woody, what do you make of that?"

Woody didn't answer. Instead, he hurried to his desk. He dropped into his chair while reaching for the computer mouse. The thin LCD monitor sprang to life. Woody fingers flew across the keyboard with quick efficient strokes.

Rhetta and Randolph exchanged glances as Woody opened a web browser and logged into a search engine. Images blazed across the screen. Woody, a self-taught computer junkie, raced from one site to another. Stopping when a familiar-looking drawing appeared, he swiveled the monitor around to display what he located.

Woody said simply, "Look at this." He turned the screen toward them. Filling the screen was a drawing eerily similar to the one on the table.

The three of them stared at a schematic displayed on the Cotton Belt Electrical Supply website with an accompanying photo of what the schematic matched: a 1500 kV ultra-high voltage transformer.

The knot in Rhetta's stomach tightened. Randolph spoke first. "What the hell are we looking at?" He jerked his chin toward the picture.

"These babies are the guts of a power substation." Woody turned back to the monitor. He typed a few more commands. A printer whirred and an image sailed off it. Woody trotted to the printer and retrieved the color picture. He carried it to the table, turning it carefully so that the picture aligned with the drawing. "I'll be damned," was all he said.

"Al-Serafi had a schematic for a power substation transformer?" Rhetta asked, glancing at the two men. "Why?"

"Why, indeed?" Randolph chimed in.

*Now Al-Serafi is dead. I'd better not jump to conclusions. I'm sure it's coincidental.* Who was she kidding? She didn't believe in coincidences. Al-Serafi was dead. He had a schematic for a power substation transformer in his car. Those were facts.

Woody gathered up the enlarged drawing they'd been examining and folded it. He snatched the original that Rhetta had filched from the car, along with the photo he'd just printed and took everything to the large walk-in office safe.

Randolph followed him.

Woody spun the combination and spoke over his shoulder. "Maybe you should call Doctor LaRose and tell him not to mention what he saw here to anyone." He set the drawings on a shelf in the safe and closed the door.

"Good point," Randolph said. "Since we don't exactly know what this is all about, it would be best if we kept it to ourselves."

Randolph began tapping Peter's number into his BlackBerry. The line rang several times before an electronic voice announced the mailbox.

"Peter said he had a meeting," Rhetta said, listening to Randolph leave a message.

"It's about the drawing, Peter. Please call me right away." Randolph disconnected.

Turning to Rhetta, Randolph said, "I think now we'd better talk to the FBI. I don't care if they didn't listen to Woody the last time. They need to know about this."

For once, Rhetta didn't argue with him.

Rhetta scanned the phone book then punched the keypad. She bounced her foot impatiently while the number rang several times. The call went to a recording. "The Cape Girardeau, Missouri office of the Federal Bureau of Investigation is closed until further notice. Please call the St. Louis office at 1-555-FBI-1000. That would be 1-555-324-1000."

Rhetta depressed the button to end the call. "The Cape FBI office is closed. Budget cuts, I guess. They directed me to a St. Louis number." She dialed it.

After following several voice prompts, a woman asked Rhetta how she could direct her call.

"I'd like to speak with Agent Cooper. He was formerly in the Cape Girardeau office." Rhetta coiled the curly phone cord as she spoke. She remembered chastising Woody for doing the same thing. When she noticed him glaring at her, she let go of the cord.

"Hold on, please," answered the all-business female voice. Rhetta found herself listening to an instrumental version of *Strangers in the Night*. The tune finished. She'd just begun humming along to *I Left My Heart in San Francisco,* when a different woman came on the line. She was much less friendly. "Agent Cooper is not available. What is the nature of your call?"

"We spoke to him about a month ago at the Cape office. We'd like to deal with him, if at all possible. Tell him that Judge Randolph McCarter is calling." Rhetta glanced over to her husband. He jerked his thumb upward, giving her a "thumbs up" approval. She hoped using her husband's title might persuade the clerk she wasn't a nut case.

"Hold, please."

Rhetta found herself on hold without any music this time. After hearing a series of clicks and some tapping sounds, a third woman's voice came on.

"I must advise you that this call is being recorded. Do you wish to continue?"

"Yes, that's all right. May I please—"

"What is your name?" the woman said, interrupting Rhetta.

"Rhetta McCarter, Judge McCarter's wife. I need to speak with Agent Coo—"

The woman began speaking before Rhetta could finish. Rhetta was about to let her know what she thought of the FBI representative's phone manners, when she realized what the woman had just said.

"Agent Cooper is what?" She felt like a horse had kicked her in the gut. "No, I don't want to speak to anyone else. Thank you," Rhetta said. "I'm sorry." She hung up.

Eyes wide, she turned to Woody and Randolph. "Agent Cooper is dead. He was killed in a hit and run accident two weeks ago." Rhetta stared at the phone. *I need a cigarette.*

"Why didn't you ask to speak to someone else?" Randolph pulled up a guest chair to sit next to his wife.

"I guess I should've, but I was so shocked at the news that I just hung up." Rhetta swiveled around to face Randolph.

"Cooper must've died right before Doctor Al-Serafi wound up in the Diversion Channel," Woody said. He began pacing and rubbing his head.

Randolph twisted toward Woody. "Hold on, Woody, what are you thinking?"

Before Woody had a chance to answer, Rhetta blurted, "Randolph, maybe the two deaths are connected." Her stomach fireball had exploded into a volcano. She fished in a desk drawer and came up with an economy-sized bottle of chewable antacid tablets. She popped several into her mouth.

"Sweetheart," Randolph said, eyeing the bottle. "I think we're all jumping to conclusions."

"I think Randolph's right." Woody rubbed his head. "After all, how could the two deaths possibly be related?"

Woody's head rubbing belied his protestations. Woody was worried, too.

Rhetta attempted to keep everybody calm. "Maybe we're jumping to conclusions about all of this."

Turning to her husband, Rhetta said, "What do you make of that schematic? Why would that drawing be in Al-Serafi's car?"

Randolph poured out two antacids tablets for himself, popped them into his mouth, and began chewing. "I don't know the answer to that, but I have an idea. I'll ask Billy Dan Kercheval about it. I'll see if he can identify the schematic."

William Daniel Kercheval, Billy Dan to everyone who knew him, was the newly retired General Manager of the maintenance division of Inland Electric Co-operative. He'd been a longtime friend of Randolph's. They'd gone to high school together. Never remarrying after a divorce many years earlier, Billy Dan had retired to a secluded wooded property west of Marble Hill, about thirty miles from Cape Girardeau.

Randolph said, "If Billy Dan confirms this is something unusual, we'll call the FBI again. We may have something concrete on our terrorist theory."

Woody nodded slowly. Returning to the safe, he withdrew both the enlarged copy and the web picture he'd printed, leaving the original schematic tucked away. He folded the papers deftly into a manila envelope, which he handed to Randolph. He returned to his desk and quickly pulled up the Missouri State Highway Patrol crash website.

He quickly located the information. "The highway patrol reported Al-Serafi's death as an accident. That could be why the document was still in the car. No one searched it."

The office door opened and a young couple trundled in. The man lugged a carrier holding a sleeping baby. Woody smoothed the front of his shirt and strolled over to greet them.

"Agnes Dalton-Evers with Tri-County Realty told us to see a man named Woody about getting pre-qualified for a home loan." The thin, blue jean clad father glanced from Randolph to Woody. His short, round wife nodded, her blond curls bouncing. It was easy to see that she had yet to shed the baby fat she'd accumulated while pregnant. Woody smiled, introduced himself, and escorted the young family to his desk.

Rhetta left them to business and accompanied Randolph to his truck. She leaned into the driver's window after he'd tucked himself behind the wheel.

"Maybe this," Randolph said, holding up the envelope, "isn't anything to worry about, but I'll go and see Billy Dan first thing tomorrow." He laid the envelope on the seat next to him.

Rhetta touched her husband's cheek. "Billy Dan can probably clear a lot of this up. I have a bad feeling about that schematic, but maybe it's just that—a bad feeling."

Randolph stretched up out of the truck window to kiss her, then turned the ignition key. The Artmobile roared to life.

Rhetta climbed into her car and sat, staring at the console. Her craving always intensified under pressure.

# CHAPTER 8

While maneuvering through the late afternoon traffic leading westward out of Cape, Randolph considered the envelope beside him. By the time he reached the edge of town, instead of turning south toward home, he continued straight to Marble Hill. Feeling an inexplicable sense of urgency, he didn't want to wait before talking to Billy Dan. Randolph assured himself that meeting Billy Dan would dispel any wrong ideas that the three of them had formed.

Randolph was perpetually skeptical, never one to jump to conclusions. Knowing that Al-Serafi possessed a schematic for a substation generator and had died in an unusual accident made the revelation about Agent Cooper's death more significant. Randolph, like Rhetta, wasn't a big believer in coincidences. Nevertheless, all of that didn't necessarily add up to a terrorist plot, either. What would be the point? How would it happen?

A glance at his watch reinforced his hope of finding Billy Dan hanging out at his new office, Merc's Diner, enjoying a late afternoon cup of java. Since his retirement, Billy Dan told Randolph that he followed a daily routine, always making his way to Merc's in the afternoon in order to catch up on the gossip and drink coffee.

Randolph pulled up in front of Merc's, a converted Tastee-Freez built alongside Crooked Creek in the 70s. Initially constructed as a small walk-up ice cream stand, Merc, short for Mercury, Leadbetter bought the business fifteen years earlier and added on a large dining room and full kitchen. He re-opened as a full service restaurant. Being situated practically on the creek bank, the cedar sided building had suffered through a few floods. Each time high water had invaded his building, Merc rebuilt and his loyal customers always returned.

Randolph found a large sycamore and parked under it, hoping the shade would keep his truck cool. Once inside Merc's, he headed straight for the smoking section in the back where he guessed he'd find Billy Dan. Glancing around, he spotted two old geezers dressed alike in faded green overalls, one sitting on either side of Billy Dan. The three occupied an oversized round table, discussing, drinking coffee, and polluting the air with an abundance of cigarette smoke.

"Judge McCarter, are you lost?" Billy Dan waved and called out upon spotting Randolph. Randolph waved back and headed their way.

"May I join you?" He nodded at the two old gents and waved the smoke aside. Randolph wondered why Merc didn't install a better exhaust fan.

Billy Dan motioned to an unoccupied seat. The old timers downed the last of their coffee, stubbed out their cigarettes, slapped a couple of bills on the table, and stood. One of the men stuffed a half-smoked cigarette into his overall pocket.

"We gotta git goin'," the first geezer said, nodding to Randolph and jamming a faded ball cap on his head. He mumbled, "Good to see ya, Judge."

"There's catfish waitin' fer us at Taylor's pond," the second one chimed in. He grinned, revealing several missing teeth.

Randolph was well acquainted with the two. He'd thrown both of them in jail for poaching. He appreciated that they weren't keen on sharing a table with him.

"I didn't mean to run off your cohorts." Randolph jerked his thumb toward the departing figures. "One of 'em left a cap here," he added, picking up a well-oiled, saggy John Deere cap and setting it to the side. He pulled out a chair and joined Billy Dan, sliding aside the used coffee cups.

Billy Dan shook his head. "You know the Hefner brothers. They have no use for politicians, preachers, or lawyers."

"Especially judges, right?"

Billy Dan grinned. "They still don't see eye to eye with the Conservation Commission." He signaled for a waitress to come to the table. "I haven't seen you in a good while, Judge. I hear you're a successful artist these days. I enjoyed that piece about you in the paper."

Randolph shook his head and smiled. The newspaper had done a feature article about his art career and had called it *Trading the Bench for a Brush.* The glowing praise for his art had embarrassed him.

Billy Dan stubbed out his cigarette and waved his empty cup at a nearby waitress. "Kathy, honey, can you bring the coffee pot? And bring a clean cup for Judge McCarter."

The slim brunette wearing a nametag on her left breast that said *Krista* arrived with a steaming stainless steel pitcher of coffee and a heavy ceramic mug. She set both on the table and whisked away the used cups. She swiped the top of the table with a damp cloth that reeked of bleach.

"Need cream and sugar?" she asked, now wiping more vigorously. She turned her large brown eyes to Randolph.

"Yes, thanks." Randolph smiled at her, holding his cup up out of the way. She retrieved a miniature stainless-steel pitcher of cream from a nearby table.

"Help yourself to the coffee." She beamed a megawatt smile back at Randolph while turning her back on Billy Dan. She trotted away to her other customers.

"Her name is Krista." Randolph stirred fresh country cream into his coffee while enjoying the view as she sashayed away.

"I know. I call her Kathy just to irritate her." Billy Dan grinned and poured himself more coffee.

"One of these days she may pour hot coffee all over you, just to irritate you back."

Billy Dan chuckled.

Turning to Randolph, he asked, "What brings you all the way to Marble Hill?" He sipped the piping hot coffee carefully before setting his cup down.

"I have something I want to show you." Randolph pushed his own cup aside. He emptied the contents of the manila envelope on to the table. He slid the enlarged copy of the schematic across to Billy Dan but left the photo Woody printed of the transformer face down.

Billy Dan scrutinized the enlarged copy for several minutes, turning it first one way, and then another. "Where did this come from?"

"Before I tell you about that, can you first tell me what we're looking at?" Randolph reached for his cup and blew across the hot beverage before sipping carefully.

"Sure. It's a schematic." Billy Dan squinted at the drawing. From his shirt pocket, he removed a pair of wobbly, wire-frame reading glasses with a broken earpiece. He attempted to balance them on the bridge of his nose. Holding the glasses in place with one hand, Billy Dan lowered his head to scrutinize the drawing.

Randolph turned over the photo that Woody had printed and aligned it next to the illustration Billy Dan was examining. "I already know that much. I also know that it's a schematic of a transformer. What I need to know is what kind of transformer?"

Billy Dan used his free hand to reach into another shirt pocket for his cigarettes. He tapped the box and a fresh one slid out. He fished into the same pocket that had held the glasses and produced a lighter. With the cigarette securely lit, he inhaled deeply. When he exhaled, he whistled softly and let out a long stream of blue smoke.

Placing the cigarette in the ashtray, Billy Dan drummed his leathery fingers on the table. Then he angled forward. "This is the type of transformer that we use in all of our power substations."

Randolph noted that Billy Dan used the possessive "we," apparently still associating himself with his longtime employer.

Billy Dan turned the drawing around toward Randolph. "What does this mean?" He pointed to the strange symbols. "What's this writing all over it?"

"I think that writing is in Arabic, and I'm not sure what it means."

Billy Dan picked up the drawing and fiddled with his glasses to study the paper again.

"See these areas with Xs on them?" Billy Dan said, holding up the photocopy. He pointed with his right index finger. "These are strategic oil points. Why are those marked?"

Randolph had previously noticed dark marks on all the areas that Billy Dan pointed out. "That's part of the mystery. Tell me, what do you think those marks signify?"

Billy Dan shook his head. He reached for his cigarette and inhaled, then stubbed it out. The partially extinguished butt gave off an acrid smell. "The only significance to me is that those areas are lubricating points. If a power transformer developed a leak or a problem of any kind at any one of these points, then that transformer could go dry and possibly burn up." Billy Dan set the copy down then tucked the glasses back into his shirt pocket. He picked up his coffee and sipped.

"What happens when a transformer burns up?" Randolph asked.

"We replace it."

"Can't it be fixed?"

Billy Dan's cigarette continued to send a spiral of smoke into the air above them. He shook his head. "We'd have to replace it. Once a transformer burns out, that's all she wrote."

"But you have backup transformers in case one fails?" Randolph bent over the drawing. The men were inches apart. He wondered if Billy Dan noticed him sweating. "Then all you'd have to do is hook up a new one, right?"

Billy Dan glanced around. He lowered his voice. "No, we don't have backups. We'd have to bring one up from Arkansas."

Randolph blinked. "How long would that take?" He stared into Billy Dan's gray eyes.

"Three days." Billy Dan held up one finger. "One day to drive down and get it." A second finger joined the first. "Another to install it," he continued. A third finger formed the complete salute. "A third day, or part of a day, to get the power switched over."

Billy Dan picked up his foul-smelling cigarette and firmly ground out the remains. "Ordinarily, we switch one substation to another to pick up the load and never have any down time if a transformer does go out. It happens automatically."

"You don't keep any spares on hand?"

Billy Dan chuckled. "Spares? Heck no. They cost a fortune. Besides, we don't ever have problems with transformers actually failing. We inspect them regularly. With routine maintenance, they last a helluva long time. In fact, we haven't had to replace one in over six years." Billy Dan reached into his shirt pocket in search of his pack of cigarettes. He slid one out, and held it, unlit. "That one only needed replacing because lightning hit the chain link fence around the substation and arced across the transformer, causing a fire in the 'B' assembly." He pointed to the schematic. "Here." The spot he identified also had an $X$ over it. "In fact, we usually get our replacements from

Paragould. It's not far, so shipping is reasonable. Even at that, they only keep one or two on hand at any given time."

"How many manufacturers are there?"

Billy Dan rubbed the back of his neck. "Only two—one's in Paragould, and the other's all the way out in Albuquerque.

"Does the one in Albuquerque keep more on hand?" Randolph removed his stare from the unlit cigarette, to peer at Billy Dan. He'd never realized until then how much his friend smoked.

"No, neither place warehouses or stocks these transformers. They build them when we order them." Billy Dan reached for his lighter, fired up the cigarette, leaned back, and took a long drag. "There isn't much call for these transformers, even nationwide. Even if every electric company who uses these would replace them, you're still only talking a few thousand." He blew a long column of smoke toward the ceiling. "Both of those factories focus on building whole house and portable gas generators 'cause that's where the bulk of their business comes from. They only build these transformers as a service to the electric companies."

Randolph took a long drink from the glass of water that Krista had brought him. His mouth had gone very dry. Everything Billy Dan said reinforced the dread settling in his gut. He swallowed more water, forcing the acid back down.

"If several transformers went down at one time, how long would it take to get replacements to the substations?" Randolph watched Billy Dan scrutinize the sheet.

They both stared at the drawing while Billy Dan, running his hands through his short silver hair, shook his head, obviously trying to calculate. "Longer than a month, probably more like six weeks."

They were interrupted by a grumbling Hefner brother who shuffled to the table and snatched up his cap. "Ferget my danged head if it weren't attached," he said, cramming the cap low over his forehead. Hefner moseyed away and continued grousing all the way to the door.

Randolph sat forward again when Hefner left. "What happens if several transformers go down at the same time? For instance, all the substations in Southeast Missouri? "

Billy Dan took a moment. "When a single substation goes down, the power is re-routed by computer within seconds. The customer barely notices a quick blink of power. If two or more substations go down at the same time, that would cause an overload on the next substation in the chain. That would in turn cause it to shut down, resulting in what's called a cascading failure, or a blackout. In fact," Billy Dan continued, his voice now barely above a whisper, "a chain reaction of shutdowns could cause not just Southeast Missouri, but the whole Midwest grid to shut down."

Randolph took a deep breath, and forced himself to stay calm. He reached for his cup and sipped coffee that had now gone flavorless. "What about the bigger cities? They don't tie in with us rural counties do they?"

"The cities like St. Louis and Kansas City and even Springfield have their own generators and don't use the same type of system we use. However, they're keyed into the same grid we are. If all our substations go down, it would create an overload. Theoretically, they'd fail too. That failure mechanism is built in to the grid system to prevent permanent damage."

Neither spoke for a minute. Then Billy Dan added in a low and serious tone. "If the Midwest grid went down, well...." He didn't finish. He didn't have to. The implications were clear to Randolph.

Billy Dan had verbalized Randolph's fear.

Randolph said, "What you're saying here is if the Midwest grid fails, then the entire country could suffer a major blackout?"

Billy Dan lit his cigarette, inhaled deeply. When his lungs were filled, he expelled the smoke while he answered. He punctuated every word with a puff of smoke. "If the tripping stations we installed to block any catastrophic cascading failure should themselves fail, well if the Midwest grid goes, yes, then it's the entire country." Billy Dan squinted around the smoke, then sat back and folded his arms.

Randolph felt his stomach clench as though waiting for a blow in a boxing match. The whiskey sours began battling with the coffee. The result was an acid war sloshing around his gut. The more he learned from Billy Dan, the worse he felt. Bile rose. He reached for his water glass, but it was empty. He ordered himself to stay calm. "Exactly how many substations are in our area?"

"There are hundreds throughout rural Missouri with six major ones in our service area of Southeast Missouri—all keyed to the Midwest grid."

"Where are they? Are they in secret locations?"

Billy Dan chuckled. His voice was back to its normal tone. "You're kidding, right? You passed one on the way out here. The others aren't a secret either."

Randolph remembered seeing a substation at Center Junction, near the Interstate. Sitting barely a hundred feet off the road, it looked so innocent, so unguarded. Although enclosed by chain link fencing, it seemed so vulnerable to him now. A determined sixth-grader with wire cutters would have no trouble snipping his way in.

Randolph stared at the notations and writing on the drawing. In front of him was evidence that somebody who wrote in Arabic had made a careful study of a transformer schematic, marking the vulnerable points on it.

Moreover, Rhetta had to be the one to find it in a dead Arab doctor's car.

# CHAPTER 9

"Tell me, Judge, where did you get this?" Although Billy Dan spoke softly, his eyes were fixed solidly on Randolph.

Randolph had half-promised Billy Dan he'd tell him where he got it, but now he really didn't want to divulge his source. Especially since the source was Rhetta.

"Let's just say that someone found it, and that same someone brought it to me." He hoped he sounded profound and judge-like, so his answer would satisfy Billy Dan.

It didn't.

"Why would anybody have a schematic of one of our power transformers? And why is there Arabic writing all over it?"

Those were, Randolph conceded, the big money questions. He stalled, folding the photocopies and picture and returning them to the manila envelope. He couldn't answer Billy Dan.

"You must've thought it important enough to drive over here to ask me about it," Billy Dan persisted. He stubbed out the cigarette that had an inch of ash dangling on the end of it. He stood and withdrew a worn leather wallet from the back pocket of his jeans. He slapped a couple of bills on the table.

Randolph also stood, reached in a back pocket of his jeans for his own wallet, and added to the funds.

"Let's talk outside." Randolph led the way.

Billy Dan followed silently. Once in the parking lot, he propped himself against the front fender of Randolph's Artmobile, stuck a toothpick in his teeth, and waited.

"You need to keep this conversation between the two of us." Randolph tucked the manila envelope under his arm while he fished in his pocket for the truck keys.

Billy Dan perked up.

Randolph unlocked his truck and opened the driver's door. He leaned against the door as he continued talking to Billy Dan. "The original drawing was found in a vehicle belonging to a foreigner. Right now, I can't tell you whose car it was, nor the circumstances. What I will tell you, though, is that you've convinced me I need to turn this information over to the FBI."

Sliding in behind the wheel and pulling the door shut, Randolph fired up the truck. While the Artmobile idled, he turned on the air and punched the window down button. Before Billy Dan could ask more questions, Randolph said, "Don't talk to anyone about this." Randolph wasn't sure why he cautioned Billy Dan, except that he felt urgently that the schematic was significant, that bad things were connected to that schematic. He and Rhetta didn't need to be mixed up in this. Nor did they need to involve Billy Dan. Randolph resolved to contact the FBI himself. That way, he and Rhetta, and everyone who'd seen the schematic, would be out of this.

Billy Dan patted the door. "I'm hearin' ya. Be careful, Judge." Then he sauntered over to his own ride, a ten-year-old two tone brown Ford Ranger with a dented right front fender. Randolph wondered when the dent had happened and when Billy Dan would get the fender fixed. He knew how particular his friend was about keeping up his equipment and vehicles. Randolph watched him ease out of the parking lot, turn right on Highway 34, and head toward his home several miles west of town.

After securing his shoulder and seat belt, and determined to call the FBI as soon as he got home, Randolph slid his own ride into gear and turned left out of Merc's parking lot. At the end of the block, he stopped for the traffic light. A dark green SUV with deep tinted windows glided out from under the tall sycamores lining the back of the parking lot. Randolph eyed it when it pulled in behind him. *Tourists.*

# CHAPTER 10

O nce the signal changed, Randolph punched the accelerator. By the time he reached the edge of town, he was up to fifty-five, the speed limit. He stole a quick look at his watch. Rhetta would probably already be home. *I should've called her. She'll wonder where I am.*

Recalling everything that had happened since Woody got the strange voicemail, he tried sorting it into a pattern. *What the hell was going on? Could there actually be a terrorist plot here in East Nowhere, Missouri?* If he read body language correctly, his friend Billy Dan Kercheval thought so.

Billy Dan hadn't told him where the other area substations were located. Randolph reached for his cell phone, but realized he didn't have Billy Dan's cell number. Instead, he selected the top name on his Blackberry's "favorites" list. Ordinarily, he didn't talk on his cell phone while driving. This occasion, he felt, was definitely out of the ordinary.

Rhetta was home and answered on the second ring.

After Randolph filled Rhetta in about his meeting with Billy Dan, he said, "I forgot to ask him where the other substations are. The only one I know about is the one at Center Junction."

"Let me Google it to see if I can find the locations." A minute later, he heard keys clattering on her keyboard.

"That information won't be on the Internet. I called so you could look up Billy Dan's number. I need to call him. Inland Electric wouldn't put that information—"

"Here we go." Rhetta interrupted him. "I found the Inland Electric web site. There are six substations listed in the service area." She began rattling off their locations. "Besides the one on Highway 34 at Center Junction, in Cape County, there's also one on County Road 637. In Bollinger County, there's one out near Glen Allen." She rattled off the rest of the locations. "There's another one two miles south of Marble Hill, one near Flatt Junction in Scott County, and, finally, one in Perry County on, let's see. . . that one's on County Road 1458."

Randolph remembered Billy Dan telling him the sites weren't secret. He wasn't kidding. They were posted on the Internet for the whole world to see. The dread forming in his mind plunged to his stomach, making it churn and burn.

He asked Rhetta, "Can you print out that list?"

"Sure. Are we going to go and check them out?" He could tell by the excited pitch of her voice that she anticipated an adventure.

"Let's talk about it when I get home. I'm leaving Marble Hill now. I'll be home soon." He topped Gravel Hill, then headed down into the river bottoms where he'd soon have no service. "I'll lose you in a few seconds." He wasn't sure she'd heard him. Two words replaced the customary five staggered bars: NO SERVICE.

He glanced in his rear-view mirror as he approached the Whitewater River Bridge. The eighty-year-old structure had low stacked rock railings along each side of the road leading up to the actual bridge. It was identical to several hundred others built across the country during the Great Depression as part of the WPA, or Works Progress Administration, during the late thirties. During the 1980s, the state had added metal guardrails on either end of the narrow approach lanes; however, the single lane across the bridge had no shoulder. Two vehicles could scarcely clear each other if they met. Everyone crossed slowly and in single file.

The SUV that Randolph noticed earlier suddenly veered out from behind him and pulled alongside. Randolph instinctively lifted his foot from the accelerator.

*The fool picks now to pass.* Randolph cursed under his breath and glanced sideways at the vehicle. He saw nothing through the dark tinted windows. Instead of speeding up to pass, the SUV maintained the same speed as Randolph, careening along parallel to his truck. They reached the bridge together. Randolph slid his foot to the brake pedal and pressed down hard. When he did, the SUV veered into him, sideswiping his front fender. The sudden impact caused Randolph's head to bounce against his door window. His shoulder harness snapped to attention, preventing a second head banging. The SUV veered and collided with him again, much harder this time.

"Damn!" Randolph cursed. He lost control. He crashed through the metal guardrail and the truck went airborne. The road vanished from under him as he sailed outward, the truck arcing gracefully before plunging to the creek bed thirty feet below. When the pickup crashed nose down, his head slammed into the steering wheel, the airbag exploded in his face, and pinwheels of light collided in his brain. Everything went black.

# # #

Above him, the SUV crossed the bridge, and pulled over. A figure in black stepped out. After checking the traffic in both directions, he scrambled down the creek bank to the truck below.

# CHAPTER 11

Rhetta stared at her phone. No answer, again. She'd already left two voice mails.

*It's been nearly two hours since Randolph was at the Whitewater Bottoms. He should've picked up service within a few minutes. It's not like him not to call right back. Where is he? He should've been home over an hour ago.*

Rhetta set her phone on the island countertop and strode across the kitchen to the back deck. When she slid open the door, she was greeted with plaintive yowling. She closed the door, headed to the pantry, and retrieved two cans of cat food. She popped open the lids and returned to the porch. Using her elbow, she slid the door open again. Three cats—two calicos and one tiger—pranced in anticipation.

"OK, babies, here's your supper." The cats threaded their silky bodies between her feet as she weaved through them to locate their food pan.

As she began spooning out the fishy mixture, the house phone shrilled. She dropped the cans on to the outside table then skidded across the kitchen floor, snatching the portable phone on the third ring. The caller ID read BLOCKED.

"Mrs. McCarter?"

She nearly hung up without speaking. *Probably a damn sales call. I'll find out who this is and report him to the attorney general's office.* She'd enrolled their home number in the national Do Not Call program.

"This is Sergeant Quentin Meade of the Missouri State Highway Patrol," said a deep masculine voice.

Her stomach lurched. She felt lightheaded. "Yes, this is Rhetta McCarter." She slid slowly to the floor. Her heart began to thud.

"Your husband had an accident at the Whitewater Bridge, and has been taken to St. Mark's Hospital. He's in the emergency room." Meade's manner was professional and dispassionate, his voice calm.

Rhetta's heart pounded harder. "Is he, is he, uh….is he all right?" She gripped the phone with both hands, dreading the answer.

"The doctors are with him now, ma'am." The officer paused. "Do you have someone who can drive you to the hospital?"

Rhetta stood and sucked in a mouthful of air. "I'm all right, Officer. I'm on my way."

"Yes, ma'am. Mrs. McCarter?"

"Yes?"

"Please drive carefully."

She blinked back a tear and clicked the off button. She gathered her purse, keys, and cell and raced for the garage. Realizing she still had the house phone in her hand, she pitched it to the counter on her way out.

Five minutes later, Cami was churning up gravel. Rhetta shifted into third. The Camaro spun out and bounced from the driveway on to the county road. By the time she reached fourth gear, she was on the highway and roaring towards Cape.

*Oh God, please, don't let him be dead.*

# CHAPTER 12

Within twenty minutes, Rhetta was standing in front of the emergency room admissions counter at St. Mark's Hospital, Cape's only trauma hospital. The blue-haired senior volunteer in a pink-and-white striped apron held up an index finger in a signal to wait. She had a phone pressed to her ear. Rhetta scribbled Randolph's name on the notepad lying on the counter and held it up in front of the aging candy striper.

The woman nodded and penned *Room 4* under his name, then pointed. Rhetta raced down the hall, skidding to a stop in front of a pair of stainless steel doors labeled, "Trauma Room 4." Following the instructions printed on a laminated sign across the doors, she punched the big red button on the wall. The doors opened silently toward her. She flew through and then stopped abruptly.

The smells of alcohol, Lysol, and vomit greeted her amid a sea of medical personnel. Some of the staff were holding clipboards, while others clad in green or blue scrubs or white smocks wore stethoscopes around their necks and rushed in and out of curtained areas.

"Excuse me," she called to a slim black woman wearing a lab coat and carrying a tray of glass vials. "I'm looking for my husband, Randolph McCarter."

The woman nodded, set her tray down, and studied a printout on the unmanned desk nearby.

"Right over there, ma'am." She pointed to an area enclosed by white curtains. Rhetta thanked her and threaded her way to the cubicle.

The metal rings along the top of the white privacy curtain rattled as she slid it along the track. Rhetta gasped, raising her fist to her mouth to silence herself. Covered in a white sheet, Randolph lay motionless on a stainless steel gurney. Caked blood matted his dark hair and streaks of blood covered his face. His eyes were swollen shut, and she could barely discern his raspy breathing over the hum of machines. A young physician clad in green scrubs looked up. "Mrs. McCarter?"

She nodded.

"Please sit. I'll be with you in a moment." He waved a latex-clad hand smeared with blood toward a blue plastic chair, a few feet away.

"If it's all right, I'll just stand." If she sat, she wouldn't be able to see what was going on. The doctor nodded and returned to Randolph.

Plastic bags containing various liquids hung from a nearby metal pole. Tubes snaked from them into one of Randolph's arms. On the other arm, a black blood pressure cuff strapped around his bicep began inflating, while an electronic box recorded the reading. Nearby, an LED monitor displayed three screens with lines that looked like a six-year-old's sketch of the Rocky Mountains. The difference was these mountains kept moving. That they were moving, she reasoned, was a good thing.

When she spotted a short, stainless-steel rod protruding from Randolph's head, she swallowed bile from her lurching stomach.

The doctor murmured to a nurse, then peeled off the latex gloves and flung them into a tall trashcan with a red biohazard diagram.

He offered her his hand. "Mrs. McCarter? I'm Doctor Sylvan."

Accepting his hand, she asked, "How's my husband?" Then when she had her hand back, she pointed to Randolph's head. "What's that rod sticking out of his head?"

"I'm afraid your husband suffered a serious head wound, but he's stable. The rod is called a bolt, and that was inserted to keep the swelling down. He's still unconscious. We did a C.A.T. scan, and should have the results any minute now. We'll be able to tell from that if he'll require surgery."

She couldn't find her voice. *Head trauma? Bolt? Surgery?* Her head began to spin. She edged toward a chair hoping to sit before she toppled.

A short, slender man with a dark complexion, thick black eyebrows, and wearing a white lab coat entered the area. He inserted a

CD into a computer. All Rhetta could make out on his nametag was Doctor Hasan something-or-other. She couldn't see the rest of the name.

Doctor Hasan Whomever and Doctor Sylvan huddled together in front of the monitor, which quickly filled with images. They spoke softly, but loudly enough that Rhetta could discern that Hasan spoke with an accent. Doctor Sylvan motioned Rhetta over.

"There is hemorrhaging, here." Sylvan pointed to a dark area on the image. "His brain is swelling from the blow to the head. We need to get him right into surgery to relieve the pressure."

"Does he need brain surgery? Will you be the one operating on him?"

He shook his head. "No, it's actually not brain surgery. We need to install a drain to relieve the pressure on his brain from the trauma. I'm the emergency room physician. Doctor Reed is the neurosurgeon on call this evening. He's on his way."

Rhetta squeezed her eyes shut and sent a quick prayer heavenward. It had been awhile since she had conversed with God. She hoped He wouldn't hold that against her. Doctor Kenneth Reed was the best neurosurgeon in the area, besides being a friend. "Thank you, God," she murmured, hoping He was listening.

Rhetta edged to the side of the gurney, clasped Randolph's limp hand with both of hers, and whispered, "I'm right here, Sweets. You're going to be all right." She prayed she wasn't lying to him. "Kenneth will be operating on you." She brushed his hand with her lips. He moaned, although she wasn't certain he could hear her. His eyes remained closed.

Doctor Sylvan touched her shoulder. "We need to get him right upstairs, Mrs. McCarter. The surgery unit is on the third floor. There's a private family waiting room up there called the Surgical Unit Waiting Room. That's where Doctor Reed will come to get you following the surgery."

She released her husband's hand. It flopped limply to his side. She let the tears stream down her face.

# # #

Rhetta paced the hall outside the waiting room, unable to sit still any longer. It had been over four hours and Kenneth Reed had yet to appear. She couldn't get an update from any of the nurses who'd come to the room to bring news to the other families also waiting there for word on their respective loved ones.

When she first arrived, there had been nearly a couple dozen people there, some reading, others talking together quietly. Gradually, the others all received news borne by the respective surgeons or nurses. The small groups, two to five people at a time, eventually cleared out of the waiting area, leaving her alone. Unable to concentrate on CNN news, she left the waiting room so she could walk off her nervous energy.

At 10:35, a figure in dark blue scrubs stepped off the elevator and crossed the hall to the waiting room. She raced after him.

The short, balding man in wrinkled scrubs and a mask that dangled around his neck turned around to face her. "Mrs. McCarter?"

"Yes, I'm Rhetta McCarter."

"My name is Doctor Helderman. I'm the anesthesiologist," he said, extending his hand. She accepted his handshake.

"Your husband has just been taken to the recovery room. He'll need to stay there for a bit, possibly the rest of the night, before he can be moved to a post-op room."

Before she could answer, the door opened and Kenneth Reed strode through.

She flew to him.

He took both her hands in his. "Randolph took quite a blow to his head. We removed a lot of fluid from his brain, and installed a drain. It doesn't appear that his brain suffered any damage, but we'll keep him sedated for a day, maybe two." Reed found a seat and motioned her to sit. She collapsed into the chair next to him.

Reed said, "Doctor Helderman will monitor his condition." Rhetta nodded and glanced toward the anesthesiologist who stood near the waiting room door, holding an electronic pad.

Kenneth touched her arm and spoke softly. "Rhetta, the highway patrol is investigating his accident. The blood alcohol test indicated that Randolph's blood alcohol level was point one zero."

She blinked. *What had Kenneth just said? Blood alcohol?*

"What do you mean? Are you telling me Randolph was drunk?"

"Very drunk." Kenneth looked solemn. "His blood alcohol level was well over the legal limit."

"That's not possible." Rhetta shook her head vigorously. "I'd been on the phone with him just before the accident, and he sounded just fine." She stood and began pacing. "How can that be? I would've been able to tell by his voice if he'd been drinking that much."

Helderman tucked the iPad under his arm, and slipped noiselessly out of the room.

"The paramedics said that when they got inside Randolph's truck, there was an empty bottle of Jim Beam on the floorboard."

Kenneth's words sent ice spiders scurrying down her spine. She began shaking. She knew positively that her husband couldn't have been drinking before his accident.

Randolph hated Jim Beam.

# CHAPTER 13

T he waiting room walls closed in. Rhetta couldn't breathe. *How is it possible that Randolph was drunk? How could there be a Jim Beam bottle in his truck?* When they last talked, he gave no indication that he'd been drinking. He told her he'd been with Billy Dan and he was concerned about the locations of the substations. He hadn't been at a tavern. He'd gone to Merc's Diner, where no alcohol was served.

Randolph was stone sober; she'd bet her life on it. *Then why is his blood alcohol so high*? She didn't have an answer for her own question.

Kenneth said no more. He tilted his head and waited.

She had to compose herself. *This doesn't make any sense.* She closed her eyes and mentally regrouped. A headache was worming its way across the back of her head to settle behind her eyes. She was sure, now, that this accident was no accident. Someone connected to the schematic was involved.

Finally opening her eyes, she gave Kenneth a long look. Then she took a deep breath and willed herself to remain tearless. "Randolph wasn't drunk."

From the look he gave her, Rhetta supposed he thought she was in denial. Kenneth knew about Randolph's history of excessive drinking. That was just it—that was all in the past. Her husband no longer gave in to binges.

Although he'd stopped bingeing, he hadn't stopped drinking altogether. Even though she suspected he'd tried to hide the fact, she knew Randolph had partaken before coming to her office earlier that day. He definitely wasn't drunk when he got there, and she was confident that he'd had nothing else to drink. Especially, he wouldn't have been drinking Jim Beam. Again, she asked herself how his blood alcohol could have tested so high

"Rhetta," Kenneth began, "I'm going to check on Randolph right now. If he's stable, I'll have someone bring you back so you can see him. He'll be quite groggy, but you can sit with him for awhile."

After Kenneth left, Rhetta sat alone on the two-person sofa, waiting for word that she could see Randolph. She tugged at a loose thread. She walked around the room, replaying the recent events—from Al-Serafi's death in his car in the Diversion Channel, to the schematic, to Randolph's accident. It played like a movie continuously repeating in her head. The more she thought about it, the more she was convinced Randolph's accident was related to his trip to see Billy Dan and especially to the schematic. This accident had to be linked to the schematic. She just couldn't make the connection.

A glance at her watch told her it was just after eleven. She wanted to call Billy Dan and ask him whether they'd stopped for drinks. Rhetta located a phone book on the counter in the waiting room. She quickly found Billy Dan's home number. Fortunately, he was the only Kercheval in the book.

She rummaged through her shoulder bag and located her cell phone. *No signal.* She walked to the window and held it aloft. Barely two bars. She tried calling, but the call failed.

She'd call Billy Dan first thing in the morning and get to the bottom of this.

# # #

At 11:30, a nurse found Rhetta slouched sideways on the sofa, dozing. The ebony skinned woman gently shook her arm. Awaking with a start, Rhetta jumped up.

"It's all right, Mrs. McCarter. Your husband is doing well. He's beginning to come around. He's been asking for you." She waited for Rhetta to gather her purse, along with her senses, then led her back to recovery.

Inside the small area where several patients lay on gurneys, separated by curtains, she found Randolph asleep. Surrounding his gurney was a forest of poles holding bags of liquid sprouting assorted tubes that snaked into his arms and hands. Nearby were several machines that whirred and beeped. Rhetta studied Randolph's bruised face. Thank God, there's no longer a rod sticking out of his head.

Pulling a chair to the side of the bed that had the least machinery, Rhetta sat. She closed her hand gently around Randolph's. His eyes fluttered and his breathing changed. He began to awaken.

"Hi Sweets," she whispered.

"Hi," he whispered, his voice hoarse. He blinked, as though trying to focus.

She smiled. She didn't want him to see her upset. Brushing her lips against his swollen cheek, she asked, "How do you feel?"

"Hurts. . . all over." He spoke slowly, making every syllable count. His eyelids fluttered.

"You had an accident and a head injury, Sweets. You had to have surgery. Do you remember any of that?"

He closed his eyes, and mumbled.

"Don't try to talk. Get some sleep. I'll be here when you wake up." She kissed him again.

His head lolled as he fell back to sleep.

# # #

Shortly before four in the morning, three nurses or orderlies—Rhetta wasn't sure exactly what they were—entered the cubicle and began preparing Randolph to be moved.

"We're taking him to a room in neurosurgery post op," said a tanned man with gelled hair. "You can come along with us while we move him."

She stood aside while they disconnected the electronic machines and efficiently wound up hoses and tubes, preparing Randolph for the trip. She followed the entourage as they wheeled the gurney to the elevator. A male nurse stayed with Randolph, while the other two returned to the recovery area.

"Is Doctor Reed still around?" Rhetta asked, as the elevator glided noiselessly upward.

"He left about midnight," offered the nurse whose badge identified him as Ray Wilkerson, R.N. "Doctor Reed left orders. I'm sure he will be in later this morning."

It took nearly an hour of preparation before Randolph was ensconced in a room on the floor above surgery, and all bags, tubes and machines reconnected. Rhetta had waited in the small waiting area at the end of the hallway. Assorted drawings courtesy of the local high school art department adorned the walls. They served to cheer up the corner with bright colors and images.

After a few minutes, Wilkerson opened the door and motioned Rhetta in. After thanking the medical team, Rhetta dragged a chair alongside the bed. She stared at Randolph's sleeping figure, his battered face; she took in the bags filled with lifesaving fluids, and the numerous machines chugging and whirring, mapping his condition in a language she didn't comprehend.

Clutching his warm, unmoving hand, she laid her face alongside his arm.

# CHAPTER 14

Rhetta jolted awake when Randolph moved. She sat up, confused. The sunlight streaming in through the nearby window bathed the room in a warm golden glow. Then the memories of the previous dreadful night flooded in.

When Randolph began stirring, Rhetta stood, walked a few steps to get the kinks out. She stretched, yawned and twisted her neck to release the knots that had congregated there. The awkward position that she had managed to fall asleep in took its toll on her neck muscles.

"Hi, Babe." His voice was weak. He reached for her.

"Hi, Sweets." Rhetta scrambled to the chair and took his outstretched hand. "Are you thirsty?"

He nodded.

Not finding any water, she pressed the button on the bedside panel to summon help. Within minutes, a nurse's aide materialized at the doorway.

"I'll check his chart to be sure he can have liquids," the young woman in a blue-and-white striped apron said after Rhetta asked for water. The aide left and the heavy room door closed slowly.

"Sorry, Babe," Randolph whispered.

"Hey, I'm just glad you're going to be okay. The Artmobile is probably totaled, but I've still got you." She squeezed his hand.

"Idiot...tried passing on the bridge." Randolph's voice was thick. He spoke slowly. "Damn fool."

Rhetta stared at him. "What idiot?"

"SUV. Dark green. Followed me from town. Sideswiped me." Randolph closed his eyes and for a moment, Rhetta thought he'd fallen asleep. He opened them a slit. "I don't remember...." He didn't finish.

"The highway patrol will want your statement," Rhetta said, her mind reeling. Did she dare ask him now about the Jim Beam bottle?

"Yes." Randolph sagged back against the pillows as the aide returned with a small pitcher.

"Start with this," the girl instructed, handing Rhetta a brown plastic tumbler filled with ice chips. "He can't drink water just yet. Let's give him some ice chips."

After standing beside the bed and feeding Randolph shaved ice, some of which he slurped and some of which dropped onto his chest, Rhetta wiped him off with a towel and fluffed his pillow. When she was satisfied that she'd made him somewhat more comfortable, she sat beside him on the bed.

Deciding that Randolph appeared strong enough to talk about what happened, she took a deep breath, and began. "Why did you have a bottle of Jim Beam in the truck?"

After the ice, Randolph's voice sounded stronger, but he appeared confused. He frowned. "What?" He blinked several times, as though trying to focus.

"Kenneth said that the highway patrol reported finding an empty Jim Beam bottle in your truck." Randolph stared at her. "And that you were drunk." She let out the breath she hadn't realized she was holding.

"I wasn't drinking." He sighed, closing his eyes.

"That's what I told Kenneth, but he said your blood level was point one zero."

"Kenneth?"

"Kenneth Reed, Sweets. He operated on you."

Randolph shook his head slowly. "Wasn't drinking," he repeated.

The door opened, and a new day shift nurse appeared with a tray of medication.

"No solid foods for awhile, Mr. McCarter," announced the matronly nurse bustling about his bed, setting the assortments of meds down on the nearby tray. "You'll have IVs for at least the rest of today." She prepared a syringe of medication and began injecting it through a port in the tube snaking into his arm.

After snapping off the vinyl gloves and tossing them into the biohazard container nearby, the nurse turned to Rhetta. "He'll be out for a while with this medication, Mrs. McCarter. Why don't you slip home and get some rest. He should be more alert this afternoon."

"Yes, I just might do that."

Rhetta kissed the top of Randolph's head. "I love you," she whispered. "I'll see you this afternoon."

"Love you," Randolph mumbled, already succumbing to the powerful painkiller.

# # #

"Woody? It's Rhetta. Randolph was in a bad wreck last night. He's in St. Mark's Hospital. He had surgery to relieve the pressure from a head injury, but he's stable now. I'm just now leaving the hospital. I'll call you later."

After leaving Woody the voice mail, she walked slowly to her car. The interior was already warm and stuffy. She turned on the ignition and laid her head back against the seat, allowing time for the air conditioning to begin cooling. Although it was only 7:30 in the morning, it was already nearly eighty degrees. The temperature was expected to climb into the nineties she learned when she turned on the car radio. According to the announcer, this was the hottest June on record.

She scrolled through her phone for Billy Dan's number. It rang several times until a recording clicked on. "If I'm not answering, I'm fishing. Leave a message."

"This is Rhetta McCarter. Randolph had a bad accident after leaving Marble Hill yesterday, and—"

Before she could continue, Billy Dan picked up.

"Rhetta, what's happened?"

She told him about Randolph's truck going over the Whitewater Bridge. "Billy Dan, did Randolph have anything to drink when you guys were together?"

"Just lots of coffee, is all. We were at Merc's. After showing me that schematic, he left with it. He was headed straight home."

Rhetta felt like an ice truck had just dumped its whole load into her bloodstream. The schematic. She was more convinced now that Randolph's accident had to do with the schematic.

"Thanks, Billy Dan. I don't know what happened, but I do know Randolph wasn't drinking."

The line grew quiet. Rhetta heard an electronic beep that she recognized as the recorder, which had kicked on before Billy Dan picked up.

"I have to go, now, but thanks." She didn't want any more of the conversation recorded.

"Please give the judge my best. I'll come over tomorrow and see him," said Billy Dan.

"Thanks. And, Billy Dan? Please be careful."

Rhetta tossed her phone on to the passenger seat and shifted Cami into first gear. Instead of heading home, she made for the interstate. She arrowed south on the interstate toward Sikeston, to the Missouri Highway Patrol Troop E Service Center. She wanted to know exactly what had been found in the Artmobile.

# CHAPTER 15

Rhetta exited the interstate at Miner on her way into Sikeston. The traffic along East Malone was light. Within thirty minutes of leaving the hospital, she stood in front of the reception cage at Troop E Headquarters. The female duty officer sat enclosed by soundproof panels topped with thick glass.

"I'd like to speak to someone about getting my husband's personal belongings. My husband is Judge Randolph McCarter. He was in an accident last night at the Whitewater Bridge in Cape Girardeau County." Rhetta spoke through a small round opening in the glass panel, addressing the officer seated at the desk. At least Rhetta presumed she was an officer. A drab grey uniform was stretched taut around her middle.

The middle-aged officer, married, if you could believe the wedding band on her left hand, advised her, "Wait over there, please," and pointed her chubby index finger to a row of wood chairs. Rhetta found a seat.

After ten minutes of scanning months-old magazines and the Missouri State Highway Patrol newsletters, a side door opened, and a tall, trim officer with dark hair clipped close to his head strolled her way.

The officer, mid-thirties Rhetta estimated, politely asked her name, introduced himself, then invited her to accompany him to his office. His black-lettered, silver badge bore the inscription, *Sergeant F. Phillips*. She followed Phillips past the cage containing the duty officer. They walked in silence down a narrow hallway and into his cramped office.

Phillips motioned her to take a seat in one of two chairs squeezed in front of his desk. When she sat, her knees thumped the front. She winced.

Phillips squeezed in behind the desk and deposited himself in the chair, then twisted around to face her. "I apologize for the small space, Mrs. McCarter. The state is utilizing every spare inch of this building. I'm told this used to be a closet." He smiled ruefully as he waved around his cramped quarters.

Behind him, plaques, awards, degrees, and various items evidencing many professional accomplishments and service organization participation covered the entire wall space above the chair.

"What can I do for you?" Phillips was all business.

"I'd like to pick up my husband's personal items."

Phillips shuffled through several file folders in an upright metal rack and selected one. He opened it and scanned a list before handing it to her. "Certainly. I'll call the duty officer to bring them up. However, we can't release the liquor bottle. That's evidence."

Deciding not to discuss the Jim Beam bottle, at least for now, she simply nodded. Randolph would have his time in court. Her husband was in no position to investigate the liquor bottle. She'd have to do it for him.

Phillips dialed a number. He requested Randolph's personal items be brought to the office.

"How is the judge doing? I knew Judge McCarter when he was still on the bench." He shook his head, almost sadly, Rhetta thought.

*I don't need your sympathy. Randolph didn't do anything wrong.*

"He had surgery last night and is stable. His prognosis is good." She held her chin up and forced herself to look past the officer. She couldn't meet his gaze. Being tired and stressed was a recipe for tears, and she was determined not to well up.

Further conversation ended with a knock on the office door. Another young male officer entered carrying a large white envelope secured with a string clasp. He placed the envelope on the desk.

Phillips unwound the string and opened the envelope. He scanned his notes before handing it to Rhetta. Along with the envelope, he handed her a lined sheet of paper

"Please sign this receipt that you've received Judge McCarter's personal items."

Rhetta peered inside the envelope. She reached in and fingered the contents—a pair of work gloves, the truck's registration and insurance papers, a notepad, several pens, and a tube of lip balm.

Missing was the manila envelope containing the schematic and the photo Woody had printed of the substation transformer.

Rhetta cleared her throat. "Is this all?"

"Yes, ma'am. As I said, the liquor bottle was confiscated."

"I'm looking for a manila envelope with documents in it."

"There was nothing else in the vehicle, Mrs. McCarter. I checked the contents against the list from the site that the sergeant included in the report." He turned the page so that she could read it.

She scanned the list signed by Sergeant Quentin Meade. His list matched the contents she held in her hands.

Clutching the envelope and shaking inside, she thanked Phillips and left.

The schematic was the key to Randolph's accident. Someone stole it from the car, she was sure of that.

Now she was positive that someone deliberately forced Randolph off the bridge.

# # #

A half hour later, with Cami's aftermarket sunroof open to the bright sunshine and hot summer air, she raced northbound to Cape. Rhetta could almost forget the reason for her trip and bask in the satisfaction she enjoyed whenever she drove fast. A quick glance down to the white envelope wedged near her console pulled her back to reality. She felt a terrible headache coming on, like the kind she got when she ate ice cream too fast. Who had tried to force Randolph off the road?

She swerved into the right lane at the first Cape exit and arrowed straight to the bluffs overlooking the Mississippi and to the county impound lot.

Eddie sauntered out to greet her the minute she rumbled to a stop in front of the office.

"Rhetta, I'm sorry about Randolph's accident. Is he going to be okay?" She didn't ask Eddie how he knew about the wreck. Obviously, he would've been the one to get the truck and haul it in.

"He had surgery last night. The doctors say he's going to be fine." She scoped out the lot. "Where's his truck? It's here, isn't it?"

"Yeah, it's here. I got called out early this morning to pick it up. Are you sure you want to see it?" He removed his ball cap and wiped his brow with his shirtsleeve before returning the cap to his head.

"I have to see it." Rhetta turned off the ignition and scrambled out of the car.

"Follow me." Eddie made for the back of the lot.

She trotted to keep up. When they stopped at the trailer holding the crushed remains of Randolph's beloved Artmobile, the twisted wreckage spoke for itself. The truck was totaled.

She took a deep breath and walked around the trailer. Unlike the last time she poked around a vehicle in this same lot, this time she didn't try to open any doors. She just stood staring at the driver's side front fender at a long gash that continued to the driver's door. Al-Serafi's car bore one just like it.

"Eddie, do you see this?" She called him over.

"Looks like the truck grazed something." He rubbed his palm along the damage. When he removed his hand, dark green paint particles stuck to his fingers.

"Don't let anyone take this truck, Eddie," Rhetta said, gazing around the lot. "Please cordon this off with tape, and don't let anyone even touch it."

"Okay, but you know the insurance adjuster will need to see it. What's going on?" Eddie also panned the lot.

"Do you remember Hakim Al-Serafi's car? I'm pretty sure it had the same kind of gash." She pointed to the Artmobile's fender. "I found it odd when I saw it on Al-Serafi's car, because there was no damage to his car when he was in our office a few weeks ago. I wouldn't have thought much about it until now I see a similar one on the Artmobile." Rhetta gripped Eddie's arm. "You know how Randolph is about his truck. There wasn't a mark on it before the accident."

Gazing around, she continued, "Is Al-Serafi's car still here?" She wanted to see that car again, compare the scratches, and make sure she wasn't imagining any of this.

"It's already gone. They came and picked it up yesterday and towed it away." Eddie removed a handkerchief from his pocket and wiped his brow.

"Who, our insurance company?"

"I guess. The guy who showed up had all the forms signed by Mrs. Al-Serafi. Art let them take the car." Art was a university student in his early twenties who helped Eddie occasionally. "There was no reason to keep it here. The insurance companies do that all the time on cars that are totaled."

"Do insurance companies usually come get the vehicles so quickly?" Rhetta fixed her gaze on the now empty flatbed trailer that had held Al-Serafi's car.

"Sometimes." Eddie shrugged. "We never thought anything about it. Should we have?"

Not wanting to say more, since she herself wasn't sure what she thought, she said, "No. I guess I'm just upset."

After thanking him, Rhetta headed for her car while Eddie returned to his office. She rested against Cami's front fender and sighed. Then she opened the door and slid into the still-cool interior. She reached across to the console, and after a quick search, pulled out a single latex glove along with her secret stash—a pack of cigarettes and a lighter. Stepping out of her car, she tugged on a latex glove, then lit the cigarette. Holding it between her gloved thumb and forefinger, she took two long, satisfying drags. She inhaled deeply, allowing the smoke to fill her lungs. Her head got light from the nicotine rush. She stepped on the cigarette and ground it out with her heel, then kicked dirt over the half-smoked butt, folded the glove, and buried her stash under a notebook, a novel, and some pens.

She hated deceiving Randolph. At times like this when she was under so much stress, she had to have a nicotine fix even though she promised her husband she'd stopped smoking a long time ago. She wasn't proud of herself for fibbing. Okay, lying. Wearing a latex glove prevented anyone, especially Randolph, from smelling the traces of smoke on her hands. Nobody knew of her secret smoking. Not even Woody.

She turned the key and while the motor rumbled, Rhetta tried to piece together everything that happened. She wasn't imagining. She clearly remembered what the gash on Al-Serafi's car looked like: it was identical to the one on the Artmobile.

Al-Serafi's and Randolph's accidents were definitely connected.

# CHAPTER 16

As Rhetta pulled into the parking lot in front of her office, the front door flew open, and Woody rushed out to meet her. His cartoon-character tie flapped in the breeze he created.

"What are you doing here?" Woody reached the car as she opened the door. "Shouldn't you be at the hospital with the judge? I can take care of things here." He held the door for her. Her arms were full with the cleaning supplies she bought three days ago, which she hadn't unloaded. Woody wound up toting the plastic sacks with pine scented cleaner, while she carted in the bags containing paper products.

"I know you can. I'm not here to work. I want to run something past you, but I need coffee first." She disappeared into the kitchen and put away the supplies.

Rhetta filled a ceramic mug from the large pot that was always on. The smell of fresh coffee always made her yearn for a cup. She was the first to admit she was shamelessly addicted.

Rhetta took her cup to the conference table. Woody poured a cup for himself, grabbed a handful of sugar packets, and followed her to the table.

"Randolph's been hurt badly. But he's going to be okay." Rhetta stared at her coffee.

Woody opened the first of the packets and emptied it into his cup. He followed that by dumping in the rest of the packets and stirred the mixture vigorously. "Take as much time off as you need. Even though LuEllen won't be back for a while, I can take care of the office."

"I need your help, Woody."

"Sure, I told you, I can take care of things here." He raised the coffee mug to his lips.

"Not the office. I know you're fine here." Rhetta stirred her coffee then took a sip. It was still piping hot, requiring her to blow across the surface of the liquid. "I need to bounce something off you."

She explained about the empty Jim Beam bottle and the pending DUI charges against Randolph, the missing manila envelope, and, most significantly, the scratches on the truck.

"Sounds to me like someone ran Randolph off the road and you think that's what happened to Al-Serafi." Woody tore open more sugar packets, and dumped them into his coffee. He stirred, the metal spoon clanking against the side of the cup. Normally, the noise irked her. Now, it didn't seem important.

Rhetta set her cup down. "That they both got run off the road is significant. This isn't a happenstance."

Woody cleared his throat. "I hate to bring this up. I heard on the news that the judge's blood level tested high."

Rhetta's stomach knotted. *Great. Now it's all over the news.* "Randolph probably had a drink or two at home before he came here yesterday, but I know he didn't have anything else to drink after noon." She shook her head for emphasis and ran her hands through her hair.

She stood, changing the subject. She didn't enjoy being the object of gossip. Woody, God love him, loved gossip. "I'm going to take that original schematic that we found and lock it in my safe deposit box at the main bank. I don't want to leave it here."

"*We* found?" Woody peered at her over his coffee cup. "Right," he said, setting his cup down a little too hard. Coffee sloshed over the side.

"Okay, okay, me. I took it. Whatever. Don't be making a federal case out of this." She snatched her purse and began rummaging through it. "Wait, maybe we should make a federal case out of this."

"Are you calling the FBI again?" Woody sighed as he mopped up the spill with a paper towel.

"Not yet. I need to ask Doctor Reed something."

Snatching her phone, which she'd set on the table, she scrolled until she found his cell number.

Reed answered before the second ring.

"Kenneth, it's Rhetta. Randolph was sleeping so I left for a bit. I'll be back later this afternoon."

"What can I do for you?" he answered, his words clipped, his voice terse. *I probably interrupted him in the middle of something important.*

She forged ahead, prevailing upon their friendship. "I need your help. Everyone is convinced that Randolph was drinking. I believed Randolph when he told me he wasn't." She went on to explain about the Jim Beam bottle. "Billy Dan Kercheval backs him up, too. Randolph had just left Marble Hill after he and Billy Dan met up at Merc's. They drank nothing but coffee."

She waited. When Kenneth didn't say anything, she persisted. "How could Randolph's blood test that high? Could the test have been skewed?"

When Kenneth didn't answer for several more seconds, Rhetta thought he must be thinking about how that could have happened, too.

She heard him sigh.

"Rhetta, a skewed test is not possible. You don't want to believe that Randolph was drunk. I'll do what I can to heal him, but talk like this will cause you nothing but trouble. I have to go now."

The line disconnected.

She stared at the receiver. His response wasn't what she expected.

*What's wrong with Kenneth?*

# CHAPTER 17

"Kenneth doesn't believe me." Rhetta set her phone down, and slid the coffee cup aside. Kenneth's tone had killed all desire for coffee.

Woody drained the last of his, then took both their cups to the kitchen. On his return, he detoured toward the office safe and withdrew the original schematic he placed there for safekeeping.

He handed it to Rhetta. "I'll go with you. Let's take a lunch break."

With that, he began penning a "Be Back Soon" note and taped it to the front door. Then he held the door open for her.

### 

After locking the schematic away in her bank safe deposit box, Rhetta drove Woody back to the office.

"I'm going to the hospital," she said, letting him out in front. On the way, they'd swung through the drive-through at Subway. She wasn't hungry. Earlier that morning, she'd persuaded the cantankerous vending machine on the fourth floor at the hospital to discharge a Snickers bar after feeding it double the amount the candy cost, and kicking it a time or two.

Woody, however, claimed to be on starvation's doorstep. He clutched his sack containing two, foot-long Italian sandwiches and a gallon of sweet tea, and climbed out. Stopping midway, he turned back. "Have you heard from Doctor LaRose?"

Rhetta rested her head on the steering wheel. "I didn't think to call him."

"I'll try and reach him. You should go check on your husband."

"Thanks. Don't scare Peter, yet somehow warn him not to talk to anyone about the schematic."

### 

She made it to St. Mark's in ten minutes. After locking Cami and remembering to drop her phone into her purse, she strode to the visitors' entrance—a set of two perpetually revolving glass doors under a brick archway containing a statue of St. Mark the Evangelist. As she stepped inside one of the doors, her iPhone began playing Woody's ring tone. She continued revolving all the way around until she was back outside.

"I can't get Doctor LaRose to answer," Woody said. "I called his office and his cell."

"Keep trying. I'm going up to check on Randolph. I'll call you in a little while. I have to turn off my cell phone while in his room. Hospital regulations."

She re-entered the revolving doors, glancing up in time to see Kenneth Reed talking on his cell, and striding across the lobby toward the exit to the doctors' private parking spaces. He hadn't seen her. She checked her watch: 1:15. She continued watching Kenneth through the all glass doors until he stopped before a parked car and pointed his remote. He climbed into a black BMW-Z4 convertible. Without lowering the top, he sped out of the lot, still talking on his cell.

*Nice ride.*

### 

The door to Randolph's room stood open a few inches. Rhetta pushed it open a foot wider and peeked in. Although it was midday, all the window blinds were tightly closed, shutting out any daylight and leaving the room in near total darkness. Randolph lay on his side, asleep. She tiptoed in, scribbled a note, and propped it on his bedside tray. *You were sleeping-be back later. XXXOOO 1:20 PM.* She pulled the door back to the same position she found it.

While riding the elevator down, she wondered if Woody reached Peter yet. When the elevator stopped, she rushed out, strode across the lobby and back through the revolving doors to the sidewalk outside.

Once there, she powered up her phone and dialed Woody.

"Never did reach Doctor LaRose," Woody said by way of hello, obviously recognizing Rhetta's cell number.

When she got off the phone, she checked her watch—plenty of time to drive to Peter's apartment.

# CHAPTER 18

Rhetta groaned in dismay as she inched her way along an overly crowded Main Street. She forgot about the three-day Rivers West Music Festival due to start later that evening. She found herself smack in the midst of music lovers scouring the streets for curbside parking near the venues. Every bar, eatery, and gallery was prepped for the occasion with most hosting a singer or a band. Every kind of music would be represented, from gospel to rock 'n' roll, and everything in between. There would be individual contests for bluegrass, gospel, rock, and jazz. All events were touted on brightly colored posters that papered every post or pole in the entire downtown.

After circling the six-block area twice, Rhetta eased Cami into a parking space in front of a bistro three blocks from Peter's apartment. She ignored the finger salutations and horn honking from a pair of festival fans who had unsuccessfully jockeyed their Dodge Neon on their first attempt into that same space. She stole the space when they pulled ahead to reposition. She didn't have time to apologize. Besides, she wasn't the least bit sorry.

The humid air crackled with strains of music seeping from every building on the street. Food and beverage vendors lined their carts up along the sidewalk. The mingling smells of cotton candy, corn dogs, and fried shaved potatoes assaulted her nostrils. Walking three blocks, Rhetta elbowed her way through the crowds and finally located Peter's building, only to discover that the stairs to his apartment were in the rear. All the walking had caused her to perspire heavily. Her hair was plastered to her skull. Instead of hoofing it another crowded block to get around to the back, she squeezed into the narrow alley between

Peter's building, which housed a cannabis collectors store on the ground floor and the boutique floral shop next to it. The distance between the two old buildings was scarcely wide enough for her to pass. The stench of stale urine grew stronger the farther she ventured. She carefully eyed where she placed her feet, mindful of what she could be stepping in.

She made a mental note to visit the cannabis store someday. *What could they possibly sell there? Isn't marijuana illegal?*

Arriving at the rear of the building, she eventually spotted the steep wooden staircase leading up to Peter's apartment. Rhetta peered skyward, took a deep breath, and began the climb. The hundred-year-old building still had the original steps, and the spacing between the narrow treads was uncomfortably steep. She was reminded of the time she and Randolph tried to climb the narrow steps to the top of the Pyramid of the Sun, near Mexico City.

At the top, she stepped onto the wooden porch and paused to catch her breath. She gazed around at the many back lots. She identified the building's parking lot with Peter's Taurus parked against the back fence. The car had been hidden from view until she'd reached the porch. If she had chosen to walk around the block instead of squeezing between the buildings, she'd have passed right by the parking lot and seen Peter's car. She prayed Peter was at home and hadn't left to join the revelers.

Near his front door, an old-fashioned white rattan rocker and glass top side table sat crowded together on the porch, which scarcely measured six feet square. Above the table, a hanging basket planter spilled brightly colored trailing petunias. Several magazines lay spread out on the table. Sighing with relief, she rang the doorbell.

No answer. She tried again. Still no one responded to her insistent ringing. Rhetta thought she spied a table lamp glowing inside the apartment when she peered through the glass panel on the side of the door. Using her knuckles, she rapped loudly on the white wooden door. No one appeared. Shielding her eyes with both hands, she squinted again through the window. She knocked even harder and was about to give up, thinking that perhaps Peter had walked downtown, when she impulsively tried the door. It opened readily. She pushed it open all the way, stuck her head in, and called out, "Peter, are you home?"

In spite of the sweltering heat of the day, Rhetta shivered. She didn't like surprising people in their own homes. She stepped slowly across the threshold, continuing to shout Peter's name. She was assaulted by the reek of rotting meat. *Not much of a housekeeper, our Peter.*

"Hello? Peter, are you here?" She took in the modestly furnished apartment and the hundreds of books stacked everywhere— on the floor, the coffee table and on a kitchen table in a narrow alcove off to the side. The cramped living room held a green plaid sofa, two TV tables, and a plasma television screen that covered the entire wall opposite the sofa. Every available space on every table also held a stack of books. She picked her way through the cluttered living room toward the hall. The stench increased.

All the window blinds were closed. It took a moment for her eyes to adjust to the dim interior. She called out again. "Peter? It's Rhetta McCarter."

Passing alongside the sofa, she noticed an open book lying face down on the arm. Twisting to get a better look, she identified the volume—an English-Arabic, Arabic-English dictionary.

The temperature in the apartment had to be nearly a hundred. *Why hasn't Peter turned on the air?* Her initial shivering gave way to fat sweat droplets dripping off her nose. She swatted them away. She heard a low buzzing noise, but the louder hum of a noisy refrigerator drowned it out. If the refrigerator was still running, then the rotting meat smell couldn't be coming from the kitchen. She threaded her way down a short hallway crowded with stacks of books. The sickening odor intensified the closer she got to a door that she suspected led into a bedroom. She buried her nose in the crook of her elbow in an effort to avoid the stink.

Again she called out, "Peter." Her voice cracked. Fear clutched her senses, commanding her to turn around and run. Instead, she took a deep breath and gagged at the foul odor that engulfed her when she pushed open the door. She was immediately beset by swarms of bottle green flies, their buzzing deafening.

She found Peter.

He wouldn't need air conditioning.

# CHAPTER 19

Rhetta's stomach revolted at the sight of the bloated body lying face down on the floor alongside the bed, nearly hidden under a cloud of flies. She was thankful she couldn't see his face. She assumed it was Peter, given the body's slender build along with what she could see of grayish, sandy colored hair.

She gagged, swallowed, and gagged again. Unable to stop her body's reflex from the overpowering stench, she bolted from the room. She barely made it into the hallway before throwing up the remnants of whatever she ate last. Stupidly, she identified it as a Snickers bar. And coffee.

Breathing rapidly, her head drenched with sweat, it took a few minutes before she finally stopped heaving. She made her way down the hall, and back to the door. Outside, she finally inhaled, clearing the stench. Judging from his appearance along with the terrible decay odor that invaded her nostrils, poor Peter had not just died. She was unable to tell what caused his death.

She glanced around as she groped in her bag for her phone. Was someone watching Peter's apartment? Her stomach began to clench again. Peter was dead. Oh, God. She felt her hand tremble as she dialed.

"9-1-1, what is your emergency?" asked a crisp female voice.

Rhetta sucked a breath in. She didn't know where to start.

"9-1-1, please state your emergency," the dispatcher ordered, more sharply this time.

"I...I.... My name is Rhetta McCarter," she began, stammering, trying desperately to remember the protocol for reporting finding a body. Then she remembered she never learned any protocol for reporting a dead body. She blurted, "I just found a dead man."

A momentary beat, then the dispatcher asked, "Are you sure he's dead? Do you need an ambulance?"

She nodded, even though the emergency dispatcher couldn't see her. "It's Doctor Peter LaRose. He's a professor at the university, and I'm sure he's quite dead." Rhetta finally gained some control of her wits.

"Address?"

*Address? I know where to tell her to come. I don't know the address!*

"Sorry, I'm not sure of the exact street number. It's the apartment above the cannabis store on Main Street," Rhetta said, and paced on the small porch. She didn't want to be so visible in case anyone was watching, but she wasn't about to go back into the apartment. She sat down on one of Peter's chairs. "The entrance is up the stairs in back. I'll wait outside for the officers."

Rhetta lowered her head between her knees and gagged again.

# # #

It took an Age of Aquarius to come and go before she heard sirens. Wasn't that one of her oldies songs? She felt like she'd been catapulted into a nightmare. How did Peter die? Was it because of the schematic? Bad things were piling up faster and faster, eliminating coincidences. Did those things indicate there was a plot to kill everyone who'd seen the schematic? She tried to convince herself it made no sense. She didn't succeed. Something most definitely was going on. But, what?

She needed to call Woody and tell him. He could be in danger, too. However, she knew she had to tell Randolph about Peter in person. Peter was his friend. Her call to Woody went to voice mail. "Woody, it's Rhetta. Peter is...." Before she could continue, her cell beeped and a "call failed" message flashed across the screen. She stared at the screen as tears filled her eyes. Her hand shook. What was going on? Who killed Peter? She choked back a sob as she heard distant sirens.

The rising and falling wailing intensified as the vehicles neared the building. In a whirl of dusty red and blue lights, two Cape police cars skidded to a stop next to Peter's Taurus in the gravel parking lot.

The sirens powered down. Two officers from each car, with weapons drawn, rushed toward the stairs.

An orange and white county ambulance, with lights swirling, materialized next to the police cars.

Radios clipped to blue uniformed shoulders crackled as the officers clambered up the stairs. Rhetta stood and fished for her wallet and driver's license, knowing she would have to offer some identification. She handed the license holder to a young officer whose pink sweating scalp glistened through a blond crew cut, and whose badge identified read *R. Germuth.*

Germuth asked her to remove her license from the plastic holder in her wallet. When she did, he took it from her, stepped away, tipped his head sideways, and spoke to his shoulder. She heard him read off her name and license number.

Two uniformed officers rushed past her into the apartment without introducing themselves. She hadn't caught any names on their badges.

A fourth officer, Sergeant Abel Risko, according to the stenciled name badge above his left breast, removed a small spiral notebook from a shirt pocket and began interviewing her. Risko was a burly man with a gravel pit voice. She guessed him to be in his early thirties. Clearly, he was the man in charge.

The two ambulance drivers wearing khakis and white uniform shirts, who had followed the officers inside, returned quickly, advised Germuth to call the coroner, and then left.

*I told the dispatcher he was dead.* Calling the ambulance had to be protocol for the 9-1-1 operator. She nodded absently.

"You knew the deceased?" Sergeant Risko asked.

*He must have thought my nodding meant I know Peter.* She focused on Risko.

"Yes, I knew Doctor LaRose." She coughed in an attempt to clear her throat, hoping she could discharge the vile odor, which by now she could taste. She plunged her hand into her purse and came out with a single piece of gum. Quickly she unwrapped it and popped it into her mouth, grateful for the burst of spearmint.

"What were you doing here?" he asked.

She hadn't thought about how to answer any questions. "I, uh, wanted to see if he was still in town," she said.

"Why didn't you call him?" The officer's pen stayed poised over the notebook, ready to jot down her answer.

"I did call, but didn't get any answer." She inhaled again, the nausea threatening a return.

"Why did you need to know if he was staying in town? Why was it so important that you had to come over here in person to find out?"

She had no idea how to answer. Shaking her head both from confusion and a desire to rid her nostrils of the stench, she said, "I wanted to tell him about my husband being in a car accident." *Why hadn't she said that first?*

"Why do you say 'still in town?' Was he planning a trip?"

*He's interrogating me as if he's the Gestapo.* "No, I don't know about any trip. It's just that when school is out, Peter has been known to travel, sometimes to Saudi Arabia." *Why did I say that? I'm so nervous I'm letting my mouth overload my ass.*

Doing her best to get her nerves under control, Rhetta continued. "He and my husband, Judge Randolph McCarter, are good friends, and I wanted to tell him about Randolph's accident."

Upon hearing that, the officer snapped the notebook closed. His tone softened. "How is your husband doing, Mrs. McCarter?"

Rhetta noticed an improvement in Risko's demeanor when he found out she was Judge McCarter's wife. Did that mean he felt better about her finding Peter's body?

"I have your statement," Risko continued, patting his shirt pocket. "You're free to leave. However, I'd like you to come by the station sometime Monday to review and sign your official statement."

"Of course." She licked her dry lips. Bile rose in her throat again and she swallowed it back. The spearmint flavor from the gum was already gone.

Officer Germuth handed Rhetta her license, which she dropped into her purse. She'd return it to her wallet later. She had to get away from Peter's apartment as soon as possible. The coroner's van had arrived. She had no desire to see the body bag being carried away.

Sliding her purse up her shoulder, Rhetta grasped the handrail, and hurried down the steps as fast as she dared. She had no desire to break her neck.

She had to call Woody. Peter's sudden death had to be connected to the schematic. *After Al-Serafi's death in the Diversion*

*Channel, we find out that Agent Cooper is dead. Then Randolph has a near fatal accident, and now Peter's dead. Someone believes that we know something that we shouldn't. It has to be linked to that schematic.*

Woody could be next, and Randolph had met with Billy Dan. They could all be in jeopardy.

She had to call and warn them.

After jogging back to her car, she beeped open the door, and slid behind the wheel, grateful that Randolph had surprised her on her birthday with a keyless entry/remote start device for Cami. Cars didn't come with keyless entry back in the Middle Car Ages. She was certain that the feature began showing up only in the 80s. She seldom started Cami remotely, but it was great to be able to unlock the car without standing at the door, groping for her keys.

She turned the AC up to its highest setting. She rested her forehead on the hard metal steering wheel and briefly closed her eyes. *Peter is dead. He saw that schematic, and now he's dead.*

She reached up to adjust the mirror before backing up. A pair of dull green eyes in her own ashen face stared back at her.

In spite of the heat, another chill rolled down her spine.

*I saw the schematic, too.*

# CHAPTER 20

It took forty-five minutes for Rhetta to escape from the craziness of the festival. People walked along the streets oblivious to the throngs of cars trying to crawl through the traffic. Most of the pedestrians carried large white plastic cups bearing the festival's logo. She suspected the cups contained fermented beverages.

Once she managed to turn north on Kingshighway, the traffic improved. However, she still managed to catch every red light between downtown and her office.

Woody was on the phone taking an application when she pushed open the door, and a young couple was on the sofa waiting to meet with him. That meant she couldn't tell him about Peter just yet.

He implored her with his eyes and by jutting his chin toward the couple. She tucked her purse into her bottom desk drawer, took a deep breath, and approached the customers on the sofa. She hoped that the smell of death hadn't permeated her clothes. She could still taste the vile smell in her nostrils.

### #

Fifteen minutes later, she'd taken their application and pulled their credit. Finally, Woody finished up and came to her desk. After introductions, Woody guided them to his desk to continue the process.

Folding her arms across her desk, Rhetta lay her head on her arms and closed her eyes. When she looked up a few minutes later,

Woody was eyeing her and furrowing his brow. She snatched a note pad and scribbled, *Got lots to tell you*. She walked to his desk, handed him the folded note, and went on to the kitchen. She glanced back at him in time to see him open it, read and nod.

Rhetta reached into the refrigerator, snatched a cold bottle of water, twisted off the top, and downed the entire contents in two swallows.

Gulping ice-cold water brought a wave of protest from her already irritated stomach. She dashed to the bathroom. After losing the water she just gulped, she bent over the sink and splashed cool water on her face.

Dabbing her face with a damp paper towel helped compose her. Rhetta returned to the kitchen where she plucked another bottle of water from the refrigerator. This time she sipped slowly. The water stayed down. She carried the bottle back to her desk.

She stared blankly at the manila folders standing neatly in her upright file holder. With everything that had happened, she hadn't had time to come into the office and work on any of her customers' files. Although she wasn't sure that she could concentrate on them now, she reached for the closest folder. She owed it to her customers to make sure their applications were going smoothly.

Opening it, she blinked, confused. A printed sheet of notes was stapled to the inside cover. Woody had gone through the file and updated it.

She reached for another and found similar notes. One by one, each of the files contained Woody's precise notes. He had taken care of all her customers.

She sat back in her chair and closed her eyes.

### # #

When she got home, the sun was still shining low on the horizon the way it does late in a summer day. That was a trick of Daylight Savings Time to fool people into believing it's still mid-afternoon, even though evening had sneaked in. Rhetta thought a better name for the spring and summer extended daylight hours would be Daylight Wasting Time, since it always served to lull the unaware into believing there was more of the day left than there actually was.

Rhetta showered, and then donned an old pair of denim jeans and a faded T-shirt. Wandering into the kitchen, she opened the refrigerator, searching for something to nibble on before heading back to the hospital, even though she wasn't hungry.

She'd brushed her teeth forcefully and rinsed her mouth with a strong mouthwash in an attempt to rid herself of the tastes of bile and death.

Earlier, after Woody had finished with his customers, she finally had a chance to tell him about Peter. He collapsed in the chair near her desk, his head beginning to glisten.

"What on earth is going on?" Withdrawing a handkerchief from his pocket, he wiped his head. "I can't believe there's a terrorist plot. That can't be happening here."

Rhetta massaged her temples in an effort to get rid of the headache bubbling at each side of her head "Hakim Al-Serafi is dead. Agent Cooper is dead. Peter is dead. Then Randolph has an accident that's a whole lot like Al-Serafi's. What do *you* think is happening?"

Woody stood and began pacing. "This just can't be a terrorist plot. I've changed my mind. It's either your imagination or it's all coincidence, or both." He left her desk and charged for the door.

Rhetta was too stunned by Woody's abrupt departure to stop him. She sighed, locked the office, and went home.

The cats had assembled on the deck, and Rhetta could hear their pathetic song of starvation. She fed them, gathered her purse, phone, and keys, then headed to the garage.

In spite of Woody's denial, Rhetta was convinced that a plot of some sort, one involving the schematic wasn't merely possible, but had already begun to manifest itself.

# CHAPTER 21

After backing out of the garage into fading sunlight, Rhetta stole a glance at her watch. Although not limited to certain visiting hours because Randolph had a private room, she'd wanted to get to the hospital early enough to visit with him before his nighttime meds. It was already almost eight o'clock. She wanted to be there for him in case he got thirsty or needed help, since the nursing staff was always busy. She knew Randolph hated being a demanding patient. Discovering Peter's body had definitely messed up her schedule.

Taking Cami up to 45 mph down the gravel road was chancy. Large rocks were deadly to the low-slung Camaro. She drove as fast as she dared, and prayed she wouldn't throw any rocks into the oil pan. She urgently needed to talk to Randolph. If he felt up to it, she had to ask him about what he and Billy Dan had discussed.

The county road crew had come through earlier that day and graded the gravel roads; the washboard ruts were gone. The realization that the county had worked on the road made Rhetta slow down. More than once following the county's road ministrations she'd managed to get a sharp rock in her tire that resulted in a flat. Changing Cami's tire in waning daylight wasn't high on her list of fun things to do. In fact, she didn't find changing a flat at anytime particularly enjoyable. She could, however, do it competently if she needed to.

Her mother, Renate Caldwell, an independent, strong woman, not unlike herself, had taught Rhetta how to jack up her car and change a flat a long time ago. The recurring loneliness tugged at her now, like it always did when she thought about her mother. Many people who knew her mother said that Rhetta favored her. Rhetta loved hearing that, although her deep green eyes were unlike her mother's cerulean orbs. Her eyes were her father's legacy, she assumed.

When an aneurysm resulting from cancer claimed her mother nearly ten years ago, Rhetta got mad at God and stopped going to the church that she and her mother had regularly attended. If her father, who had abandoned them right before Rhetta's second birthday, had heard of Renate's death, he didn't bother showing up for the funeral. Rhetta prayed all right—prayed that she'd never run into him and prayed he was dead.

She forced her melancholy back to its dark place and concentrated on her driving.

She made it safely to the highway and opened Cami up.

Flashing blue lights filled her rear-view mirror. A glance at her speedometer revealed the needle nosing past 65, ten miles over the posted limit. Slowing down did not stop the flashing lights. The police car, now right behind her, blasted once on the siren. Understanding exactly what that meant, she coasted to the shoulder and stopped.

The highway patrol officer exited his car and donned his flat brimmed Mountie-style hat. With flashlight in hand, he approached her driver's door. Rhetta powered down the window.

"Good evening, ma'am." The officer, a sergeant, touched his hat. "You were driving a little fast when I met you. I clocked you at 68."

*Crap.*

He shone the flashlight beam around inside the car.

Before Rhetta could answer, he said, "May I please see your operator's license and car's registration?"

While waiting for her to rummage through the glove compartment and then to fish through the black hole of her purse for her wallet, the officer scanned around the outside of her car, then back inside.

She was proud of how beautiful Cami was. She and Randolph found the car four years ago and had gutted the stock interior and redone it in navy blue with white upholstery. The two-tone blue-on-silver blue exterior glimmered. Maybe the officer was admiring the car.

Rhetta removed her license from its case for the second time that day. She handed it, together with the registration, out the window to the officer. Her heart skipped when she read the name on his badge: Sergeant Q. Meade. *The officer who responded to Randolph's accident.*

With her license and registration in hand, Sergeant Meade turned to walk to his patrol car. She knew the normal procedure would be to run her car's plate numbers along with her license number, then write up the citation. After just a few steps, Meade, who had begun to examine the license in the narrow flashlight beam, stopped, then returned to Rhetta.

"Mrs. McCarter?" Meade asked, needing to bend his tall frame at the waist to talk through the window.

"Yes?"

Meade handed the license and registration back to her without an accompanying ticket. "How is your husband?"

Rhetta exhaled. "He had surgery for a head injury. The doctors tell me he will recover completely." *Thank you, God.* She dropped the license and registration into her open purse. "You were the officer who responded to his accident?"

Meade nodded. "Yes, ma'am."

She peered at his rugged tanned face. Even in the dim light, she spotted faint lines at the corners of his eyes. Meade had to be at least forty. "The report says you found an empty Jim Beam bottle, so you must have searched the interior. Did you find a manila envelope?"

"No, ma'am."

A quick scan of his expression told Rhetta he was telling the truth. *Where did the darn thing go? Could she ask him if anyone else was standing around the accident scene?*

"Thank you for your help at the accident, Sergeant." He touched the brim of his hat, and turned away. Rhetta called after him. "Excuse me, Sergeant, can I ask you something else? Were there any witnesses who saw the crash?"

"No one came forward claiming they saw exactly what happened. A family from Marble Hill heading to Cape glimpsed the taillights down in the creek bed when they crossed the bridge. Luckily, the wife made her husband pull over. That's when they spotted a truck nose-down at the bottom of the creek."

Hearing Meade say "nose-down" resonated with Rhetta.

*That's exactly how Al-Serafi's car was found.*

Meade continued. "They flagged an oncoming car to call 9-1-1, since their cell didn't work on the bridge. They stayed and waited until I showed up." He switched off the flashlight, and tucked it into the keeper on his belt. "Nobody was around the truck, because getting to it required climbing down a steep embankment. The emergency team thought they might have to airlift your husband, but they managed to haul him up the embankment on a stretcher."

Rhetta forced herself to smile. "I appreciate your help and everyone else's too. Thank God someone spotted him so quickly." She shuddered at what might have happened had the family not stopped.

*Randolph could've died.*

# CHAPTER 22

In her side mirror, Rhetta watched Meade return to his patrol car. When he opened his door, she turned on her left blinker and eased back out onto the highway. She managed to hold Cami to the speed limit the rest of the way to the hospital.

A glance at the dash clock told her that she had left home nearly an hour ago. She lucked into a parking spot close to the door and ran to the building.

Once through the hospital's revolving doors, she surveyed the main floor in search of a faster route to the fourth floor post-op area. A stainless steel door marked STAIRS and AUTHORIZED PERSONNEL ONLY appeared to the right of the main door. Without hesitation, she strode to the door and pushed it open. She didn't know exactly where the stairs led, but providing they went up four floors, she calculated that she should come out very close to Randolph's room. Avoiding the labyrinth that was the medical complex in order to reach the elevator was worth any effort of the stairs. Climbing them didn't bother her. She was used to running every morning. Inhaling, she grabbed the handrail and began.

Through the glass on the second floor doors, she recognized the rear of the emergency room triage area. The revolving doors she used to enter the hospital were on a level lower than the main floor level where the ambulances pulled in. The hospital complex had so many additions that it had become a maze of specialty wings connected by a warren of hallways and stairs.

Reaching the fourth floor, Rhetta paused to fish a tissue out of her purse to dab the sheen off her forehead. The stairwell, she noted, didn't enjoy the frigid air conditioning of the rest of the hospital. With shoulders back, she pushed through the door with an air of importance, as though she was 'authorized' to be using those stairs. She needn't have bothered. No one was around to notice. She quickly got her bearings and was pleased to find herself one door away from Randolph's room. She fist pumped. *Outstanding shortcut!*

Randolph's room was quiet—lights low, machines humming softly. As she began tiptoeing past his bed, a piercing alarm shrilled, causing her heart nearly to explode. Afraid that she'd set a machine off by tripping over a cord, Rhetta searched frantically to identify which one of the several machines clustered around Randolph was screaming.

Seconds later, a nurse threw open the door and immediately switched on the lights, flooding the room from the powerful overhead fixtures. The entire time the woman scanned the machinery, adjusting and checking knobs and dials, Rhetta noticed that Randolph didn't stir. The piercing wail should have awakened not just him, but all the other patients on the floor, and a few souls from the nearby cemetery. Rhetta felt helpless. Her pulse raced in fear. All she could do was step back and let the nurse take charge.

Finally, after interminable shrilling, the machine fell silent. Randolph lay motionless. Hand flying to her chest, Rhetta whispered, "Is he all right? What's happening?"

"Mr. McCarter is not responding, ma'am. I've paged the doctor."

Rhetta's head pounded. She willed herself to remain calm. "Not responding? What does that mean?" Randolph lay very still, his breathing shallow.

"We'll have to wait for the doctor." After checking the computer and making notations on a chart hanging on the foot of his bed, the nurse frowned. Her hands found the wireless mouse, which she slid back and forth to bring the monitor to life. With fingers flying over the keyboard, the nurse quickly located a computer file. Then the nurse read the screen, which Rhetta couldn't see. She next reached for the chart and compared the chart to the screen.

A slender blond man wearing a lab coat over navy dress slacks and a stethoscope dangling from his lab coat collar, hurried through the door. From his awkward gait, Rhetta guessed the man had a wounded leg or a handicap. His ID badge read Henri Marinthe, M.D. He barely nodded to Rhetta before checking Randolph's vital signs.

"I am Doctor Marinthe," he said to her, after examining Randolph. "When did you first notice your husband was unresponsive?" His soft voice had a lilting, musical quality.

"I had just come into his room when the alarm, or whatever, began going off," she said, gripping the rail alongside Randolph. "Just a few minutes ago."

Marinthe nodded. "I will have blood work done and follow that with an MRI to see what is going on in his head. As you can see, he is unresponsive. He appears to be in a coma. I shouldn't think there could be brain swelling now, but we must not overlook that possibility."

Rhetta collapsed into the chair. Propping her elbow on the arm, she pressed her forehead into her palm. "What does this mean, Doctor? What's going on?" Unable to stop a tear, she slapped it away with the back of her hand. "He was doing so well when I was last here. What could've happened?"

Marinthe turned toward her. "This isn't good. We'll scan him immediately. Then we will know what we are dealing with." The nurse had unplugged the machines, which continued running on the battery back-up units as evidenced by periodic beeping.

A lab tech holding a tray of dozens of rubber-stoppered tubes used her elbows to push the door open enough so that she could enter. She deftly snapped a rubber tube around Randolph's arm, swabbed the inside of his arm with a cotton ball she removed from a jar, and inserted a needle into the bend of his arm. Three vials quickly filled with his crimson blood. She finished labeling and hurried to the door. "I'll be running these the moment I get to the lab, Doctor," she called. Her blue lab coat billowed behind her as she sailed out of the room.

Doctor Marinthe approached Rhetta's chair. She peered up at soft blue eyes that radiated caring and kindness. He patted her shoulder. "I will be here all night, and I will monitor your husband personally," he said.

She nodded, registering for the first time that his English, while flawless, had a soft accent. She wondered where he was from.

"I will contact Doctor...." He leafed through the file. "I see here Doctor Reed is his surgeon."

Rhetta nodded.

An orderly with shoulder-length dreadlocks hustled through the door, announced he was from radiology, then pushed Randolph's bed out into the hall. "Please wait here, ma'am," he called over his shoulder, wheeling Randolph expertly toward the elevator.

"Will you still be on duty when my husband returns from having the MRI?" Rhetta asked as Doctor Marinthe's fingers flew across the keyboard.

"Yes, certainly. I have a call in to Doctor Reed, too." He slid the keyboard drawer back into place. He rose slowly, avoiding any weight directly on his left leg. She noticed then that his left leg appeared to be shorter than the right.

"Where are you from?' Rhetta asked, finally succumbing to her curiosity. "I can't place your accent."

"I am from Libreville, which is in Gabon, a country on the shore of Western Africa. Have you heard of it?" He turned to smile at her.

"I'm not very familiar with Gabon, but I have friends who live in France who spent a dozen years there," Rhetta answered, remembering her college roommate and her husband who moved to Gabon to work for Shell Oil.

Marinthe nodded. "My parents were from Antibes in the South of France and emigrated to Gabon also to work in the oil business. They moved there because it was one of the few French-speaking oil producing countries. At that time, it was also a Muslim community that welcomed French Muslims." *Of course, his accent is French.*

Marinthe glanced up when he heard the speaker page him to the nursing station. "I will be back whenever your husband returns from the testing, Mrs. McCarter." He turned off the computer and limped to the door.

The room fell deadly quiet—no machines whirring, no activity, no Randolph.

# CHAPTER 23

The slap of magazines hitting the floor startled Rhetta awake. If she believed the round clock with a large white face and oversized black numbers, Randolph had been gone nearly an hour. After the lab had taken him for testing, she found a current *Newsweek* and had tucked herself into the recliner alongside his bed. Before she read three pages, fatigue cascaded over her and she fell into a deep sleep.

*Randolph should've been back by now.* Irritated at herself for dozing, she snatched her purse, intending to walk to the nurses' station and find out about her husband. Her purse was partially open, and her phone slid to the floor. She stooped to retrieve it, realizing that she forgot to power it off. Although she hadn't heard it ring, her screen indicated she'd missed two phone calls and had two voice mails.

The first message was from Mrs. Koblyk, their Hungarian-born neighbor.

"Ah, Miss Rhetta? This is Anna Koblyk, your neighbor? I'll go to your house and check on your cats? I heard Mr. Randolph was in the hospital?" Her voice rose at the end of each statement, like she was asking a question. "I will take some cat food over while you stay with him so you don't have to come back to your house? Please do not worry about them? Mr. Koblyk has been watching over your house, too, ever since that green car went up your lane today? I am at home if you need me? Goodbye." Her accent was more noticeable on the phone in spite of her obvious effort to speak slowly and clearly. Although Mrs. Koblyk had lived in America for over fifty years, she retained a good bit of her Eastern European accent.

With everything that had been going on, Rhetta had forgotten about her cats. *The poor things. Thank God for Mrs. Koblyk.*

Then she realized what the woman had said. *Green car? What green car?*

The next message was from Woody. "I, uh, sorry about today, Rhetta. Call me and let me know how Randolph is." That was as close as Woody would get to apologizing for storming out in a huff. She smiled humorlessly. *I suppose now he doesn't think all of this is part of any plot. Purely random occurrences. Right.*

*Maybe Woody's right. Maybe I should forget about everything except getting Randolph better.* Her heart lurched. Where was Randolph? She quickened her pace toward the nursing station.

At the sight of a frowning, tall woman with wild grey hair marching purposefully toward her, Rhetta dropped her phone into her purse. She knew she should've turned the thing off, but she didn't and wouldn't. Rhetta didn't give the nurse the opportunity to begin scolding her about the phone. "Excuse me," Rhetta said, stepping into her path and intercepting the woman. "I'm waiting for my husband, Randolph McCarter. He still isn't back from getting an MRI."

Before the nurse could answer, a soft ping signaled the elevator's arrival. The doors slid open and a tall man wheeled a bed toward the hallway. Rhetta recognized the dreads and rushed alongside the rolling bed.

"What did you find?" Rhetta asked, while fixing her eyes on a still unconscious Randolph.

"The doctor will have to go over everything with you, ma'am," the attendant said, his tone sympathetic. "I believe Doctor Marinthe is on his way."

Once inside the room, the MRI technician wheeled Randolph's bed back into place. The scowling nurse appeared and with the technician's help, they began reattaching all the devices. Her scowl melted away as Doctor Marinthe rapped lightly on the door and entered. Rhetta smiled at the nurse, but received none in return. She reminded Rhetta of mean Nurse Ratched in *One Flew Over the Cuckoo's Nest.*

Withdrawing a small flashlight, Doctor Marinthe sat on the bed, facing Randolph, and bent over him. Using his thumb, he gently raised Randolph's eyelids. He continued his probing and examining in silence. The blood pressure monitor that had been re-attached to

Randolph's arm inflated noisily. When it had released the pressure and deflated, Marinthe studied its results, then logged onto the computer. When he finished typing, he turned toward Rhetta.

"Mrs. McCarter, we have good news, but also, maybe some not-so-good news. There is no further brain swelling. In fact, the swelling is much reduced. That is the good news. The not-so-good news is that we must wait for the lab results to confirm why your husband is not responding." He checked his watch and added, "I expect the results any moment."

Puzzled, Rhetta said, "Confirm what? Why do you think he's not responding?"

Marinthe's beeper sounded before he could answer. After scanning the message, he turned to the computer, pulled out the keyboard and typed quickly. He studied the screen several moments before speaking.

"I just got a text to check the results. There is a high concentration of barbiturates in your husband's blood." He turned to face Rhetta. "I don't see anything in his chart indicating that such drugs were prescribed for him." Marinthe stood, and began moving quickly, pulling a blanket up from the foot of the bed and wrapping Randolph in it. Then he summoned a nurse and returned to the computer screen. His fingers flew over the keyboard.

"What?" Rhetta stood, bewildered.

"I am going to give him an infusion of naloxone to counteract the effects of the barbiturates, along with putting him on oxygen." Marinthe withdrew nasal tubing from a drawer, and began attaching it deftly to the oxygen port above Randolph's head.

Nurse Ratched appeared with a syringe and injected its contents into a heparin port on Randolph's hand.

Marinthe motioned toward a chair. "Please sit, Mrs. McCarter. You might want to stay here with your husband tonight. He was in a deep sleep, probably a coma, and it will help if you are here to talk to him when he awakens."

"Tell me what's going on. What the hell just happened?" Rhetta knew her tone sounded short, but fear made her go on the offensive.

Marinthe pulled up a chair alongside her. "When the MRI was normal and the blood work revealed the high level of barbiturates, I realized that your husband may have been given an anesthesia medication like we use for surgery, but in a larger dose. The naloxone should help to get rid of the effects. The oxygen will help to remove the medication from his blood."

"Who gave that to him? Will he be all right?" From what Marinthe just told her, she realized someone must have intentionally put Randolph to sleep, maybe even tried to kill him. Was it someone here, in the hospital, someone on staff? Who? Why? The questions bounced around inside her head. Could this, too, have something to do with that damned schematic?

Doctor Marinthe rose carefully, putting his weight on his good leg, measuring his balance before continuing. "Fortunately, Mrs. McCarter, you were in his room when the alarms began going off. Those alarms indicate a drastic change in blood pressure. A drop in blood pressure can occur as a result of the barbiturates." He limped to the computer and paused briefly before turning around. "I don't believe the drug had been in his system long."

His blue eyes fixed on her. "There is no record in his chart of any such medication being ordered, especially in his condition."

After a beat, he said softly, "It could have killed him."

# CHAPTER 24

R hetta's mind reeled and her head began pounding. She could barely absorb what had just happened. She felt sickened, like she had descended into a nightmare of hell.

Doctor Marinthe started toward the door, but instead, turned and made his way back to her. "I will get to the bottom of this," he said, putting a hand on her shoulder. "I will report this. I think someone made a mistake in the medication. I will initiate an investigation."

Rhetta nodded mutely, unable to find her voice. Her gaze followed Marinthe as he walked slowly toward the door, opened it, and then vanished. She stared at the closed door a moment before fixing her eyes on Randolph. He lay still but was breathing regularly. His pale face was partially hidden by the cocoon of blanket around him. Who did this to Randolph? Should she call the FBI? Peter is dead, the FBI agent is dead, and she was sure someone had tried to kill Randolph— twice. Was it someone who worked in the hospital, and was Randolph in even more jeopardy?

Her stomach burned as she agonized over Randolph, not wanting to leave. Glancing at the door to be sure Nurse Ratched wasn't on her way back, Rhetta pulled out her phone, then called Kenneth Reed. Her hands felt clammy. Fear did that to her.

Her call went straight to Kenneth's voice mail. She didn't leave a message; she was paranoid that the wrong person might get the message intended for Kenneth. Instead, she asked him to call her back. She slid the phone back into her bag.

She pulled her chair to Randolph's bedside and grasped his hand. Randolph moaned lightly, and his eyes began to flutter.

"Hi Sweets, can you hear me?" she whispered. Her heart raced and the ball of bile grew larger.

He moaned again, but didn't awaken.

# # #

An hour later, she was still staring intently at Randolph's sleeping form. Her mind churned over everything that had occurred since Al-Serafi had been killed, her trip to the impound lot, and the start of her world turning on its butt. She replayed everything like a movie looping continuously through her head. Everything was there, like pieces of a puzzle. The most important piece was missing—the key. The reason.

If only she hadn't gone to the impound lot to see Al-Serafi's car for herself. What exactly was she thinking? That Al-Serafi was a terrorist? Her curiosity was the real reason she went. Moreover, she'd dragged Woody along to participate in her nosiness. Al-Serafi had cashed out a large amount of money from refinancing, true, but that didn't make him a terrorist. The phone call on Woody's phone? Maybe Woody was right, although he agreed with her initially, that it was suspicious, now, she decided that maybe she overreacted.

Another knot punched her in her stomach. *What about Peter LaRose? He's dead. He saw the schematic. And what about Randolph? When he began asking questions, he had a suspicious car wreck. Now, someone here, at the hospital, for God's sake, gave him an overdose!*

Gently, she placed her husband's hand on the bed. She stood and began pacing. If pacing helped Woody think, maybe it'd help her to think, too, to work out this crazy puzzle.

Al-Serafi's wrecked car bore a gash identical to the one on Randolph's truck. Didn't Randolph say a green SUV had tried to pass him? After all her mental meanderings, she arrived at the same conclusion—that since she had discovered the schematic, Peter was dead, and anyone who had any contact with the schematic was in peril.

She slipped into the private bathroom and pulled out her phone. Glancing at her watch and discovering it was nearing midnight, she hoped Woody was still awake. He'd told her many times he was a night owl.

The instant he answered, she knew he hadn't been asleep.

"Rhetta, what's wrong?" Woody's voice boomed through the phone.

"You won't believe what's happened." She told him what Randolph had just been through.

"You can't leave the judge alone. Let me come up there, so you can get home and shower, change clothes, take a nap. You need to sleep. But don't you think you ought to call the police?"

"Woody, the police aren't going to investigate something here at the hospital until we know what's happened. Dr. Marinthe is all over this. I trust him. I'll wait until he finds out who's behind this.

"Ok, then. I'm on my way," Woody said.

She returned to the chair.

# # #

"I'm sorry but visiting hours ended at nine. Only family is allowed in now." From the tone of the shrill voice, Rhetta knew the woman speaking wasn't a bit sorry. Two sets of footsteps trekked down the hall toward the room.

Hearing a commotion just outside the room, Rhetta opened the door to find Nurse Ratched attempting to block Woody from entering the room. Ratched squeezed ahead of Woody and placed both arms on the doorway, as though guarding the entrance to King Tut's tomb. Woody glared at her and stepped around her. "I'm family," he said, lying with a straight face. He pushed past her and went on in. Woody's demeanor must have intimidated Ratched. She didn't follow him into the room.

Instead, the woman whirled around and left for parts unknown. *The witch probably returned to her lair.*

Stopping abruptly at Randolph's bed, Woody stared at the array of machinery. He whistled softly. "Sure are a lot of machines." He found the guest chair and lowered himself into it. Rhetta stayed fixed at Randolph's bedside. She merely nodded.

Woody cleared his throat. "I'm sorry about walking out on you earlier. I, uh, I just couldn't wrap my head around a…a terrorist plot." He peered at Randolph. He cleared his throat again and whispered, "How's he doing?"

"He's fine for now, but still hasn't awakened from the overdose," Rhetta said. She began massaging the outside of Randolph's arm.

Still massaging, Rhetta turned to Woody. "Thanks for coming here. Someone's trying to hurt Randolph. It has to be connected to the schematic."

Woody held up a palm to stop her. "Wait, you know his blood alcohol level was high, and—"

Rhetta interrupted him, whispering loudly. "Randolph wasn't drunk, Woody, and I intend to prove it." She laid Randolph's arm gently on the bed, then edged to the window, where she gazed down at the bright lights of downtown Cape. The world below hummed along just as though nothing was out of the ordinary, and no one was trying to kill her husband. And, like there was no terrorist plot. She began doubting herself again. Was she right? She knew whatever was going on had to involve the schematic, but how? Had she stumbled upon a plot by finding the schematic? If so, what was it? She massaged her temples, trying to ease the headache worming around inside her brain.

Peter's death was not her imagination. That sobering reality jolted her back on track.

Rhetta said, "He should sleep for a couple more hours. I'll run home and shower and change, and be back." She left her spot at the window to retrieve her purse, which was hanging on Woody's chair. "Call me right away if he wakes up?"

"Of course," Woody said, scooting aside to release the purse strap he'd sat on.

"Thanks," she said, touching Woody's shoulder. He nodded.

Leaving the room, she didn't see Ratched or anyone else so she ducked into the AUTHORIZED PERSONNEL ONLY stairwell. She trudged down the stairs to the next floor. Before pushing the doors, she peered through the window to see if the coast was clear.

The triage area was alive with medical personnel attending to a gurney wheeled in from the ambulance and backed up to the open emergency room doorway. A young man lay unconscious on it, his head and arms bloody. She heard someone call, "Accident victim, possible DUI. We'll have to draw blood for a B.A.C."

She recognized her friend Doctor David Islip, the emergency room physician who was attending the patient. A phlebotomist materialized with her kit of tubes and dabbed the victim's inside arm with iodine. The technician inserted a vacuum syringe and began withdrawing blood. When finished, the technician gently lay the man's arm down on the gurney. The patient's chest rose and fell erratically. He murmured incoherently.

Rhetta stared at the injured man's arm, at the orange stain marking the location where the blood had been withdrawn.

She shut the door and sprinted up the stairs.

Bursting into Randolph's room, she startled Woody, who leapt up, nearly knocking the chair over.

She snatched Randolph's covering back and gaped at his left inner arm. Then she rounded the bed and peered at his other arm.

Both of his arms were clean.

# CHAPTER 25

"Woody, look at his arms. They're clean, no orange stain," Rhetta said.

"So?" Woody looked confused. His gaze swiveled from Rhetta to Randolph's arms.

"See, here?" She pointed to Randolph's inner elbow. "There's no iodine stain. Whoever pulled his blood for the blood alcohol test didn't use iodine." She pushed the call button.

"What are you doing?" Woody sat back in the chair, and rubbed his head with his handkerchief.

"Calling Doctor Marinthe. I need to ask him about this."

Ratched appeared, lips pursed and raising an eyebrow at Rhetta. *How can she scowl and raise an eyebrow? That must take practice.* Rhetta didn't wait for the nurse to speak. "I need to see Doctor Marinthe, right away." The woman's scowl morphed into a façade of concern as she padded up alongside Randolph's bed. Her manner had also changed to one of efficiency. She checked his pulse, then scanned the machinery. When she finished, she looked up, seeming puzzled. "What seems to be the problem, Mrs. McCarter?"

Woody answered for Rhetta, staring down at Ratched from his full height. "My sister, here, needs to speak to the doctor right now. Please get him."

Ratched merely nodded and hurried out. Woody must have had authority in his voice, for within minutes they heard a page for Doctor Marinthe.

When Marinthe arrived moments later, Rhetta tugged him to her husband's bedside. The doctor wore a look first of surprise, then one of concern.

Presenting her husband's arm for his assessment, Rhetta asked, "Do you notice anything?" She lifted her husband's arm and pointed.

Marinthe appeared puzzled, glancing from the arm to Rhetta. "What is it? Is he all right?"

"He's the same, Doctor. What I want you to see is that my husband's arms are clean." She heard her voice rise and fought to keep it under control. "He hasn't had a shower, or anything, yet."

"Yes, I see that." Marinthe frowned. "I'm sorry, I'm not following you. What is the significance to you that his arms are clean?"

Rhetta lay Randolph's arm down, and tucked the sheet around him. "I just saw a lab tech draw blood on an accident victim downstairs. She used iodine to swab the area before she pulled blood for a blood alcohol test. That's when it hit me that Randolph's arms didn't have any orange iodine stain from where blood was pulled from him." She stared at Marinthe and continued. "If alcohol was used instead of iodine to disinfect the skin before pulling blood, couldn't some of the alcohol be transferred into the sample?" Her right temple pounded, and she reached up to massage it.

Marinthe answered, "That's possible, of course. The protocol is to swab with iodine when testing for B.A.C." He picked up Randolph's arm and rubbed the inside. He did the same to the other.

"There has been no iodine on his arms," he said, and turned to Rhetta.

"Let's do another B.A.C. right now," she said.

Marinthe glanced at his watch, then at the chart at the foot of Randolph's bed, which had the patient's name, room, and bed number and the time he was admitted.

"It's been too long. The test will not reveal anything now," Marinthe said. "It's been over twenty-four hours. If there was any alcohol in his blood when he came in, it would now be gone from his system."

Marinthe glanced from Rhetta to Woody, who spoke first. "So there's no way of double checking the test?"

"We have to go with what they have?" Rhetta asked. She sat and lowered her throbbing head to her chest and used both hands to massage her temples.

"Judge McCarter is screwed," Woody said, and began to pace.

"No, Woody, he's not." Rhetta set her jaw. She willed her headache to dissolve.

Turning to Marinthe, she said, "To quote two American icons, Lenny Kravitz and Yogi Berra, 'It ain't over 'til it's over.' And, Doctor Marinthe? I assure you, it ain't over."

# CHAPTER 26

To an exhausted Rhetta, the dark county road leading to their property stretched endlessly. Eventually, she spotted her driveway. Before continuing down to the house, she stopped at the big country mailbox and withdrew a bundle of mail. She tossed it onto the passenger seat. Then she drove slowly up their long gravel drive. Ahead, her home glowed warmly from landscape lights surrounding the walks and driveway. The sight normally filled her with pleasure. Tonight, however, the lighting filled her with overwhelming sadness as she thought about Randolph lying in the hospital, and the possibility of never having him home again.

*No, that's not going to happen. He's not going to die. I won't let him!*

Rhetta glanced up into the cloudless night sky filled with a million points of starlight. *I'm so tired. I'm going to lay my head down for a few hours.* Looking into the vast Milky Way had always brought issues into perspective for her during many other low points in her life. Like when her mother had died and she'd wept uncontrollably. She'd been an only child and had no one to turn to for comfort. A wave of hate for her father began to roll over her, but she stopped it short. She whispered to God, hoping she'd gotten back into His good graces. "God, if you can hear me, let Randolph be okay. Let this nightmare stop."

Rhetta intended staying home just long enough to shower, change clothes and grab a sandwich before heading back to the hospital. She parked Cami near the front door, instead of using the garage.

Once inside the house, she never made it to the shower. She collapsed, fully dressed, across the sofa and fell instantly asleep.

### # # #

Figures and shapes hovered around Rhetta. She stared down at the body on the floor. It wasn't Peter LaRose lying there in the hot downtown apartment. She began to recognize the face. It was Randolph.

The hospital was complicit in the charade. It wasn't Randolph, but Peter, who lay in the hospital bed struggling for his life. Why did the charts say McCarter? If Randolph was dead, shouldn't she be making funeral arrangements?

*Why is a phone ringing? Where is the phone?*

She groped around until she located her cell phone under a couch cushion. Staring at it with sleep-blind eyes, she couldn't understand why it kept ringing. She pounded the answer bar.

Finally, the fog lifted from her brain and, like mist in the morning sun, the bad dream began to dissolve. The insistent ringing was coming from the front doorbell, not the cell phone she cradled stupidly.

She struggled to her feet, shaking her head to chase away the last of the nightmare. The schoolhouse clock on the fireplace mantel glowed 6:28.

When she peered through the window, Rhetta barely recognized Mrs. Koblyk. The neighbor's normally smiling face wore an expression as abject as a bird dog that had lost its quarry.

"Hello Missus, how is the good judge today?" the woman asked by way of greeting after Rhetta sighed and opened the front door. Rhetta shielded her eyes with her hand against the bright morning sun.

Mrs. Koblyk jutted her chin towards Cami. "I see the pretty blue car, which means you must be here, so I come to see what I can be doing for you." She peered around Rhetta into the still dark house. Rhetta hadn't opened the blinds.

"Thanks, Mrs. Koblyk, I appreciate your taking care of the cats. Everything is fine now."

*What a lie. Nothing's fine.* Rhetta finger combed her messy hair. *I must look a sight.*

Looking almost disappointed, Mrs. Koblyk turned to leave. "All right, Missus. But if you need my help, I can come again today to feed the poor things."

Rhetta smiled. "I'll feed them this morning, and they should be fine until I get back later." She began to close the door, yearning for a hot shower and even hotter coffee.

"I ask the man in the green car, or truck you know, a big car like a truck, if he is family, and how is the judge. But he didn't answer me, only turned around in your driveway and sped away, sending up the gravel, too." She clicked her tongue in disapproval.

Rhetta thought she'd missed part of the conversation.

"What man? Was it an SUV?" She opened the door wider and stepped out onto the porch, peering around.

"Yes, that's it, as you say, SUV. The same car, two times, I see it. The second time, he doesn't go all the way to your house."

The Koblyks' tidy bungalow nestled in a copse of cedar trees along the county road, directly across from the McCarter driveway.

"We don't know anyone in a green SUV. Please, Mrs. Koblyk, you shouldn't be talking to anyone you don't know." Instantly, Rhetta regretted telling her that. The woman was easily alarmed.

Mrs. Koblyk's pudgy hand flew to her mouth. "Oh, my. I will be telling that to Mr. Koblyk. We call the police if they are coming back?"

Rhetta paused a beat before answering. She didn't want to frighten the woman, but then, there shouldn't have been anyone on their property, either. "Yes, Mrs. Koblyk, you should call the sheriff's office. Whatever you do, please stay away from that car and whoever may be in it."

Mrs. Koblyk's neat grey curls bounced in rhythm with her bobbing head. "Yes, I will do that, Missus. Oh, my." She wrung her hands. "Oh, my," she repeated.

Rhetta took both of her neighbor's hands in her own. "Mrs. Koblyk, you must call the sheriff if they come back, all right? Those people have no business on our property." Rhetta tried to sound calm in spite of the sudden surge of fear that had invaded her stomach.

The woman nodded and turned to shuffle down the steps to her own car that she'd parked behind Cami. She waved briefly before climbing inside, backing up, and then inching forward around Rhetta's car. She completed a turn around the circle drive in front of the house, before heading down the long driveway to the county road.

Once Mrs. Koblyk left, Rhetta made a pot of coffee, and headed for the deck to feed the cats. When she called to them, she was greeted by a symphony of plaintive yowling. "Who are you trying to impress? I know Mrs. Koblyk fed you while I've been gone. You aren't starving." The three felines milled around her feet and legs, purring and meowing their innocence. "All right, you win. I'll get some breakfast for you."

The feeding done, Rhetta darted through the kitchen and began peeling off her clothes on her way to the bedroom, leaving a trail of discarded items behind her. She managed to be fully naked by the time she reached the master bath. She turned the shower on full blast and stepped in. Steam from the shower rose around her, and hot water sluiced down her face. Rhetta worried who could have been in the strange car. Her heart began thudding. She twisted the water knob off and grabbed a towel. Green SUV. Mental head slap! She should've asked Mrs. Koblyk if the strange SUV was damaged in any way around the front or the fenders. She visualized the traces of green paint on the Artmobile and Al-Serafi's car. She leapt out of the shower, snugged a towel around her and snatched her phone off the sink. She dialed the St. Louis number for the FBI.

"Federal Bureau of Investigation."

"I need to speak with—"

She was interrupted by the automated voice that continued, "If you know your party's extension, you may dial it now. For a directory, please dial 2, for assistance, please dial 3."

She punched the number 3.

When a male voice answered, she immediately reported the SUV being on her property.

Before she could explain its significance, the man interrupted her. "I'm sorry, ma'am, but if someone has trespassed on your property, that would be a matter for the local authorities. I suggest you call the police or sheriff's department in the county where you live. Have a nice day." He hung up.

"Damn," she said. She scurried across the bedroom, snatched the phone book from her nightstand, and dialed the sheriff's department.

She was met with the same indifference.

"Do you have a license plate number for this SUV?" the female dispatcher asked.

"No, we were unable to get that," Rhetta said. "My husband was recently run off the road by a green SUV."

"I'm very sorry, ma'am, but there isn't anything we can do for you. If you can get the license number, you may report it again."

Damn again. The police were no help. Her heart pounded against her ribcage. She remembered the trip back from Eddie's impound yard the day she found the schematic. Someone nearly ran them off the road.

She was sure, now, that the same someone had come to pay her a visit.

# CHAPTER 27

S he spotted her iPhone dancing across the edge of the sink to a tinny rendition of the *William Tell Overture*. She put down her toothbrush and grabbed it.

Woody. She'd changed his ring tone to the Lone Ranger theme because Woody liked to refer to himself as the Loan Arranger. She thought it was cute. Woody preferred *Who Let the Dogs Out,* but she wasn't persuaded to change it.

"Hey, what's up?" she said, doing her best to sound cheerful, while chewing her fingernails in worry.

"Good morning to you, too," Woody said, his tone light.

*This is a good sign. If Randolph had taken a bad turn, Woody wouldn't sound so cheerful.*

"Someone wants to talk to you."

Before she could answer, she heard a raspy voice that she immediately recognized.

"Hi," was all he said. She didn't have to ask who it was. Relief flooded her and she sank into the chair near the bed. The towel slid to the floor.

"Hi, Sweets, how are you? It's so good to hear you."

"I'm…I'm okay," he said, his voice ragged.

"I'm getting ready to come to see you." She glanced down then, and pulled up the towel. "I'd better get dressed first. I just got out of the shower and I'm still naked."

"I love it when you talk dirty," he said and coughed.

She laughed. It felt good to laugh. "I'll be right there."

"Come as you are," he said and began to chuckle. He coughed again.

"Okay, my dirty old man, I'm on my way."

"He's awake, hungry, and giving me grief." Woody was back on the line. "I'll stay until you get here."

"Thanks. I'll be there soon." She flung aside the towel, and disappeared into the walk-in closet. She came out wearing a pair of soft faded jeans, a pale green tee, and white tennis shoes.

# # #

Since her stomach was rumbling, Rhetta veered through McDonald's drive-thru and ordered a bacon-egg-and-cheese biscuit and a large coffee. She balanced the coffee between her thighs since Cami didn't have a cup holder, praying fervently she wouldn't have to stop suddenly and wear the coffee. Evidently, no one ever drove while eating or drinking back in the 70s.

The pleasure and excitement from speaking to Randolph soon waned as Rhetta remembered the barbiturates and the blood alcohol test. She was more determined than ever not to leave Randolph alone while he remained in the hospital. What she couldn't figure out was what Randolph was caught up in. It became clear that someone wanted to make sure Randolph didn't go home. Was it connected to the schematic? She lost her appetite. She tossed the still wrapped breakfast biscuit aside.

# # #

Pulling into a nearly empty hospital parking lot, Rhetta concluded that Saturday morning mustn't be a busy time for visitors. She easily snagged a good spot close to the door. Balancing the coffee, her purse, and her keys, she started to push the driver door closed when she caught sight of the breakfast bag lying on the seat. She ducked back inside to retrieve it for Woody. Woody could eat anytime.

While she stretched to reach the sack, the heavy car door continued closing and caught her squarely on her butt. The coffee exploded out of her hand and spewed onto every surface inside the car, all over the white upholstery, front and rear, white door panels, the inside of the windshield and the top of the dash. Cursing under her breath, she groped for the box of tissues she kept in the back seat and began to mop up the mess.

*Why does coffee expand exponentially when spilled? There must be a mathematical equation for that. How else could sixteen ounces of coffee cover the entire interior of a car?* She glanced up then and saw light brown spots on the white headliner.

She sighed, put her purse on the concrete floor of the parking structure, along with the coffee cup that amazingly still had about a third of the liquid left, and dug in the console for the baby wipes.

When the interior was sufficiently clean so that Rhetta felt there would be no permanent stains, she wadded up the fistful of used wipes and toted them to a nearby trashcan.

She'd have to live with the baby powder smell for a while. She wrinkled her nose.

She  never had any children, nor had she ever baby-sat much when she was a teenager, therefore had never acquired a fondness for the baby powder fragrance. She'd looked for unscented wipes the day she picked those up at the supermarket, but baby wipes was all she could find.

Back at her car, she slid her purse onto her shoulder and retrieved the Styrofoam cup. She downed the last of the coffee and headed for the hospital door. She tossed the coffee cup into the trashcan along with the coffee stained wipes.

Once inside the main door she turned right and ducked through the now familiar AUTHORIZED PERSONNEL ONLY doors.

And came face to face with Doctor Kenneth Reed.

# CHAPTER 28

"Rhetta, what are you doing here?" Kenneth Reed said, frowning.

"I'm on my way up to see Randolph. Do you have a minute to talk to me about him?" She figured that the "here" he was referring to was her AUTHORIZED PERSONNEL ONLY violation, not the fact that she was in the hospital. She let it go.

He consulted his watch, a Rolex, Rhetta noticed as he bared his wrist.

"Yes, I, uh, wanted to get with you too. I don't have Randolph's chart with me. I'll come upstairs and meet you in his room."

"You don't need a chart to remember that Randolph was drugged, do you?" Rhetta never hesitated speaking her mind. She didn't understand Kenneth's attitude. He was supposed to be their friend. He studied her briefly before answering. She wasn't sure of his expression, but she hoped he clearly understood hers.

"I haven't had the opportunity yet to read all of the notations in Randolph's chart, but I understand that there was an issue with some barbiturates."

"Issue my butt!" she exploded. "Someone dosed him with barbiturates, he could've died, and you call it an 'issue?' For God's sake, Kenneth, Randolph is your friend." Rhetta groped into her purse for a tissue. She hated it when she got so mad that her eyes teared up. She wasn't going to cry, and she wasn't about to let Kenneth think for a moment that she was. She blew her nose instead.

For just a second, he looked properly chastised, but he recovered quickly. "Of course Randolph is my friend, as are you,

Rhetta." He rested a fine-boned hand on her shoulder. "I don't think we need to jump to unwarranted conclusions."

She shrugged his hand away, her temper rising. "Then act like his friend, Kenneth," she snarled at him. She fought the urge to pop him, just for the hell of it, for his cold, supercilious attitude.

"I know how upset you've been since the accident. Please trust me. I will check into all of this myself." He put both hands on her shoulders and bent his slender frame to stare into her eyes. "Please believe me, Rhetta. We all want to get to the bottom of this."

Rhetta closed her eyes and sucked a deep calming breath. She couldn't find her quiet place. Measured breathing would have to do instead. "Yes, of course you do, Kenneth," she said, exhaling.

"Go up to his room and I'll be there shortly." Kenneth consulted his watch again.

"Nice watch," Rhetta said, eyeballing his timepiece, then angling for the stairs. She trotted up the next three floors. Kenneth never did chide her for using the private stairs.

# # #

Rhetta pushed open the door and found Randolph sitting up in bed, but still connected to several machines. His color had vastly improved, and his eyes, although still swollen, were open and alert.

He slowly turned toward her and smiled. Woody used the distraction to snatch the remote and change the channel. "I can't take any more Court TV." Woody scowled. "You'd think he would've had enough court in his life." Woody found *The Food Channel*.

"Hi, Sweets." Rhetta folded her arms carefully around his neck and gently kissed his bruised face. Woody mumbled.

She tilted her head toward Woody. "What did you say?"

"Nothing." He grinned.

Handing Woody the bag containing her breakfast sandwich, Rhetta said, "Thought you might want this."

"What happened to the bag?" Woody held up the coffee-stained sack.

"Don't ask." She tugged a chair alongside Randolph's bed and tucked one of his hands into hers.

"Just one?" Woody feigned disappointment after upending the bag. Instead of more food, only napkins floated out.

She sighed. "All right, I'll confess. I didn't think of you at all. I bought that for myself. I lost my appetite and didn't eat it. If you don't want it, give it over. I can eat it now." She reached toward him, waggling her fingers, palm up.

"No deal, sister." He unwrapped the sandwich and stuffed it between his grey whiskers. "Umm," he said after he swallowed. "Thanks."

Randolph, who had begun chuckling at the banter between Woody and Rhetta, coughed. Rhetta handed him a tumbler of water, which he slurped noisily, and without a straw, she noted.

Randolph handed her back the plastic glass, and asked Woody, who was snarfing up the last morsel, "Are you still hungry?"

Woody dabbed his beard with one of the napkins that had dropped from the bag. "Those other two breakfast sandwiches were at least thirty minutes ago."

Before Rhetta could retort, Kenneth strode into the room.

With his arms thrust into the pockets of his starched white lab coat, Kenneth stopped alongside Randolph's bed. He withdrew one hand and patted Randolph's arm. "How're you doing? Do you feel like eating?" Without waiting for Randolph's answer, Kenneth turned on the bedside computer and began typing. When he finished, he glanced back at Randolph.

Woody strolled to the window and stood gazing out. From his stance, Rhetta knew he only pretended not to be listening.

Randolph pointed toward the hanging bags of liquid dripping medicine and nutrition steadily into his arm. "That sure doesn't taste like steak."

Rhetta could tell from the return of his sense of humor that Randolph was feeling better.

"I don't know about steak, but you can order from the limited menu." Kenneth pointed to the plastic meal card on the bedside table. "You need to build up your strength."

Kenneth returned to the computer, keyed in some data, then turned it off. Even craning her neck, Rhetta was too near-sighted without her glasses to decipher what he'd typed.

Kenneth's sunken eyes gazed from Rhetta to Randolph.

"All in all, the surgery went well, and you've been recovering as you should." He held up a hand, stopping Rhetta before she could speak. She'd started to sputter in protest. "The setback of the barbiturates wasn't great. You should be well enough to move to the regular unit today. No one prescribed those drugs, Randolph, and there is no record of who administered them," he continued, focusing on Randolph. He ignored Rhetta. "This is an unfortunate hospital error. We're investigating and will get to the bottom of this."

Rhetta wasn't to be ignored. She grabbed Kenneth's arm. "This was meant to be more than a setback, and you damn well know it." Kenneth flinched slightly. He stared pointedly at her hand. She removed it.

Kenneth finger combed his grey-tinged hair. "I don't believe anything of the sort." His direct stare pierced her gaze. "There was a mistake made, and we will find out who made it." He strode to the door, hesitated, and turned around. "Rhetta, I know you think someone tampered with the blood alcohol test, and that there is someone after Randolph. You're working too hard, and I believe you're under too much stress. You're acting paranoid."

He turned to the door, pushed it open, then marched out. The door glided silently shut.

"Paranoid? I'll show him paranoid." She stomped her foot.

# CHAPTER 29

"What the heck was that all about?" Woody said, leaving his position near the window to come to Randolph's bedside. His gaze shot from Rhetta to Randolph.

"Damn if I know what's going on with Kenneth," Rhetta said, recovering from the doctor's sharp comment.

Randolph said nothing, merely closed his eyes, and lay back against the pillow.

Crooking his finger at Rhetta to follow him, Woody edged back toward the window.

"I haven't told Randolph about Peter LaRose yet," he whispered. Rhetta's stomach fluttered. She wasn't sure she could hold up telling Randolph right now. She nodded to Woody, and then sidled back to Randolph. She grasped one of his hands with hers. With her free hand, she tugged the nearby chair closer to the bed. She sank into it.

"I love you," she said, covering Randolph's hand with both of hers.

He winced. "I love you too."

Rhetta took a deep breath. There was no easy way to break the news, except to tell it like it was. Randolph was a strong man.

"I have bad news. Peter La Rose is dead." She exhaled.

Randolph merely blinked. *Did he hear me?*

"And I was the one who found him in his apartment yesterday afternoon."

Randolph gripped her hand. His strength surprised her. He whispered, "What happened?"

She patted his hand, then left his bed and went to the bathroom in search of water—for herself this time. She splashed water on her face and dabbed it dry with paper towels. When she returned, she perched on the side of the bed.

She told him everything that had happened.

When she finished, Randolph frowned. "Do you know how Peter died?"

"No. The coroner said there would be an autopsy. I know I sure couldn't tell anything. I didn't stay in the bedroom very long and I sure didn't want to examine him. There's the matter of messing up a crime scene. That is, if it's a crime scene."

Randolph pushed a button on the panel of his bed, making the head of the bed rise slowly.

"Are you all right?" he asked, after he squirmed into a more comfortable position.

"Yes, but I gotta tell you, I'm still feeling queasy. That was almost as bad as seeing you with a bolt sticking out of your head." She took in a deep breath. "Sweets, if you're up to it, we need to talk about that damn schematic. I have to know what Billy Dan told you. Did he know what all the markings signified?" Rhetta reached behind her husband and plumped his pillows.

"Can you get me some ice?" Randolph licked his lips then swallowed. "My throat is still sore." Rhetta located the pitcher and poured some of the melting ice and water into the plastic cup, and held it for him. He slurped the icy mixture. Nodding at her when he was satisfied, she set the tumbler on the tray near the bed and waited.

He leaned back against the pillows. Slowly, he related everything that he and Billy Dan had discussed.

After he finished, Rhetta asked, "A cascading power failure occurs when too many substations go out at the same time?"

"Billy Dan said if that happens in a concentrated area, then the power can't be taken up by any other station, and the grid could go down and maybe cause the entire Midwest grid to fail." Randolph closed his eyes briefly, then opened them and stared at her earnestly. "If the Midwest grid should fail, then the other grids could also start to fail and soon, the entire country could be without power." He sighed and closed his eyes, his brow furrowed as though in pain.

"So...what you're telling me is that with the Midwest grid down, it could be lights out everywhere?"

She turned to Woody. "Think about what the ramifications of that would be, besides the immediately obvious. Should there be a national blackout, then our entire monetary system, national security systems, satellites, telephones, cell phones, all communication...." She trailed off. "Everything crashes."

Woody just stared back at her silently.

She didn't wait for Woody's opinion. She turned back to Randolph, her voice cracking. "Could that be what they're up to, Randolph?" She stood, not waiting for her husband to answer. "The sons-of-bitches are going to take us without even firing a shot." She left the bed and began pacing. "What can we do?"She snatched her purse and began searching for her phone. "I need to call Billy Dan."

Randolph touched her arm. "And the FBI."

"Sure, the FBI. Why not? They were so helpful this morning." She told him about her earlier call.

"You need to call them again. This is urgent."

"Of course, you're right. I'll call them. She rose to leave with the phone clutched in her hand when the door opened, and Doctor Marinthe appeared. She slid the phone back into her bag.

"Good morning, Mrs. McCarter," he said, making his way slowly, his limp more pronounced this morning. Turning to Randolph, he said, "Good morning, Mr. McCarter," and continued toward Rhetta.

Clearly, he was not here to see Randolph.

"Doctor Marinthe, it's good to see you," Rhetta said and plopped into the chair she'd just vacated. Stopping beside her, he turned to face both her and Randolph.

"I have some news." He leveled his brilliant blue eyes at her.

# CHAPTER 30

"I tracked down who administered the barbiturates. It was a second-year intern, and we are in the process of questioning him about it."

Marinthe withdrew a small sheaf of papers from his pocket, examined the top page, and continued. "I have also located the technician who withdrew Mr. McCarter's blood sample when he was in the emergency room. We are trying to solve the riddle of how the blood sample was pulled." He replaced the papers into his pocket. "All I can tell you at this point is that we are questioning two people about what happened to your husband. I will tell you more when I know more."

When Rhetta started to thank him, he held up a hand to stop her. "Please understand that I don't want you to say or do anything at this point. I am telling you this, perhaps prematurely, since the investigation isn't yet completed, so that you won't worry about leaving your husband in our care without bringing someone else to watch over him." He glanced sideways at Woody while he spoke. Woody returned his gaze.

"You do realize, Doctor Marinthe, that my husband is facing a DUI as a result of that blood test?"

"I do. That's why I am investigating this along with the barbiturates." He handed her his card. "Please call me if you have any more concerns."

Rhetta nodded and tucked the card into her purse as the slightly built French doctor walked to the door, his left leg dragging slightly.

Woody let out a low whistle. "What do you suppose he thinks is going on?"

"I don't know, but for some inexplicable reason, I trust Doctor Marinthe."

Randolph said, "What's going on, Rhetta? What's that about the blood test?"

Rhetta hadn't told Randolph about the need to use an iodine scrub to pull blood for a blood alcohol level test. When she told him, Randolph examined his own arms.

"No trace of iodine," he said and met his wife's gaze.

"Right." She peered at Woody, who sauntered over to peer over her shoulder at Randolph's arms.

"Look, guys," Rhetta said, glancing from Randolph to Woody, "the court will use the test they pulled. However, if we can prove they took it incorrectly, then the test should be thrown out, and there goes any proof that Randolph was drinking."

Woody inspected his shoes, then examined his fingernails. He looked everywhere but at Randolph.

"I wasn't drunk, Woody," Randolph said.

Woody glanced up. "Sure. I know." He shoved his hands into his pants pockets.

Randolph sighed and reached for Rhetta's hand. She wrapped both of hers around his.

"Woody doesn't believe me," Randolph said to Rhetta.

"I...it's just that, you know, it's hard to believe that in a hospital somebody messed up these tests, but I believe you," Woody said. He began pacing and repeated, "I do believe you. Especially now, after this incident with the barbiturates. I guess anything can go wrong anywhere, including at a hospital."

Rhetta stretched across the side of the bed and planted a kiss on her husband's cheek.

"I'm going outside to call Billy Dan. I'll be back soon."

Woody gathered up the wrappers from his breakfast and deposited it all into the trashcan. "I'm going to head to the house. Jenn's mom and brother, and his new wife are coming by today for a cookout. I need to get home, and get stuff ready."

"Thanks for coming here, Woody," Randolph said, extending his hand. Woody shook it, gave a little wave over his shoulder and left.

Randolph said to Rhetta, "Babe, can you change it back to Court TV?" before lying back on the pillow and closing his eyes.

# # #

Rhetta found Billy Dan's landline number in her contacts list and dialed. She counted eighteen rings without an answer or an answering machine. She disconnected. The time on her iPhone read 10:35. She'd call him back at noon.

# # #

The rattle of the food trays coming down the hall ended Randolph's nap. He appeared delighted to discover real food on his meal tray, even if it consisted of fruit Jell-O and soup. Rhetta had to smile. He was not normally a fan of Jell-O.

She fluffed pillows and adjusted Randolph's bed upward, which made it easier for him to eat. "I can't believe everything that's happened since I found the schematic, including your accident, is all coincidence. Especially, Peter's death." Rhetta shuddered, recalling the image of Peter lying dead on the floor of his apartment.

They were interrupted by the booming voice of an overweight man in an ill-fitting suit, shuffling uninvited into the room. "How are you feeling, Judge McCarter?" the man said and stopped by the bed. Randolph made no effort to accept the business card the man held out. "I just want you to know I'm available to help you with your little, ah, problem, Judge." The unkempt man with hair overdue for an oil change dropped the card on the nearby tray table, then produced an oversized handkerchief and mopped his sweaty face.

"Albert Claymore. My wife, Rhetta." Randolph nodded toward Rhetta.

"Pleased, I'm sure, ma'am," answered the unkempt man, whose foul body odor permeated the room. He offered her a stubby hand with ragged fingernails. Rhetta glanced at her husband, then back at Claymore. She accepted his handshake but quickly removed her hand, fighting an urge to run to the bathroom and scrub up.

"I won't need your services, Albert. Have a nice day."

"If you change your mind...." The grubby man lumbered to the door.

As soon as the hulk cleared the doorway, Randolph said, "Not even if hell freezes over."

"Who in God's name is that creature?" Rhetta called from the bathroom as she washed her hands.

"That's the one and only Albert Claymore, attorney at law," Randolph answered.

"Did he want you to hire him?" Rhetta returned to Randolph's bed, where she picked up the card by its edge and examined it.

Randolph said, "He's an ambulance chaser. From what I know, he specializes in representing drunk drivers. He checks the hospital records daily to see who's been admitted with a possible DUI."

"That's disgusting," Rhetta said, pumping a generous dollop of antibacterial gel into her hands from the dispenser on the bedside table. She massaged her hands vigorously.

"I wouldn't hire him if he were the last attorney in the county, or on the planet, for that matter," said Randolph and reached for the ramekin of fruit-flavored gelatin cubes.

Rhetta whispered, even though no one else was in the room. "I'm worried about Billy Dan. I can't reach him."

Randolph grimaced before he swallowed a bite of the red gelatin. "Billy Dan gets up at the crack of dawn. He's probably already had coffee and breakfast in town and is out fishing on that big lake of his." Billy Dan's house nestled deep in the woods, within casting distance of a well-established fifteen-acre lake built fifty years earlier. It brimmed with bass, channel catfish, bluegill, and crappie.

"His voicemail doesn't even pick up." Rhetta reached for her phone, peered down the hall to be sure no one was approaching, then speed-dialed Billy Dan's number again.

When he still didn't answer, Rhetta opened the drawer on the bedside table and rummaged around until she found what she wanted. She thumbed through the phone directory and found the number for Merc's Diner. She couldn't help feeling uneasy about not reaching Billy Dan. With everything that had happened to Randolph, she hadn't called Billy Dan earlier. Now she chided herself for not calling him. Billy Dan saw the schematic and was with Randolph just before the accident. Her gut told her Billy Dan could be in danger, too.

Again making sure no staff was approaching, since she'd been clearly informed by Nurse Ratched not to use her cell phone in the room, she dialed Merc's.

A woman answered. "Merc's Diner, this is Krista." Typical kitchen sounds filled the background. "Can I help you?"

Rhetta spoke up louder, so that Krista would hear her over the restaurant noise. "This is Rhetta McCarter, and I need to reach Billy Dan Kercheval. Is he there?"

"No, ma'am, he's not here. As a matter of fact, I haven't seen Billy Dan all morning," said Krista. "Do you have his cell number?"

"No, I don't," Rhetta answered, fumbling for a pen and slip of paper. She located a pencil and notepad in the drawer. She scribbled the number the girl rattled off and repeated it before hanging up.

Once disconnected from Merc's, Rhetta tapped in the number for Billy Dan's cell. This time, the call went straight to voice mail. She left her name and number and asked Billy Dan to call back right away.

Rhetta frowned, and Randolph spoke before she could say anything. "It's not like Billy Dan not to be at Merc's first thing in the morning. That worries me."

"Why don't I go out there?" Rhetta said, already gathering up her purse.

Randolph agreed. "You should do that. I'll be fine. I need a nap anyway after that big meal." He jutted his chin toward the empty Jell-O dish.

She glanced up. The clock above the door said 1:15.

Remembering the schematic and the misfortune that befell everyone who had seen it made Rhetta's stomach flutter. She urgently needed to know if Billy Dan was all right. Before reaching the door, she stopped. "I turn left at County Road 1140, don't I?"

In the last couple of years, she and Randolph had been out to Billy Dan's fishing several times. Although she was sure she knew the way, she occasionally mixed up County Road numbers. She wanted to be sure she had the correct route in mind before heading out. Her Google map wouldn't help her much unless she knew the road number. Rural Bollinger County addresses didn't appear on her iPhone map.

Randolph nodded. "Yes, that's his road number." He reached for her hand. "I love you. Be very careful."

Rhetta grasped his hand, and leaned in to place a kiss on his still-swollen cheek. "I'll call you when I know Billy Dan is okay."

Randolph caressed her cheek with the back of his hand. She turned his hand over and kissed his palm. "I love you, too." She swept out before Randolph could notice the extra moisture in her eyes.

# CHAPTER 31

A brisk wind blew as Rhetta pushed the revolving door leading out to the parking lot. Leaves from the nearby trees fluttered to the sidewalk and swirled with the dust devils. From all appearances, a summer thunderstorm was marching in.

Rhetta emerged from under the emergency room porte-cochère to fat, cold raindrops smacking her in the face. She broke into a run, reaching the covered parking garage just as a torrent of rain descended. By the time she reached her car, she was drenched.

She grabbed more baby wipes for the second time that day and wiped off the splashes. She turned up her nose at the lingering baby powder smell. "I'll have to treat these seats with Armor All." After their hard work replacing the interior in Cami, she didn't want to suffer stains on the immaculate upholstery.

While the car idled, she snatched her phone and scrolled to the weather application. She hadn't recalled any rain in the forecast. Then she realized that she hadn't even heard a weather forecast for several days. Sure enough, AccuWeather displayed little lightning streaks indicating severe thunderstorms for the afternoon. It also predicted a clearing by early evening.

If Billy Dan was indeed fishing as Randolph suggested, he should have sought cover, probably in his house, when the storm erupted. She scrolled through her recent calls to Billy Dan's number and called it again. Still no answer. *He probably went into town for coffee.*

Before she could put Cami into gear, an old man shuffled in front of her car, stopped, and placed a hand on the hood. He stood there, palm still on her car, staring at her through the windshield. Her heart pounded. The man seemed familiar. Or did he? A former customer? No, she didn't know this guy. She threw open the door and got out, staying behind the big door for protection.

"Hey mister, I think you need to move. I'm kind of in a hurry."

"Hello, Rhetta," the old man said. His raspy voice tugged at dark recesses in her memory. She stared at the man coming toward her. He was much older now than he was in the only picture she had of him, the one with him smiling and an arm draped across her mother's slender shoulders.

He stopped when he reached the door. She stared into the green eyes she'd inherited.

Her father.

Rhetta's mouth went dry and her hands began to sweat.

"Do you know who I am?" her father asked, his hands dropping to his sides. He stood there, a shriveled old man in faded blue jeans and a tattered blue T-shirt. His thinning white hair stood askew from the gusts that swept through the garage.

The way he spoke, along with the realization that the man she most hated in the world was inexplicably standing in front of her car, made a long-buried fury rise from the depth of her bowels.

"I know exactly who you are. You're the son of a bitch that walked out on us. Get the hell away from me."

The old man reached a trembling hand into a shirt pocket and pulled something out. He walked to the driver's door and offered it to her.

Rhetta didn't look at it, didn't take it.

"Get out of here. Get away from me!" She began pulling the car door closed. He touched the door. With surprising strength, her father held the heavy door firmly. "Please take this. It was your mother's."

Rhetta stared at his hand. In his palm nestled a gold, heart-shaped locket on a thin, gold chain. She reached for it and closed her hand over it.

"Where did you get this?" Rhetta popped the catch with her thumbnail. The heart split open, revealing a faded black-and-white picture of her beautiful mother holding a towheaded baby.

She stared at her beloved mother, smiling. Tears filled Rhetta's eyes. Memories of her mother washed over her.

"I'm sorry, Rhetta." The old man shook his head. "I know you can't forgive me. I'm sorry I wasn't part of your life." He looked down at the concrete floor. "I loved you both."

"Loved us? You had a peculiar way of showing your love, Daddy dear. What do you call that? Love by absence? Where the hell have you been all my life?" She trembled with long-buried fury that bubbled to life.

He shuffled from one foot to the other. When he spoke, his voice was raspy, like a man who smoked and drank too much. "When I came back from my first tour in 'Nam, your mother had taken up with someone else." He let go of the car door and stepped back. "She told me never to see her or you again. My heart was broken, but I had to go back overseas. I got shot in my second tour and spent three years in and out of hospitals. After that, I gave up, hit the bottle, and did a lot of things I'm not proud of."

"I don't believe you. Mama never married anyone else. She told me you left us. And, in case you haven't noticed, it's been a long damn time since Vietnam." Rhetta spat out the words, fervently wishing they were knife blades that would pierce his heart.

Rhetta shook, unable to think clearly. Why had her father searched her out? And what lies was he telling about her mother?

"Your mother and I never divorced, Rhetta. We were always married."

That news hit Rhetta in the gut. She clearly didn't know anything about what had happened between her mother and father, but how dare he stand there and lie to her?

It had to be about money. That must be why he was here now. Probably wanted her to give him money. "What do you want? You think there's money since Mama's gone? Well, think again, buster, 'cause there isn't any. Mama was broke when she died." Rhetta clutched the gold locket to her heart, her hands trembling. "And speaking of that, why didn't you come to her funeral?"

The old man's eyes welled and he slapped away the tear that threatened to fall. "I don't want any money, Rhetta. I just came to say goodbye." He shook his head. "I couldn't make your mother's funeral because they wouldn't let me out to come," he said, his bloodshot eyes staring into Rhetta's. "The only reason I'm here now is because I'm gonna die." His mordant laugh changed into a deep cough. He sucked in a wheezy breath before continuing. "Prisons are too crowded. They need the space. They let me out. Compassionate discharge, they call it. They kicked me out to die."

Anger flooded into Rhetta, washing away any pity that may have remained. "Get the hell away from me, old man."

Slamming the car door, she dropped the locket into her purse and sat, shaking. She stared at him, the tears blurring her focus until her simmering rage exploded. She threw Cami into gear, and took off. An unholy urge compelled her to turn around. She u-turned and aimed straight for the old man—her father, a man she hated all her life. He stood silently, a specimen of vermin that didn't deserve to live another day. Cami's brakes squealed. Smoke spiraled around the hood as Rhetta came to her senses in time to skid to a stop a scant foot in front of him. She threw open the door. Jumping out, she found her trembling legs unable to support her. She slumped back into the driver's seat and slammed the door.

"Go ahead and finish it, Rhetta, you'd be doing me a favor," her father said, unflinchingly. He remained riveted to the spot.

"You aren't worth getting my car dirty." She spat the words at him as she shifted Cami into reverse and spun out backward with tires squealing. She swerved around him and raced down the ramp into the street.

# # #

Torrential rain pounded the roof of her car, then cascaded down the windshield. Rhetta sat, staring at watery images of swans paddling around the park pond as happily as if the sun were shining.

When she left the hospital garage, she was too upset to drive, much less head out in the raging storm. Instead, she pulled into the park across the street and parked, turned off the engine, and stared out the window. Gradually, she stopped shaking as the fury drained.

Hatred had nearly overcome her. She wanted badly to run over the detestable old man who called himself her father. Her hands still trembled. She gripped Cami's steering wheel and tossed her head back and forth in an effort to shake the entire terrible scene from her head.

Her purse lay on the passenger seat. Pulling it to her, she fished around until she found the precious locket. Holding it against her cheek, she let the tears flow unchecked.

Her father. The only person in the world she hated. He was there. He told her things. Were they true? Who was her mother? The strong woman that had raised her, who had worked nights, who'd saved up enough money to buy a new Camaro, who'd taught her daughter to be independent. Was it all phony? And, who was Rhetta herself? A crazy woman who'd just wanted to run over her own father.

Rhetta wept for her mother, for her father, and for herself.

She grabbed a tissue and blew her nose.

Kissing the locket, she tucked it securely into a zippered pocket inside her purse. Closing her eyes, she swayed slowly from side to side, willing her emotions to drain, and her nerves to calm. She breathed deeply, the way she learned in a yoga class.

Her senses and her life came back into focus. Randolph. She had to get to Billy Dan's.

Hatred had to wait until another day.

# CHAPTER 32

R hetta eased Cami into first gear, rolling slowly along the narrow one-way park road in the rain. At the intersection, she stopped, facing the hospital. She blew a kiss toward the building, directing it to sail upward to her husband. Then she merged into the slow moving traffic along William Street.

The golden arches of McDonalds beckoned to her just as her stomach growled. She realized she was famished, and swung a quick turn through the drive-thru. She came out with a Big Mac, fries and a chocolate shake.

After gulping down most of the sandwich, all of the fries and slurping up the last bubbles of milky ice cream at the bottom of the shake, she made her way quickly across town and soon found herself on Highway 34, the two-lane highway leading to Marble Hill. She also calculated how many miles she'd have to run to work off her dietary splurge.

The fierce summer storm must have discouraged most of the Saturday drivers; she didn't spot any other cars. She throttled Cami as much as she dared on the slick, curvy roadway. In an effort to keep the images of her father from creeping back into her head, she switched on the oldies station. The sun always shines in radio land.

A quick glance skyward through her windshield revealed a threatening sky as dark as night, even though it was barely 2:30. She located the knob for the driving lights and pulled them on since Cami wasn't equipped with automatic headlights. She knew every inch of her car and didn't need to take her eyes off the road to locate the switch.

She recalled the recently enacted law proclaiming headlights on was mandatory while driving in the rain. More specifically, the law stated that lights were "mandatory while using windshield wipers." Did that mean that if anyone was dumb enough not to turn on wipers in the rain, they weren't required to turn on their headlights? Just how does that law get enforced? Does the windshield-wiper enforcement brigade lie in the road ditches, waiting for an offender to slosh by?

The heavy rain runneling down her windshield taxed her wipers and snapped her attention back to the slick roadway. She turned off the radio. She could focus better in the quiet. She could also think better. Why did her father show up at the hospital? She was so angry, she hadn't even asked how he'd found her. Didn't he say he'd kept up with her over the years? How did he do that? She regretted now that she let her anger overwhelm her. Not that she wanted anything to do with her father, but he told her some strange things. What if they were true? It would turn her memories of her mother upside down.

She forced her thoughts back to Billy Dan. He'd seen the schematic and talked to Randolph. Snaking her hand across to the passenger seat for her phone, she held it aloft, stole a glance at it, then tapped the last number she'd called. Billy Dan still didn't answer. Just as she did, she spotted flashing lights ahead and braked. Her rear-wheel drive Camaro began fishtailing across both lanes. Sliding her foot from the brake to the gas pedal, she accelerated into the direction of the swerve until Cami straightened. With a death grip on the wheel, she steered back to her own side of the road.

She sucked in a breath then tapped the brake pedal. This time her Camaro slowed evenly.

*I'm going to get antilock brakes*. Her friend and mechanic, Ricky (short for Veronica) Lane had advised Rhetta to get antilock disc brakes when they had first bought the car. It was equipped with the factory drum brakes in the rear, with disc brakes only in the front. Drum brakes weren't as reliable as disc brakes.

Rhetta vowed to get hold of Ricky and take care of changing out the brakes.

Of the two women, Rhetta was usually the fashionista, while Ricky tended to look as though she'd crawled out from under a car, which was normally the case. Although a real estate agent by trade, Ricky, divorced and still single, lived to mechanic and fix up muscle cars. The friendly redhead usually tucked her long hair under a ball cap and wore magnifying safety glasses when she worked on cars. Whenever it was time to show houses, she popped in her green contact lenses and let her shoulder-length hair fall loose.

Rhetta eased past a van with its emergency lights flashing that had pulled over onto the shoulder. The right front end squatted low to the ground, a sure sign of a flat tire. As she passed, she glanced around for the van's driver, but spotted no one. Once safely past, Rhetta sped up. Her stomach was in a full-blown cramp from her near wreck.

*Thank God, no one was on the other side of the road.*

Beads of sweat popped out on her forehead in spite of the air conditioning. That, she knew, was due entirely to fear.

# CHAPTER 33

By the time she arrived at the four-way stop in Marble Hill, the rain had quit. The menacing storm clouds were beginning to part, revealing a smattering of the sun's rays.

The city limit sign both welcomed her and warned of a twenty-five mile per hour speed limit. She drove agonizingly slow along the main street. The highway went straight through town, effectively splitting it, so she had no choice but to drive through town to continue west to Billy Dan's. Randolph had warned that the second generation Camaro would attract enough attention on its own merit without roaring through town. She eased up on the accelerator, not wanting the Flowmaster exhaust system to turn a cop's head.

Merc's sat directly ahead on the right. She pulled in. She needed to know if Billy Dan had shown up yet at his "office." Also, she badly needed to find a ladies' room.

She'd just parked Cami when four leather-clad bikers on Harleys rolled in. They parked in two slots alongside of her. One of the riders, a large man sporting a black leather vest over a hairy chest, jerked his thumb toward her car, grinned, and gave her a two-thumbs-up salute.

It wasn't unusual to attract a crowd whenever she and Cami cruised into the small towns around Southeast Missouri. Whenever she and Randolph had first restored the Camaro, she seldom drove it, limiting her excursions to a few area car shows and hot rod cruise-ins at the local drive-in restaurants. When Ricky replaced the original stock 350 motor with a tuned port injection LS1 Corvette motor, Rhetta turned Cami into her daily spring, summer, and fall ride.

The rainstorm had apparently discouraged many of the local fishermen from going to the ponds and creeks. Several pickup trucks with johnboats in tow parked along the back edge of Merc's parking lot. Swirling leaves that had blown from the tall sycamores still littered the asphalt lot. The clean, fresh smell of summer rain teased her nostrils.

She held the door to Merc's open for two older women, then followed them in.

One of the blue-haired matrons easing her way in slowly behind an aluminum walker said, "Nice ride, young lady."

"Thanks," Rhetta said and smiled. That elderly woman may have required a walker, but she clearly kept up with the current vernacular.

Inside Merc's, she spotted dozens of overall-clad men sipping coffee and klatching around several large circular tables. Billy Dan was not among them.

Using one hip, Krista pushed open the swinging door from the kitchen and emerged holding a coffee pot in each hand. One pot was filled with decaf and bore a green stripe, while the other contained regular, if one was to believe the orange stripe. "Hi, Mrs. McCarter," Krista called out as she sailed by. "You can sit anywhere."

"Thanks, Krista, I'm not staying."

When Krista paused to refill coffee mugs held up by a half-dozen men at the nearby table, Rhetta asked, "Has Billy Dan been in since I called?"

"Why, no, he hasn't," Krista said, stopping and gazing around the restaurant. Turning to a table of overall-wearers, she shouted, "Have any of you boys seen Billy Dan today?" Several heads shook. A few gents muttered, "Nope," and continued their conversation.

"Thanks," Rhetta said and headed to the rest room. Feeling better after using the facilities and applying some cool water to her face, she made her way through the many tables and headed for the door. On her way, she caught snatches of the old boys' banter—mostly colorful assessments of current political candidates.

Once outside, she tried Billy Dan again. Still no answer. She hiked her purse up her shoulder and trotted to Cami. The hairs prickled on the back of her neck.

It wasn't from static electricity.

# CHAPTER 34

O nce outside the city limits on the west side of town, Rhetta floored it. Cami hugged the road, the speedometer chased 70. She glanced at the dash clock—not quite 4:00.

The sun's rays broke decisively through the cloudy sky to dry the soaked pavement. Only a scattering of puddles remained along the sides of the narrow state highway. Traffic was light. She met a smattering of cars as she raced westward. Glancing at her speedometer, Rhetta prayed one of them wouldn't be a highway patrol officer.

Instead of finding five bars and a big "3G" when she again picked up her cell phone, she glimpsed an unsteady two bars followed by the letter E. She groaned. She'd soon be running out of cell service. Then she brightened. *If there's no service out here, maybe that's why I can't reach Billy Dan on his cell.*

Mental head slap when she reminded herself that she'd also tried Billy Dan's house phone.

Up ahead, on the left she recognized an old country store bearing a hand-lettered sign above the front door. The words *Green's Grocery* were barely decipherable on the weather-beaten board. The square, wood slat store building was topped by a corrugated steel roof. A sagging front porch awaited the customers who came through the front and only door. The old place was reminiscent of a tavern in a western movie set.

She knew from past visits that the porch was sturdy. She and Randolph had stopped there to buy night crawlers the last time they'd been out to Billy Dan's to fish. They also discovered Green's Grocery made the best fried bologna sandwiches in the universe.

Remembering that the road to Billy Dan's would appear quickly on the left after passing Green's Grocery, Rhetta slowed in anticipation. Ahead, partially hidden by the boughs of a tall cedar, she spotted a crooked green sign with three white numerals, 1, 4, 0. The space in front of the first "1" was a darker green. Probably where the other numeral "1" had been when it had completed the 1-1-4-0. It must have recently fallen off the sign.

She turned left, and Cami bounced on to the county road. Although the road was gravel, it wasn't the firm grey limestone gravel like the surface of their road in Cape County. Instead, this Bollinger County road gravel was boulder-sized, the rocks undoubtedly mined from a local creek. Deep puddles littered the road and there were too many potholes to count.

Her initial mutterings of displeasure turned to cussing when she heard loud pings and splats from the mud attacking the low-slung Camaro. She hadn't realized how close to the road surface her car traveled, especially now that she was inching over a rough gravel road like this one. She and Randolph had always driven the four-wheel drive Artmobile on previous visits to Billy Dan's.

She was driving so slowly that the speedometer didn't register, going just fast enough to avoid stalling. Not wanting to ride the clutch, she eased the Camaro forward a little faster. "Sweet mother of God," she mumbled. "I'll definitely have to wash the car tomorrow."

She prayed that Cami would only need a bath, and not a new oil pan. Rounding a steep curve to the left, she met a dark green truck careening toward her. It swerved across the middle of the road, hogging not only its side of the narrow road, but hers as well. She jerked Cami's wheel hard to the right to avoid colliding with him. He veered in the opposite direction, causing him to fishtail along the edge of the road and sending a spray of gravel skyward. She accelerated hard, managing to escape the worst of the cascading rocks he left in his wake.

"Damn," she cursed as some of the raining gravel bounced off her trunk. "What an idiot." She cringed, visualizing the damage to the hood and paint.

In her rear-view mirror, she glared at the back of the offending vehicle speeding away. It wasn't a truck after all, but an SUV, probably a Ford Explorer, she guessed. *A green SUV*. She snapped her head around to see if she could catch the license plate number. The SUV was, however, long gone.

Billy Dan's driveway came into view ahead on the right. Slowing to make the turn in, she noticed two sets of fresh deep ruts in his driveway. From their appearance and direction, she guessed that the first set of tracks were made by a vehicle entering, followed by another set of ruts made when it left. That SUV had to have been at Billy Dan's. Her stomach knotted again and her hands grew clammy. Was someone now after Billy Dan, or her?

Billy Dan's house wasn't immediately visible. He'd built his home at least a half mile away on top of a small hill overlooking his lake. He bragged that being well away from the road suited him perfectly. No one could accidentally find his house. One had to be determined to visit Billy Dan to find his house.

She took a deep breath and eased Cami up the long driveway, dreading an expedition along an even worse path than what the county road was. Billy Dan kept his private lane so well maintained that even after the rain, she was grateful to discover that it wasn't anywhere near as bad as the county road. She exhaled a sigh of relief. The public road had already taken its toll on Cami. She was loath to add to any more damage to her undercarriage. If the driveway had been bad, she was prepared to stop, park Cami, and hoof it the rest of the way to the house. The driveway was quite smooth. Billy Dan had imported Cape County gravel for his personal lane. She sped toward the compound at the top of the hill.

Billy Dan referred to his home site as a compound because of the many outbuildings that were nestled close together behind his house. A wide porch surrounded his cozy two-story, cedar-sided cabin. The wood veranda offered a stunning view of the lake. About twenty yards behind the house, stood a modern grey metal-sided building topped with a bright red metal roof. The building was larger than the house. This was Billy Dan's workshop. In it, he also had storage for his tractor, mowers, and assorted other machinery. He kept all of the equipment in one end, while his shop was at the other, heated with a wood stove, and cooled by a window air conditioner.

A miniature version of the shop stood next door. Billy Dan used this building exclusively for his fishing gear. Above the entry door to what he called his fishing shed was a hand-lettered sign that warned, *"Non-fishermen enter at your own risk,"* and which was illustrated with a rendering of a largemouth bass that bore an exaggerated open mouth baring man-killing teeth. Overlooking the buildings stood the turn of the twentieth century cattle barn—a two story wood structure. Its tin, roof glistened in the sunlight Billy Dan didn't keep cattle any more, and he kept that barn as tidy as the rest of the property.

Rhetta glanced around, marveling at how the place was as fastidiously groomed as a state park. With the recent state funding cutbacks, Billy Dan's property was probably in better condition than most of the state parks.

She jogged up the steps to the porch and rang the doorbell. When no one answered, she rapped on the doorframe and called out, "Billy Dan? Are you here? It's Rhetta McCarter." Nobody answered her. After a third unsuccessful attempt to raise Billy Dan, she scurried down the steps.

Her mind raced. She wasn't about to try the door. The last time she entered someone's home unbidden was at Peter's apartment, and look how well that turned out. Continuing to shout Billy Dan's name, she sprinted toward the outbuildings.

The workshop was closed, with no sign of activity. The air conditioner unit, which protruded from the window next to the entry door, was silent. In this heat, Billy Dan wouldn't be in the shop without cool air. She skipped that door. No sense in checking there.

The fishing shed door stood ajar. A quick inspection revealed only shelves of neatly organized fishing tackle. No Billy Dan.

After a search around the barn, she was again disappointed. There was no sight of Billy Dan anywhere. Images of Peter's body drifted in unbidden. She shook her head to chase the memory off. This was different. Billy Dan wouldn't be lying dead inside his house. She couldn't be having that bad a day. He had to be out somewhere on the grounds or at the lake.

She turned back to investigate the shop. She'd try to get a peek inside. If the Kubota tractor was gone, Billy Dan could be out in the fields mowing, although she doubted that he would mow immediately after a hard rain. The ground was much too muddy. She paused to listen for a tractor that might be chugging nearby. She heard nothing but the eerie calm that descends after a violent storm. There wasn't even any birdsong, as though the birds weren't sure they could come out from wherever they'd sheltered during the storm. The entire place was deathly quiet.

After trying both walk-through doors and the roll-up doors to the workshop and finding them locked, she peered through a window in a side door. There sat the big Kubota parked next to a grader blade, a finish mower, and two or three riding mowers. She craned sideways and spotted a four-wheeler and several small wagons.

Billy Dan definitely wasn't mowing.

She turned away from the building and gazed up at the house, then fixed her eyes on the lake. She remembered his voicemail message that if he didn't answer the phone, he was fishing. She stared at the water. Around her, the trees were still; no wind rustled the leaves. No crickets or tree frogs sang. She shouted once again, but only half-heartedly. She wanted to turn and leave. Billy Dan was nowhere on the property, of that she was sure. Unless he was in the house, hurt or....

Rhetta shook the unfinished thought away, afraid of thinking the worst. Then she gathered herself together, remembering the reason she came here. She swallowed hard and turned toward the house. She'd try every door. If she found one unlocked, she'd go in. She couldn't possibly find another body, could she? What were the odds?

# CHAPTER 35

A fter trying the front door knob, then ringing the bell and knocking again, Rhetta eased around to the side of the house, searching for other doors. She tried the door to the breezeway between the house and the garage. Locked. After walking around to the sliding glass basement door, she found it locked as well. No one answered her pounding. *Maybe he's just not home. Maybe I'm over-reacting.*

She cruised around the house and hopped back up on to the porch to again survey the surroundings. From Billy Dan's porch, she had a good view of the lake. Strange, how every door on the place was secure with the exception of the fishing shed. That door wasn't only unlocked, it stood wide open. Billy Dan must've gone fishing, yet he was nowhere around his property that she could tell.

She scanned the grassy slopes surrounding the lake. Nothing appeared out of the ordinary. At the foot of the hill below the house, the wooden dock stretched a good 20 feet out over the water, an extension of the stone walkway leading to it. Tied to the dock was Billy Dan's paddleboat. Nothing unusual there.

After trotting down the back porch steps, she picked her way along the rock walk to the lake, studying the ground, the grass, the dock, the paddleboat. She stepped gingerly on to the dock and walked to the end of it. The water was so still it didn't even lap around the pilings. Cupping her hands around her mouth, she shouted Billy Dan's name again and was shocked to hear her amplified voice bounce back to her. Her "Hello-o-o" skimmed across the water, where it reverberated through the trees on the other side of the lake.

The clouds scudded off, leaving brilliant late afternoon sunshine in their wake. Rhetta shielded her eyes as she stared westward across the glittering blue water of the lake. She shouted again. "Hello, Billy Dan?" No answer.

A faint noise, a bumping sound, floated up from the water. Following the sound, she spotted an overturned johnboat in the water close to the edge of the lake. After calling out one more time, she heard another faint thump, as if in response.

Rhetta exploded into a sprint, shouting Billy Dan's name as she ran. She drilled her stare on the overturned flat-bottomed boat. Billy Dan had to be underneath it. She was sure of it. For some reason, he couldn't get out and was answering her shouts by pounding. She pumped her legs to the max.

About twenty feet from the spot on the shore closest to the boat, a white oak tree root snagged her toe as she flew by, catapulting her face first on to the damp grass. For a second, she couldn't fathom what had happened until the pain from her ankle shot to her brain. She moaned and cursed at the same time. Propping herself up on her grass-stained elbows, she scrabbled backward enough to free her foot. Her ankle began throbbing. Her right ankle. Her driving foot.

"Crap, that hurts," she yelped. She hoisted herself up to her knees, then slowly stood. Her ankle sent a jolt of pain each time her heart beat. She sucked in deep breaths. Her head swiveled toward the boat. She heard the faint thump again. She examined her swelling ankle, daring to touch it. It felt hot and started to swell, and began throbbing as she limped along.

"Billy Dan, hang on. I'm coming," she shouted. Another response thump from the boat. "Oww," she cried when she tried to hurry and pain shot up her leg.

Reaching the spot on the bank nearest the overturned boat, she shouted again. "I'm here, Billy Dan, hang on." The boat bobbed upside down and was no farther than ten feet from shore. A muffled moan escaped from under the boat. The groan was followed by a weak tap, tap, tap. "I'm coming out to you," Rhetta shouted, and dipped her good foot into the water at the shore, where the water was ankle deep. The bank sloped sharply the farther she slogged out toward the boat. Moving carefully so she wouldn't slip and fall, she slid along the slimy mud bottom. She cried out again from the pain reverberating from her injured ankle.

By the time she reached the small boat, she was waist-deep in the water. Mud had sucked off the tennis shoe on her injured foot. She didn't care. This time when she called out to Billy Dan, he answered her with a groan.

"Billy Dan, it's Rhetta McCarter. I'm going to get you out from under there, okay?" She didn't ask him if he was all right. That was a stupid question. If he'd been all right, he wouldn't have been clinging to the underside of his small fishing boat.

He mumbled something she didn't understand, but which she interpreted as a "yes."

She didn't have a clue how to get him out.

"Where are you hurt?" she shouted.

Another muffled sound followed by a moan.

"Can you turn loose of the boat and I'll push it away?"

"No," came the distinct reply.

*Now what?*

She started to tug the boat toward shore. She stopped abruptly when she heard Billy Dan yelp in pain. "No, stop," he cried.

*All right, go to Plan B. What the hell is plan B?*

She'd never had to rescue someone from under a boat before. Was there a protocol for this?

"I'm going to push down and try to turn the boat over."

"No!" came an even sharper reply.

*Of course not.* What was she thinking? *Why not? What's wrong with Billy Dan?*

The only way to know how to free him was to get under the boat with him and see what she was dealing with.

She ducked down, bobbed her head under the water, and came up alongside him beneath the boat. Although sunlight streamed across the water, underneath the boat was dim. Little light penetrated. She willed her eyes to hurry and adjust to the dark.

Squinting around to get her bearings, she identified the streaky dark splotches spattering the underside the boat. Blood everywhere. Rhetta inhaled sharply. An upside-down portion of the hinged upholstered seat that normally covered the bait well dangled into the water. The two wooden bench seats, one in the bow and one in the stern, served to hold the little johnboat steady after it had turned over.

"Billy Dan, oh my God, what happened?" Billy Dan, wedged firmly between the stern seat where he'd been sitting, and the middle seat, didn't answer. He groaned, his mangled right arm trapped in the bait box. His lower body sloshed in the water. The cover of the bait box dangled, splintered in two. One piece hung loosely into the water, while an enormous shard pierced Billy Dan's arm, pinning him to the boat. "Dear God, I've got to get you out of here!" Frantic, she looked around for something she could use to help Billy Dan.

She had no idea how to free him.

# CHAPTER 36

R hetta ducked back under the water and surfaced on the other side of Billy Dan. She found herself in the small space next to the bait box, inches from the middle seat. Billy Dan was hurt. Hurt too badly to free himself. He clung to the bottom of the boat with his good arm, exhaustion evident. She could easily see that he was barely able to hold on.

Glancing around, she was unable to determine what had caused his injury or the boat to capsize. She'd save those questions for later. Right now, she had to figure out how to get Billy Dan out from under the boat. She saw that the first thing she had to do was free him from the shard.

"All right, let's get you loose." She began tugging on the wood shard that pinned him to the boat, but stopped quickly when he cried out in pain.

"I need to figure out which pieces of this thing," she said, pointing toward the bait box, "that I can remove to free you." He grunted.

If she loosened some of the other pieces instead of the one in his arm, she might have enough room to maneuver Billy Dan and free him from his impalement.

She groaned with the effort of pulling an unwieldy wood slab with one hand, while gripping the rim of the underside of the boat with the other. She turned loose of the boat, grabbed the splintered piece with both hands, and jerked as hard as she could. The piece broke loose and she stumbled backward. Losing her balance, she went under the water again. Flailing and churning forward, she propelled herself back under the boat. The process seemed to take forever, like she was moving in slow motion, caught in a bizarre dream. When she finally surfaced, she sputtered, spitting out muddy water.

Minutes later, she was able to free him. The moment she loosened Billy Dan's injured arm, it floated limply in the water. Billy Dan seemed unable to control it. His head lay against his good arm, as he gripped the underside of the boat. His strength had waned and he turned loose of the boat. She feared he was unconscious.

"Billy Dan, can you hear me?" She was inches from his face. He didn't respond. His eyes were nearly shut. "Billy Dan, answer me," she commanded. His eyes fluttered open and he grunted.

"I'm going to hold on to you and pull you under the boat. Then we're going to shore." She'd figured she'd wrap her right arm around his waist and pull him downward to clear the boat.

"Uh...," he mumbled faintly and began heaving himself outward. His movement, she quickly saw, was a hindrance.

"Stay still and let me get a grip on you," she ordered. She slogged up alongside him and encircled as much of his waist with her right arm as she could reach. Although Billy Dan wasn't tall, his muscular build made him a lot larger around than she was. Rhetta's size—barely five feet two and one hundred ten pounds—made her feel like she was grasping a giant.

"On three," she said. "Then let go." She sucked in a deep breath. "One, two, three!" With all her strength, she pulled Billy Dan downward into the water. When she ducked to clear the boat, her painful ankle gave out. She stumbled backward, lost her balance, and tumbled into the water. She also lost Billy Dan.

When she righted herself, she began panicking. She couldn't locate him. He hadn't surfaced. He was still underwater.

*Oh, God, where is he?*

All she saw was muddy water churning all around her. She'd made most of those billowy mud clouds herself. The boat drifted away, a sure sign that Billy Dan was no longer holding on to it.

She stabbed the water with both hands, searching frantically. She couldn't find him. *Where did he go? How could I lose him in three feet of water?*

She lunged toward the spot she last saw him, but grabbed only muddy lake water. Holding her breath, Rhetta ducked under the surface of the water and spotted him a few feet from her, face down, his limbs floating loosely, and a dark trail of blood oozing from his head. He was floating to the surface, no longer attached to anything. *He hit his head. He's unconscious!*

Sloshing toward him, she circled both arms around his upper torso and propelled him upward until his face cleared the water. Although it felt like she was wading through quicksand, Rhetta managed to hold on to him.

She lugged him the longest ten feet in the world to the shore. When his head lay safely on the grass, she gulped for oxygen. Billy Dan's legs rested in the water. After her chest stopped burning, and she was finally able to breathe, she locked both her arms around his chest and tugged him up on the bank, clear of the water. Kneeling alongside him, she gasped for air. Using the last of her strength, she shoved as hard as she could, managing to roll him on to his back. She propped herself on her elbows and hovered over him, panting. She'd used up all her strength.

Rhetta crawled into a sitting position alongside Billy Dan. She was dripping wet, with mud and slime gluing her jeans to her legs. A now unrecognizable tennis shoe covered in mud stuck to her left foot. She sloshed whenever she moved. Her right foot was bare. She panted, still fighting to catch her breath.

Rhetta changed positions and kneeled over Billy Dan. She tilted his head sideways, then ran two fingers around his mouth to clear his airway. She began mouth-to-mouth resuscitation. After a few agonizingly long minutes, he sputtered and coughed.

He was breathing!

When Billy Dan came around, he began to moan softly. Rhetta squeezed her eyes shut, hoping to stop the tears before they fell.

*I nearly killed him trying to save him!*

Coated in muck and dripping wet in the hot afternoon sun, Rhetta's shaking ratcheted up to earthquake proportions.

# CHAPTER 37

"Billy Dan, can you hear me?" Rhetta panted as she gripped the sodden man around his shoulders and helped him sit up. After a bout of coughing, sputtering, spitting out water and mud, his rapid breathing finally slowed, and he nodded. She sat back on her heels, observing him.

"Thanks," Billy Dan said trying to talk. He coughed violently again, unable to finish his sentence.

Rhetta peered at Billy Dan's left arm, which had begun swelling around the ugly protruding shard.

"I need to call an ambulance."

He barely nodded.

"I have to go up to your house," she said. "No cell. All your doors are locked," she added.

"Back porch, key under…the…geraniums." He managed to get that out without more coughing.

Rhetta stood, and tugged off the tennis shoe and dropped it to the ground. She winced as it came free of her swollen foot. "I'll be right back. Don't move. Stay still"

Hobbling barefoot on her injured ankle, she scrambled up the slope to his house. Sliding on the first wood step caused her to snag a splinter in her left heel. "Oww," she muttered, barely slowing down. *Crap. Now I'm hurt in both feet!*

Glancing frantically around the porch, she couldn't find any geraniums. Eventually, she spotted a huge pot of red flowers near the heavy oak back door. It took two hands to shove the pot aside to reveal the key underneath. After two unsuccessful fumbling tries at the lock, she took a deep breath, counted to ten, and tried the key again. This time the lock yielded easily.

Inside the house, the air was cool. The afternoon sun filtered through the slatted blinds on the large window over the sink, bathing the spotless kitchen in a warm golden glow. She located the phone, a base unit with a portable headset, sitting atop the granite kitchen counter. Upon hearing the reassuring dial tone, she punched 9-1-1 into the keypad.

The emergency operator immediately asked for her address.

"Address?" she asked, stymied. *Don't they know where I am?* "Uh, don't you have the address on your screen?"

"No, ma'am, this isn't enhanced 9-1-1. Please tell me your name, and where you are." Was that impatience in the operator's voice? *What did that mean, no enhanced 9-1-1?*

"This is Rhetta McCarter. I'm at Billy Dan Kercheval's place on County Road 1140, and there's been an accident. He's badly hurt."

"Thank you, Mrs. McCarter. We know where Billy Dan's property is. Hold please." Rhetta heard the operator dispatch an ambulance and a patrol car.

The operator returned. "Is Billy Dan conscious?"

"Yes, but just barely. He injured his arm. He's lost a lot of blood."

"The ambulance is on the way. Please stay with him until they arrive."

"Of course." Rhetta disconnected. She glanced around the kitchen, hoping to find a pair of Billy Dan's sneakers, or moccasins or even flip flops that she could borrow. She dismissed the flip-flops. She couldn't picture an outdoorsman like Billy Dan wearing either sandals or flip-flops. Finding not a single shoe of any sort in the kitchen area, she rushed down the hall to the bedroom, leaving muddy footprints tinged with blood on the wood floor along the way.

In his bedroom, a large wood four-poster bed, neatly made, sat against the wall opposite a large window. A matching dresser and a tall armoire containing a TV filled the rest of the room. A deer head with an enormous set of antlers graced the wall across from the bed. She shuddered, thankful that Randolph didn't hang dead deer bodies on their walls at home.

Stepping into the large walk-in closet, she studied the orderly rows of clothing items on racks that wrapped around three sides. Below the clothes, on the far wall, several pairs of shoes and boots were lined up like soldiers awaiting marching orders. She spotted a couple of pairs of possible replacement shoe candidates—a pair of blue canvas deck shoes and a pair of well-worn sneakers. Favoring the sneakers, because she could tie them on, she sat on the floor, slipped them on, and tied them snugly. They were too big, but they'd have to do. When she stood, she left a muddy spot on the floor from her soaked rump.

Snatching an armful of towels off the chrome racks in the bathroom, Rhetta plopped across the house, down the steps, and back to Billy Dan.

# CHAPTER 38

"The ambulance is on its way," Rhetta said, hoping her voice sounded soothing enough to reassure Billy Dan, even though she was panting from her trek. "It'll be here soon. You're going to be fine." She patted the arm that wasn't injured.

Billy Dan, lying on his back on the grass, made a soft moaning sound.

"What happened?" she said, dropping into a crouch alongside him. "Can you talk to me?"

"Shot," he answered simply, turning toward her with a great effort. He inhaled, and his lungs whistled and wheezed. "Tried to take cover. They shot at me." He panted, short of breath. "Got the bait box and my arm, same time."

*Shot?* His answer wrenched a knot in her gut. *What? Why?*

Once he said it, she how the bait box had splintered. The gaping wound in his arm hadn't only been caused by the shard that still protruded. She began to feel ill. "Who shot you?"

A slow head shake. "Don't know. Didn't see 'em."

Then she remembered the vehicle that she'd met on the road. *The green SUV! They had to be the ones who had made the ruts in the driveway on their way in to kill Billy Dan. Had he not been in his boat....* She had to tell the cops about the green SUV.

"I'm going to hold this tight against the bleeding until the ambulance gets here," she said, wadding a towel and pressing it firmly over the angry wound. She was doing her best to sound calm, hoping to keep Billy Dan quiet. She wrapped another towel around the part of his arm with the shard, and tucked the towel ends under him.

Billy Dan didn't answer. Under his injured arm, the blood pooled, staining the grass a dark crimson, and darkening the white towel. Using the heel of her palm, she increased pressure on the wound. He moaned. Billy Dan was losing consciousness. *He's losing a lot of blood. Where the hell is the ambulance?*

# # #

Billy Dan hadn't spoken for several minutes. Rhetta was sure he'd passed out. She'd taken another towel and wrapped it around his upper arm in a makeshift tourniquet. She twisted it and held it for a few minutes then released, repeating the tightening-release-tightening technique. She thought the bleeding was diminishing, but maybe it was her wishing it were so. She couldn't be sure. Although the towel became soaked and blood covered her hand, she continued the systematic tightening and releasing required of a tourniquet.

Finally, she heard the distant wail of a siren. Gradually it grew louder and closer. Then it powered down, followed quickly by the sound of crunching gravel and slamming doors. She glanced up and saw two EMTs on the back porch of Billy Dan's house.

"Down here," she yelled, waving one arm. She wasn't ready to release the tourniquet yet. The EMTs scrambled down the steps and rushed toward her.

When they reached Billy Dan, she released the tourniquet and stepped back, getting out of the way so they could work.

"I think he's unconscious," she said, and felt brainless as soon as the words crossed her lips. Of course, he was. They'd be able to tell that right away. Weren't they medical personnel? Her nerves were frayed.

One of the emergency techs asked her what had happened. While he talked, he began his efficient ministrations, checking Billy Dan's pulse, and then examining the horrific wound. When he gently unwrapped the makeshift pressure bandage Rhetta had applied, she was relieved to see that the blood, which had been spurting like a geyser, had slowed. The EMT instructed his companion to bring more supplies. The other tech ran back to the ambulance.

"He told me he got shot," Rhetta said. "He was fishing in his johnboat, and someone shot him. When I got here, he was under the boat. I'm not sure how that happened."

The tech plugged a stethoscope into his ears and listened to Billy Dan's heart and lungs. He merely nodded at her in acknowledgement. The EMT who'd run to the ambulance returned with a rolled up stretcher, bandages, and a bag of clear liquid and tubing. Within seconds, he'd deftly inserted the tubing into Billy Dan's arm. They loaded Billy Dan on to the stretcher and handed her the bag.

"Carry this. Hold it up as high as you can while we take him out of here," he said. Luckily, the bag had a molded handle that she could grab.

The EMTs scurried up the bank. It was all she could do to keep up. While the EMTs loaded Billy Dan into the back of the ambulance, another vehicle skidded to a stop alongside them.

Sheriff Frizz Dodson heaved himself out of the passenger side of a white Chevy Tahoe bearing foot high black lettering on each front door that said, *Bollinger County Sheriff*. Deputy Gordon Caldwell, leaner than the sheriff by fifty pounds, leapt out from behind the wheel.

After exchanging words with the ambulance driver, Dodson slapped the side of the ambulance in a signal for them to get rolling. They sped away down the driveway, sirens wailing.

The Sheriff's tan uniform shirt bore large half moons of sweat under the arms. His radio crackled from his shoulder and he paused, slapping at the transmitter to reply before approaching Rhetta. She heard him relay his location.

Rhetta wasn't sure what the Sheriff's real first name was, because everyone called him Frizz, due to the mop of wiry dark hair that sprang outward from his head.

Dodson was wheezing by the time he reached her. He pulled a large red paisley handkerchief from a rear pocket and mopped his brow.

"Afternoon, Mrs. McCarter," he said politely, appearing to overlook the fact that she was covered in crusty dried silt and Billy Dan's blood. He glanced first at her clown-sized sneakers, then at her hair, mud-plastered to her head.

"Sheriff," she said, greeting him in return.

"Can you tell me what happened?" he asked, swiveling his big head, taking in the surroundings. He wiped the absurdly oversized handkerchief across his wide forehead one more time before stuffing it into his back pocket.

Rhetta replayed everything that had happened after she arrived at Billy Dan's. She also told the sheriff she'd nearly been run off the road by a green SUV.

"Did you get the license plate number?" Dodson asked, removing a damp, pocket-sized spiral notebook from a breast pocket.

She shook her head. "No, I was pretty busy keeping Cami on the road."

"Cami?"

She tilted her head toward her car. "My Camaro."

"I see." He flipped the notebook closed. "It's a good thing for Billy Dan that you got here when you did, but can I ask what brought you out here today, Mrs. McCarter?" His bovine eyes stared down at her.

Rhetta sighed. She propped herself against the rear fender of the Tahoe. "I wanted to ask Billy Dan about his last conversation with my husband, Randolph. They were together before Randolph had his accident. I tried calling Billy Dan. When I couldn't reach him, I decided to come out here."

"All the way out here from Cape just to ask him about a conversation?"

Rhetta heard the skepticism in the question. *I guess every law enforcement person in Southeast Missouri knows about Randolph's accident.*

"Sheriff, I believe something bizarre, like a terrorist plot is going down in our area. My client, Doctor Hakim Al-Serafi died in an accident in the Diversion Channel. Then, my husband suffers a similar, nearly fatal accident, and Doctor Peter LaRose died in his apartment. The FBI agent that we first talked to is also dead. Now, Billy Dan gets shot. I think it all has to do with a schematic I found in Doctor Al-Serafi's car. All of us have seen the schematic, and something terrible has happened to everyone except me." *And Woody, who may be next. I have to get out of here and warn him.*

"A schematic? Terrorist plot? FBI? What in blazes are you talking about?" Frizz raised his thick eyebrows, fished out the notebook again and fanned himself with it. For a moment, she thought he might write down what she said. Not so. He only needed the notebook for a fan. "Doctor who?" he said and flapped the notebook harder.

"Randolph showed Billy Dan a schematic I found in the car that Doctor Hakim Al-Serafi died in." Frizz's eyebrow shot up again.

Before he could ask how, exactly, she came to have said schematic, she continued. "Billy Dan told Randolph it appeared to be a schematic of the transformers used in all the power substations. On his way home from meeting with Billy Dan, Randolph's car was run off the Whitewater Bridge, and now somebody tried to kill Billy Dan." She folded her arms and waited for Dodson to answer.

Frizz Dodson couldn't have looked any more confused than if someone had just rattled off *Fermat's Last Theorem*, the most difficult math problem ever solved, according to the Guinness World Records.

"More likely someone in the woods over yonder was poaching and a stray bullet clipped Billy Dan," Frizz said. "Besides, I heard your husband had a high B.A.C., so I doubt if anything fishy happened to him."

From the condescending tone of Dodson's voice, Rhetta concluded there was no use in continuing with her terrorist theory. Feeling defeated, she merely rubbed her temples and stayed quiet. *I need to warn Woody.*

When Deputy Caldwell jogged back from where Billy Dan had lain, Frizz glanced up at the late afternoon sky, then at his watch. The setting sun spread long orange fingers deep into the horizon. "Dang, it's after seven. No wonder my stomach's growling."

Caldwell cut a sideways glance at the sheriff, rolled his eyes, and ambled to the driver's side of the Tahoe. Frizz aimed for the passenger door and Rhetta eased away. Frizz yanked open the door. Before pouring himself into the seat, he turned back toward her. "Stop by the office in Marble Hill so we can get your statement." It wasn't a request.

"Sure thing" she said raising her hand in a small wave. *Yeah, I'll get right on that.*

The Tahoe backed, made a Y-turn, and left.

Rhetta stared at the plume of dust that marked their descent to the county road. The hot afternoon sun had finally dried out the surface of the gravel road, erasing any memory of the earlier storm.

She trudged to Cami, pulled open the driver door and groaned. She eyed her muddy clothes, then the spotless white interior.

# CHAPTER 39

H er shakiness calmed, Rhetta knew she had to get to a phone again and warn Woody. She returned to Billy Dan's kitchen and called Woody's cell phone. Good thing she'd gone back. She had failed to lock the door earlier. The call didn't go through. If Billy Dan had a long distance carrier, Rhetta didn't know the dialing code. Frustrated, she tried again, using 1, the area code then Woody's number. And received the same error message.

No more time to waste. After securing Billy Dan's house, she headed to Cami, and tugged open the door. She would have to use her cell phone to warn him as soon as she had service. She paused before sitting. In spite of the urgency, Rhetta couldn't make herself climb in and sit on the white seats with her muddy clothes.

She limped to the back of the car, opened the trunk, and stared inside for something to throw over the seats. The small trunk contained only the stereo amp along with a donut-sized spare tire and jack. *Cami wouldn't make a very good Mafia car. Couldn't stuff a body in the trunk.* Silly thoughts tended to invade her brain when she was nervous.

Remembering the unlocked fishing shed, she limped down to it. She was glad that she had. The door stood ajar. She needed to lock the building. She ventured inside, inhaling the mingled smells of plastic, paint, and a remnant of fish odor. To her relief, she found a new bright blue plastic tarp still in a bag, tucked away neatly on a shelf. Snatching it, she pushed the door closed and snapped the padlock shut.

Limping back to her car, Rhetta found she couldn't tear open the plastic package with her hands. Using her teeth, she tugged at a corner and succeeded in ripping it enough so that she could pull it open with her hands. She unfolded only as much of the tarp as she needed to drape over the driver's seat. When she was satisfied that the seat was sufficiently protected from the filth of her clothes, she climbed in. Groping around the passenger seat, she located her cell phone. Still no signal. She turned the key, and Cami rumbled to life.

Darkness had begun to replace the waning rays of sunlight when at last she reached the county road. Pausing at the end of Billy Dan's driveway, she tuned in her oldies station. She hoped the familiar music would work its magic on her frazzled nerves. After cautiously checking both directions for speeding SUVs and finding none, she eased out. She returned to the main highway, driving even more carefully than when she'd come in. She dreaded checking out what damage might have been done to her beautiful car.

This time, the rock'n'roll tunes didn't help her. She couldn't chase away the images of the afternoon of bizarre events that paraded across her mind. Everything swirled together. She'd been distracted, thinking about her father when she'd met the SUV that had nearly run her off the road. She tried to recall more details about the vehicle. She wished she'd seen the license plates. Surely, the county authorities were searching for it.

Who was she kidding? When she started talking about a terrorist plot, Frizz Dodson's eyes glazed over. From his expression, he definitely wasn't interested in her theory, preferring to believe that Billy Dan suffered a poacher's stray shot. She didn't believe his poacher theory for a second. She was lucky the lawman didn't want to haul her in for smoking wacky weed. Course if he did, he wouldn't get home in time for dinner. Dodson had priorities, for which she was grateful.

*Then who shot Billy Dan?*

A dread as cold as an Arctic blast washed over her. She knew the answer. It was whoever was driving the green SUV. The tracks she saw in the driveway had to be made by the shooters. She'd ask Frizz to check out the tread marks. That is, if they hadn't been obscured by all the traffic.

*The terrorists wanted rid of Billy Dan because somehow they'd known that he'd seen the schematic and understood what it meant.*

Pulling out on to Highway 34, Rhetta marveled at all the twinkling lights glittering around her. Although she was several miles west of Marble Hill, she realized that the area wasn't nearly as isolated as she'd always thought. Anytime she'd ever come out this way before, it was daytime, and the landscape of trees and pasture always seemed to stretch for miles. Tonight, lights blinked and winked at her from both sides of the highway as she gunned Cami, rapidly reaching, then exceeding the speed limit.

Cami glided effortlessly around a gentle curve, and Rhetta had just begun to relax when a flicker caught her eye. She glanced to the side. House lights and pole lights winked out. The same happened across the highway. She stole a glance in her rear view mirror. She saw nothing but pitch darkness behind her. She'd just passed *Green's Grocery*. The sign had been awash in light from four old fashioned light fixtures that arched out over the sign from the top, reminding her of gooseneck desk lamps. Now, there was only darkness where the bright store lights had been.

*A power outage.* Her heart thumped until she decided that it wasn't that unusual during hot days and heavy summer usage. A single substation could easily overload and cause a temporary brown out.

As she raced eastward, the phenomenon of extinguishing lights continued. She felt disoriented. There were no other cars on the road, no headlights or taillights to give her a sense of the roadway. The inky blackness made her feel like she'd driven into the *Twilight Zone.* She felt eerily alone, as though everyone had left the planet and turned off the lights on their way out. Her heart rate sped up again. *This ongoing blacking out shouldn't be happening!*

Reaching the edge of Marble Hill, she sped past the *Welcome* sign before realizing that the normally illuminated sign was dark. In fact, the whole town was in darkness.

This was no brown out.

An announcer interrupted her tunes. She turned the volume up. "There appears to be a major power failure in rural Bollinger County in Southeast Missouri. Listeners have reported an outage that stretches from Grassy east to the Cape Girardeau County line. We are unable to reach Inland Electric. As soon as we can confirm the cause, we will interrupt with a report. For now, we take you back to our regular programming." *The Guess Who* resumed belting out *American Woman.*

Rhetta reached over and lowered the volume.

A quick glance at her cell phone confirmed that she had three bars. At least the cell towers were still working. She had to call Woody. This blackout had to be part of the plot involving the schematic.

She didn't stop at the sheriff's office in Marble Hill to sign her statement. She doubted anyone had worked on it. Besides, Frizz Dodson would have his hands full with the power out all over his county. She sped on through town. Approaching the east edge of town, she slowed, remembering an intersection. At Merc's, dozens of patrons spilled out of the restaurant, heading for their rides. Several clusters of people milled around, as though unsure what to do.

At the four-way stop, the traffic signal was out. Although dozens of vehicles were maneuvering through the intersection, no one honked and no one appeared to be impatient. Everyone acted calmly, each driver giving the other a turn at going through. That, she reasoned, was a benefit of the friendship and camaraderie of a small town. It still took forever for her turn. She drummed her fingers on the steering wheel as she inched forward.

Finally after several long minutes, she made it through the intersection. She raced along highway 34 toward Cape. Reaching the power substation at Center Junction, she downshifted, slowing for the five Inland Electric trucks parked along the shoulder with their emergency flashers on. A dozen men in hard hats had gathered around the darkened substation. After she was safely past, she shifted again, and Cami throttled forward.

*They'll get the power up soon.* She'd never known these summer outages to endure more than a few hours.

"Not this time," argued a voice inside her head. Her gut agreed. This was more than temporary.

Flying across the bridge where Randolph had wrecked, Rhetta cringed, not daring a look over the side where his truck had gone. She checked her rear view mirror for the hundredth time since leaving Billy Dan's. At any moment she fully expected a green SUV to fill the reflection.

Her thoughts flew to Randolph. What about the hospital? Was it also without power? She held her phone aloft and pushed the button to illuminate the screen. She needed to talk to him, but all she saw was "No Service." She tossed it to the passenger seat.

A few minutes later, Rhetta approached the city of Jackson, just west of Cape. She stared mutely through the windshield, a horrible sense of déjà vu washing over her. The city's lights began disappearing. Soon, the city itself all but vanished. The only remaining visible light came from a radio tower. She'd heard the towers had battery backup in case of a power failure, allowing the position lights to remain lighted so that planes wouldn't run into them. Here and there, an isolated light winked on. Probably from home generators that began kicking in.

She and Randolph had purchased a whole house propane-powered generator three years ago after suffering a five-day loss of power during an ice storm. She wondered if it had kicked on. What had the installer said? It was supposed to kick in after ten seconds, or something like that. They'd never needed it since the ice storm.

The car radio fell silent. She fiddled with the knob, turning the volume up. Nothing but static. She hit the *search* and finally found a weak broadcast from a Memphis station. The sporadic crackling made the announcer difficult to understand.

Except that she clearly understood when he said, "Major blackout in the Cape Girardeau, Missouri area."

### # #

Crawling along with the snarled traffic on Jackson Boulevard, the main east-west thoroughfare through Jackson to Cape, Rhetta took time to snatch her phone and speed dialed Woody. Approaching a vacant lot, she pulled in to talk on her phone. With no traffic lights operating, the traffic was much worse in Jackson than it had been in Marble Hill and the drivers much more impatient. Horns blared, and headlights blinked as motorists expressed their unhappiness.

The call went through!

"Woody, it's happening," she said when he answered.

"What? What are you talking about?" She could hear radio or television static in the background.

"The power grid. It's going down. It's the terrorists. Don't you see?"

"God, Rhetta, what are you saying? You can't believe that." Rhetta heard shuffling and knew Woody held a hand over the phone while he shouted, "Jenn, the generator is in the garage. I'll get it."

When he came back, his voice was strained. "Look, it's crazy here. I gotta go and hook up the generator."

She couldn't let him hang up. "Woody, wait, I'm telling you, it's happening. I haven't told you about Billy Dan. I think the terrorists are implementing their plan right now and—"

Woody interrupted her. "What? What about Billy Dan?"

"Someone shot him this afternoon. I found him badly injured in his boat. Look, I'll tell you about it when I see you. I'm almost to Cape. I'm on my way to your house right now."

She pulled back on to the highway and gunned Cami. The Corvette engine delivering four hundred horsepower gave her plenty of punch to roar ahead of a Dodge minivan.

"Find your hunting rifle, Woody and get it ready. We have to stop them."

# CHAPTER 40

O nce past Jackson, Rhetta flew up the on-ramp to the interstate and pushed the Camaro toward Cape.

Woody hadn't said anything after she told him that Billy Dan had been shot, probably because she hadn't given him the chance. She disconnected after informing him she was on her way. She needed Woody with his 30-06 rifle and his military expert marksman skill. She'd thought about detouring home and getting some of Randolph's hunting rifles and shotguns, but they were locked in the gun safe. She couldn't remember where Randolph kept the key. Besides, Woody's house was closer.

Rhetta was certain that the power substations were under attack. Likewise, she realized that only she and Randolph understood what was going on. And Woody. He understood. He was just in denial. They were the only ones left who'd seen the schematic. *Is that why Randolph was run off the bridge? Because someone knew he'd seen the schematic?* Only she and Woody were in a position to do something. Time after time, she tried getting the law to help her. Law enforcement didn't believe her. It was up to her and Woody to get to the substations and stop the terrorists.

With the blackout occurring first in Bollinger County and now moving to west Cape County, she remembered the list of substations that she'd memorized. She had to visualize the map, and determine where the next outage would occur. By her calculation, there were still three substations left. The one in Glen Allen was out, as was the one on Highway 34 at Center Junction. Just now the one serving Cape

Girardeau County and City, which was the one on County Road 637, had surely gone down.

She and Woody needed to get to the next substation ahead of whoever was responsible. There were two left. They needed to decide whether to go to Perry County or to Scott County. Those two substations were at least fifty miles apart.

There had to be a team of individuals responsible for the substations going down. How else could that many transformers fail so quickly? One man or a pair of men couldn't be traveling to all of them that quickly. Would she and Woody be too late to save any of the substations?

Had that team originally included Al-Serafi who died with a schematic in his car? How did he die? And why? So many questions, so little time.

The FBI had ignored her and Woody, and Sheriff Dodson today had treated her as if she was on crack. Even so, she decided to call the FBI again. She reached for her cell phone and punched it the St. Louis number that she'd memorized. The number rang until it went to voice mail. She disconnected without leaving a message. Then she tried 9-1-1, hoping to reach the local police or highway patrol. She wasn't sure where her cell phone call would go. She remembered reading somewhere that cell phone 9-1-1 calls were seldom routed locally.

A dispatcher answered on the fourth ring. "9-1-1. What is your emergency?"

"Is this the Cape Girardeau police?"

"Yes, ma'am. What is your emergency?" asked the female dispatcher, her voice harried and clipped.

"Can I speak with Sergeant Risko? It's about the power outages. I think I know what's causing them."

"Hold please." Rhetta heard the familiar clicking sounds indicating that her call was being recorded.

She thought about what she and Woody needed to do. Her stomach tightened into a knot. Could she get the police to help them? Did Woody believe that they were under attack? She'd find out soon enough.

A voice came on the line. "What is your name please and what is it you want to report?"

"I'd like to speak to Sergeant Risko."

"I'm sorry ma'am, we have no way to reach Sergeant Risko. This is the 9-1-1 call center. This is Officer Len Brightwell. I can try and help you. Please state your name."

"Rhetta McCarter." She took a deep breath, frustrated at having to start her story yet again, but plunged forward. "The power substations are going down because there's a terrorist plot to take out the Midwest power grid by damaging the power transformers in each of the substations." She waited for him to ask her to elaborate.

Silence.

"Did you hear me?" Rhetta said, her voice rising.

He sighed. "Yes, ma'am. I did." Then with reluctance evident in his tone, he continued, "Who did you say is taking out these power transformers?"

"I didn't say. I'm not sure who, and I'm not sure why. What I can tell you, is that there are maybe three substations left, one south of Marble Hill, one at Flatt Junction in Scott County, and one on County Road 1458 in Perry County, although I think the one south of Marble Hill is out by now."

"All right, ma'am. We'll look into that. Thank you for calling."

The line went dead.

He didn't believe her. Perhaps if she'd been able to talk to Risko, he'd have remembered her from interviewing her at Peter LaRose's apartment and not dismissed her so quickly.

It was obvious. She'd get no help from the police.

Rhetta badly needed to hear her husband's voice, to get his assurance that stopping the cascading power failure was the right thing to do. Especially, she needed to know that he was all right. She speed dialed the hospital.

"All circuits are busy. Please try your call again later." The tinny sounding message repeated in a loop. She tossed her iPhone into the console. The phone system appeared to be down. She'd keep trying.

She whispered, "Randolph, you have to be all right. I can't come right now. I got stuff to take care of. I love you."

*I got stuff to take care of* was an expression her mother had always used when called Rhetta to tell her she'd be home late from work. Many nights Rhetta, an only child, fell asleep on the couch waiting for her mother to come home from one of her two regular jobs. Sometimes her mother never showed up, and Rhetta woke up to an empty house the following morning.

She pushed her memories away and accelerated to a hundred miles an hour.

Within minutes, she braked for the first exit into Cape. On the left, three blocks from the exit ramp on William Street sat St. Mark's Hospital. To her relief, she saw lights. *The hospital must be getting power from its own series of massive generators*. She sent a silent prayer heavenward to keep Randolph safe. For someone who'd quit going to church and who'd been mad at God, she'd sure been sending up a lot of prayers lately. What was it they said about there being no atheists in foxholes? She felt like she was definitely in a foxhole now.

Woody lived about two miles farther, near the university campus. Rhetta merged into the eastbound traffic on an eerily dark William Street. Normally, the four-lane boulevard was as brightly lit as the Las Vegas Strip, especially near the Interstate. Now, the various fast food restaurants, hotels, bars, and the shopping mall where Jenn worked were cloaked in inky blackness. Rhetta had never seen anything like this.

The chaos she found herself in was straight out of a horror movie. Cars, pickups, SUVs, taxis, and busses all clamored for the right-of-way through every intersection. Again and again, brakes screeched, followed by the sickening sounds of metal crunching metal.

She was forced to stop at the Kingshighway intersection barricaded by angry motorists. Although the other side was where she needed to be, she wasn't going to get across any time soon. She also couldn't turn around. She decided that once across, she'd get on a side street away from the main thoroughfare, or Cami would wind up a crushed tin can.

Finally, she was able to inch her way across Kingshighway. In a desperate attempt to get out from the confusion of cars on William Street, she took the first right. In two blocks, the street dead-ended. She veered left. There was little traffic. She found herself in an unfamiliar neighborhood, one that she recalled hearing about, where women shouldn't travel, especially after dark. She should've turned left off William Street, not right. She'd gone the wrong way.

Two blocks later, she veered left on to West End Boulevard, an old-fashioned divided four lane with a median full of trees and flower beds. Although the traffic squeezed bumper to bumper on the street, at least everyone on her side of the median was traveling in the same direction.

Just before arriving at the cluster of traffic that signaled a return to William Street, a late model Cadillac Seville poured out of a side street and cut her off. It sped across both lanes as it headed for a left-hand turn lane ahead. Rhetta slammed her brakes, barely avoiding a collision. After the black Seville rocketed past her, she pulled up to William Street, stopped, and waited. The endless traffic wouldn't break long enough for her to cross. Impatient, and unable to bear waiting another minute, she turned right, even though she was surely going out of her way. She plodded along slowly, forced to stop several times before managing to worm her way into the left lane. Woody lived on the other side of William. The agonizingly slow traffic ate up precious minutes.

Where were the terrorists heading next? If she and Woody couldn't stop them, the Midwest grid would completely crash.

That realization spurred her to floor the gas pedal. Imitating the Seville, she tore off left across two lanes amid loud honking and screeching of brakes. She careened on to Henderson Street, which snaked past the university campus and on to Woody's house. Approaching the campus, she eased up, fearing another crush of traffic and wanting to avoid another right turn. Could she make all right turns and still go left? She didn't think so.

Surprisingly, traffic away from William and Kingshighway wasn't bad. She turned left, and then zigzagged right. Only one more traffic hurdle ahead, the intersection at Independence Street. She needed to go a block past it, to the corner of North Park and Whitener, where Woody lived.

As she feared, Independence, always one of the busiest streets in Cape, was swarming with traffic. Hundreds of students aboard scooters wove crazily between the horde of cars. At least the vehicles were moving. There was no traffic backed up. She soon discovered the reason. The intersection was manned by a stocky campus police officer directing traffic. When he signaled her turn to go, she floored Cami.

# CHAPTER 41

The darkness disoriented Rhetta. When she crossed Independence, she didn't recognize anything and didn't know for sure where she was. She couldn't look to the familiar green patina of the lighted coppered dome on Academic Hall on the Southeast Missouri University campus to get her bearings. The entire area was pitch black. No dome anywhere in sight. Was she heading the right way?

After six blocks, Rhetta realized that she had passed Woody's house. Irritated at the time she wasted getting lost, she spotted a driveway and quickly used it to turn around and backtrack.

Mercifully, there was almost no traffic on the side streets. She wasn't honked at or forced to dodge wayward vehicles aiming for her. There was also no light. She slowed down, willing her eyes to recognize Woody's house.

Finally, she recognized his bungalow and roared into his driveway. The moment she stopped, Woody appeared at her driver door. She rolled down the window.

"I heard you coming from down the block," he said.

"Do you have your 30-06? C'mon, we gotta go." Rhetta hit the accelerator and revved the motor. Cami responded throatily.

"I'm not going with you, Rhetta. I can't leave Jenn here alone."

Jenn stepped out from behind Woody. She cradled a large hunting rifle and a box of shells. "Here, Woody. Go." Jenn thrust the rifle at Woody. "I'll be fine. I have a .38 and know how to use it." Jenn, nearly as tall as Woody, but a hundred pounds lighter, deposited the rifle into her husband's arms.

When he took it, Jenn tucked a strand of her long blond hair behind her ear and nodded. She blew him a kiss, then whirled around and disappeared into the shadow of the house. In a moment, Woody's back door slammed and she heard a metal latch clattering into place.

"I can't believe this blackout has to do with terrorists," Woody said, making no move toward Cami's passenger door.

"We're being attacked. It's up to you and me, Woody. We're the only ones that can stop it. We have to get to a substation ahead of whoever is doing this and stop them." Rhetta kept her voice as calm as she could. She knew Woody well enough to know she had to stay calm, or he'd bull up and walk away from her. She didn't have time to drive to her house and find Randolph's weapons, then head to the substations. She needed Woody to shut up and get in the car.

"I tried calling the police, but they wouldn't listen to me. I can't reach the FBI office in St. Louis either." She put Cami into neutral and held her foot on the brake.

"You still haven't told me about Billy Dan. What happened? You said he got shot?"

Why did Woody just stand there talking?

She sighed. "Yes, he got shot, by somebody driving a green SUV. Sound familiar? Get in and I'll tell you about it."

She wasn't positive about the person or persons driving the green SUV being responsible for shooting Billy Dan, but she'd bet her next paycheck on it.

Jenn stepped out on the front stoop and shouted, "Woody, go with Rhetta. Right now." Woody obeyed, crossed in front of Cami and opened the passenger door. He slid the rifle and a box of shells on to the floor and covered them with the surplus tarp that draped from Rhetta's seat into the back. The bright overhead LED interior light spilled all the way to the outside of the car. She was glad that Ricky had added the LED. The old-style yellowish interior light wasn't strong enough to draw moths.

Woody stared at Rhetta. When she saw his expression, she touched her hair and frowned. She must've looked like a yard gnome that had fallen into wet concrete. And then the concrete dried.

"Hurry up and get in. We have to plan our strategy."

After the passenger door closed, Jenn returned to the house.

"Don't you look cute. Is that a new fashion trend?" Woody gestured to Rhetta as he fastened his seat belt.

She didn't answer him.

He glanced sideways at her. "What are we going to do?"

"Here's how I have it figured. We've already lost three, maybe four substations, starting with the two in Bollinger County and one at Center Junction. I think maybe the other one in Cape County is out because everything around us is dark as the devil's breath. That only leaves two. We have to decide whether to go to Scott County or Perry County."

"What do you plan on doing to stop them, whoever they are?"

"First we need to decide the where, then the what," Rhetta said and slammed Cami into reverse.

At the end of the driveway, Rhetta pulled out on to the street and stopped. Cami's engine rumbled.

"Since we're in Cape Girardeau, I figure we're about the same distance away from either Perry or Scott County. The interstate connects all three communities in a straight line. Right now, we're in the middle. The issue is the traffic. Not to mention, choosing which one to go to first. Our choice could mean the difference between success or total failure." She turned and stared at Woody. "It might be a crap shoot, but I favor going north to Perry first because it's easier for the perps to reach that one from the substation in Cape County." She waved her hand around. "We know they've been to Cape County. They can easily use a back road instead of the interstate and get to Perry County. Otherwise, they'd have to fight traffic to cross town, then head down south on the interstate to Scott, then drive back track up the interstate to Perry."

She waited for a comment. Woody didn't say anything. When she slid a glance his way, she swore she saw him nod. She took that as a positive sign. Maybe he was finally persuaded.

"Perps?" Woody said, and a slow smile sneaked across his face.

Rhetta felt relief. Woody was with her. "Let's hit the substation on County Road 1458 in Perry County," she said and shifted into first.

They screamed down Woody's dark street. Rhetta shifted, downshifted, made two turns, and headed to the old Farm-to-Market Road.

"We'd never have made it to the interstate. There's too much chaos," Rhetta said, tearing through another turn and roaring on to State Highway 127, which the locals still called the Farm-to-Market Road. In spite of the road disappearing into a hill, she knew it continued north, straight into Perry County.

"What's the plan?' Woody asked. He passed a bare palm over his slick head.

"Is that rifle loaded?" Rhetta pointed to the back seat. She thought he nodded, although she couldn't see him clearly. "Are you still an expert shot?" She knew all about his numerous marksmanship awards from the military.

"Yes, and yes."

"All right. Here's the plan. We get to the substation and stop anybody inside the fence that shouldn't be there. We'll hold them until the police get there. Maybe if we catch these guys, the cops will pay attention."

"They aren't going to stand there meekly while you call the cops."

"Right. That's why you have the rifle."

Although she couldn't see him shaking his head, his silence spoke his uncertainty.

"Have you got a better idea?" Rhetta's glare was wasted. Most of her face was probably concealed by the darkness.

"I don't know." He shook his head. "I don't know what the Sam Hill is going on any more than anyone else does. We can't shoot these people."

"You do, too, know what's going on, Woody. These people are trying to take down our country. You and I both know this is a terrorist attack. And it's up to us to stop it."

Woody sighed. "Jenn believes you're right. We had a huge argument. Just before you got there."

Rhetta smiled in spite of the terror she was feeling. *Good for Jenn. At least she has some sense. Maybe I should've brought her instead of Woody.*

Inside, Rhetta felt like a bowl of jelly. On the outside, she needed to appear strong so Woody wouldn't waver. She knew he'd been forced to kill during his stint in the war, and that had contributed to his PTSD.

"Is Jenn a crack shot like you?"

"What? No. Well, yes, she can shoot. She's not a marksman. Or is it markswoman? Whatever." He rubbed his head with a handkerchief he'd pulled from a back pocket.

Rhetta steered the subject back to the plan. "County Road 1458 runs down to the river. The substation is on the bluffs overlooking the river. We'll turn off on Gabriela Road. That crosses County Road 1458 about a mile after we turn. Then we head toward the river."

As they sped along the two-lane highway, Rhetta filled Woody in on how she found Billy Dan shot under his boat. And how Sheriff Dodson didn't believe her.

"Woody, it's down to you, me, and Randolph. We're the only ones left of everyone who saw the schematic. And poor Randolph is out of commission."

Woody didn't answer, although she thought she heard him grunt his assent. She cut her glance sideways but was afraid to take her eyes off the dark, twisting road to stare back at him. Especially since Cami was flying at over eighty through the twists, turns, and hills.

Topping a steep crest on the outskirts of Perry County, they were met with a glorious sight. The landscape ahead was dotted with lights. All around, the lights from houses, farm dusk-to-dawn lights, and street lamps glimmered. The view looked wonderfully normal.

"Look, Woody!" Rhetta shouted, even though he sat a mere two feet away. "We're not too late. They haven't knocked the substation out up here yet."

She gunned the Camaro and dared not consult the speedometer.

"Maybe we're all wrong about this," Woody said. "Maybe it really is just a massive power failure in Cape."

"Are you forgetting about Bollinger County and Billy Dan? Right after Billy Dan got shot, the power in Bollinger County started failing. Then the power in Cape went out. That's not random."

"I know, I know, you don't believe in coincidences, but still. The power substation going out in Bollinger could have caused an overload in Cape."

Rhetta spotted Gabriela Road up ahead. The whole area looked so bright and normal that she began to wonder if maybe Woody wasn't right.

She swerved a hard right on to Gabriela Road. In about a mile, she spotted the sign for County Road 1458. She pulled up and stopped.

"Why are you stopping?"

"If there's cell phone service here, I need to call the county sheriff or the FBI again," Rhetta said. She located her iPhone on top of the console and powered it on.

A red bar replaced the usually green battery indicator. The battery was nearly dead. She groped around in the console for her car charger cord. "Damn, where is it?" she said, and pulled everything out of the small storage bin. She riffled through a mileage logbook, three pens, a small spiral note pad, and several paper napkins. No cord. She didn't take out the cigarettes and latex gloves.

"Let me have your phone," she said to Woody. She held out her hand.

"I don't have it. I guess with all the arguing with Jenn, I forgot to grab it."

"Crap," Rhetta said and sifted again through the console.

"All right, forget it. We're on our own." She snapped the lid closed. Gravel flew as she turned right on the unpaved county road.

She raced along County Road 1458 for nearly a mile before Woody spoke.

"Uh, didn't you say the power substation was near the bluffs?"

"Yes." Her eyes were glued to the road.

"You're heading away from the river," Woody said. His voice was calm. "You need to turn around.'

"Damn," Rhetta said, screeching to a stop. A cloud of dust swirled around the car as she executed a Y-turn. She tore off back from where they'd just come. Sailing past the intersection where she'd rummaged for her charger, she said, "How could I have gone the wrong way? We may be too late." Couldn't she find anything tonight?

Woody glanced out the side window.

"Uh, Rhetta, all the lights are still on so we're okay."

He no sooner said it when lights began winking off. Just like in Bollinger and Cape counties.

The countryside around them plunged into a hellishly familiar blackness.

# CHAPTER 42

*S*o much for getting here on time!
Rhetta slammed the brakes and pulled to the side of the county road.

"What are you doing?" This time it was Woody shouting as he threw out his hands to brace himself against slamming into the dash. The shoulder harness snapped tightly against his chest, pinning him against the seat.

Rhetta threw Cami into reverse. "We can cut across and get back on Gabriela Road. It connects to the interstate just south of Perryville. Maybe we can beat them to Scott County if they don't know this short cut."

Woody fiddled with the shoulder harness until it finally yielded some slack. "How come you know your way around Perry County but get lost in the Steak 'n Shake parking lot in Cape?"

"I once dated a guy that lived on a farm up here," Rhetta answered. "We used to drive all these back roads." She swerved hard to the right. Woody braced again. "Who told you I got lost in the Steak 'n Shake?"

"So, how come you went the wrong way back there, looking for the Mississippi?"

Rhetta ignored him.

### # # #

As Rhetta had predicted, once they hit Gabriela Road they were within five minutes of the interstate.

Hustling down Gabriela Road, she swerved right when she spotted the interstate. Woody again braced against the dash. Cami's modern shoulder harnesses were getting a workout.

It took only a dizzying few seconds to complete the near circle of the on ramp. Soon they were racing on to the interstate. This was their last chance to stop a total grid failure. They had to get to Scott County, to the last substation, before the terrorists did.

There were few vehicles on the divided interstate. Mostly, she saw only over-the-road trucks with trailers. Once she locked into the inside fast lane, Rhetta opened Cami up. Her speedometer displayed a maximum top-end speed of 160 on the face. She didn't dare look at it to see how close they were to burying the needle.

The interstate wasn't much different than it was before the blackout, since there was no highway lighting in this part of the state. She stole a glance at Cami's fuel gauge. To her shock, she had less than half a tank of gas left. All that crazy driving from Glen Allen and then through Cape to get to Woody's had taken its toll on the nearly full tank she'd started out with. Her pet Camaro was a gas hog.

Rhetta reached up and patted the dash. "Come on baby. Don't let me down. I can't stop for gas. We've got to go another 50 miles."

*Please God, we've got to stop them.*

"It wouldn't do any good to stop at a gas station, anyway," said the ever-practical Woody. "There's no power, remember?"

"Yes, Woody. I'm aware that there is no power and therefore we won't be able to get any gas."

"Then don't run out."

*Honestly. Does he think I planned it this way? Grr….*

"Why are you growling?"

She wasn't aware that she'd growled aloud. "I'm just getting frustrated, that's all."

"Yeah, well, me, too." He twisted around and gazed out the back window. "Have you seen any cars in your rear view? Maybe we should be on the watch for a car that's driving suspiciously fast down the interstate. Besides us, I mean."

Woody made sense. She glanced in her side view mirrors. No other cars. Theirs was the only car rocketing along.

Peering at the speedometer, Woody said, "You're liable to get pulled over for speeding, you know."

*Good grief, was he being deliberately obtuse?*

"That would actually be wonderful." She slapped the steering wheel. "If only!" She felt herself getting exasperated. Had he not paid attention when she told him about her unsuccessful attempts at contacting law enforcement? Getting pulled over might get them some help, damn it!

"Can you get out the map from the glove box?" Rhetta angled her chin in the direction of Woody's death grip on the dash. "Under your right palm."

"Why do you need a map?" He sounded worried as he fiddled with the catch to open the glove box.

"Turn the knob to the right," she instructed after seeing his impatience. He'd already slapped the glove box door twice.

"I got it," he said and rooted around. Instead of a map, he produced a leather holster with a neat pearl handle showing through.

"What's this?" He held it between his thumb and index finger.

Rhetta slid a glance his way and recognized the .22 pistol Randolph had bought at the gun show last month.

"Randolph bought that at the gun show. I guess he forgot to take it out of the glove box."

"Good, we could use another weapon, even if it is just a toy."

"We can't use that one. It's not loaded."

Woody set the holster down on the console between them. Rhetta changed lanes and the gun slid to the floor near Woody's feet. He groped around his feet, searching for the gun.

"Never mind the pistol, Woody. Find the map."

Triumphantly, like he'd found a scavenger hunt object, he finally held up the folded Missouri map. He left the glove box open to utilize the small light to read the map. The Camaro had no map lights, only the overhead LED dome light, which didn't have a switch.

He opened up the large map and spread it out over his lap. "What do you want me to find?"

"Look for Flatt Junction. It's in Scott County. I think it's east of Old Miner."

"Old Miner? Where's that?"

"It's considered a part of Sikeston now."

"Then why didn't you say Sikeston?"

She groaned. *He has to be provoking me on purpose. Woody isn't that dense.*

That's when it hit her. His reluctance had to do with his PTSD. She stole another sideways glance at Woody, hunched over, examining the map. His head glistened with droplets of sweat in spite of the air conditioning. His shirt was soaked with sweat. Woody was a nervous wreck. She prayed he wasn't working up to an episode. She didn't have time to deal with it. It was up to her to keep both of them under control. *Stay calm.*

She took in a deep breath, and tried to go to her quiet place. She couldn't find it. She hoped her brain would at least benefit from added oxygen. She inhaled two more times. She willed the oxygen to cleanse her heart, her blood, her brain, go to her nerve endings, and slow her pulse. Each time she let the breath out quickly, in order to dispel the carbon dioxide.

"Why are you panting?" Woody broke the reverie she'd induced in hopes of keeping calm.

"I'm not panting. I'm taking cleansing breaths," Rhetta said.

"Sounds like panting to me. By the way, it isn't just your breaths in need of cleansing. That dried mud all over you is getting pretty ripe in this cramped space."

In spite of the tension, or maybe because of it, Rhetta giggled. Woody chuckled. Then, they both laughed. Like during a preacher's sermon in church, even though laughing was inappropriate, neither of them could stop.

# CHAPTER 43

Woody and Rhetta zoomed past the last Cape Girardeau exit heading southbound. Sikeston lay twenty miles ahead. Woody held the large paper map to within inches of his face, staring intently.

Woody said, "I don't have my reading glasses. From what I can tell there's a Sikeston exit at Highway 62 that says Miner. There's also one south of Sikeston at the Highway 60 exit that also says Sikeston. Do you know which one we need to take?"

"We'll get off at the Miner exit, and go east. See how far it is to Flatt Junction."

"Flatt Junction isn't marked," Woody said after scanning the map. He began folding it. "I need to get this down to a manageable size." He folded it over twice more.

"Flatt Junction should be on Highway 62 just before we get to Bertrand. I looked it up when Randolph called me the night of his accident. We have to turn left on a state road. Do you see a state road marked there? Not a number road, a letter road." Rhetta referred to the mysterious system Missouri had of identifying its roads. Some state roads had letters while others had numbers, according to a pattern no one could understand.

A flashing blue light in Rhetta's rear view mirror caught her attention.

Woody held the map closer to the glove box light and then he leaned back, holding it at the end of his reach. He squinted and then tilted forward again. "Why didn't I bring my glasses?" he mumbled. Then, tapping the map, he asked, "Could it be Highway O?"

"That's it," Rhetta said. "How far to O after we get off the interstate?"

The blue light had now pulled up behind her. The lights had doubled. There were now two flashing blue lights and they were ablaze atop a highway patrol car.

Rhetta downshifted, pulled over to the shoulder, and stopped. The patrol car pulled in about twenty feet behind her.

"Looks like you got your wish," Woody said, closing the glove box.

"Maybe he'll help us." Rhetta kept Cami idling in neutral, her foot on the brake. The officer took his time getting out of his car and making his way to her driver's side. She rolled her window down before he got there.

"Officer, I'm glad you're here," Rhetta began before he had a chance to recite the customary, *Good evening ma'am. Going a little fast there, weren't you?*

The officer looked surprised. He aimed an excessively bright flashlight beam directly into Rhetta's face. She squinted.

"We need you to follow us," Rhetta said. "It's an emergency. We're going to the power substation at Flatt Junction, near Sikeston."

Apparently, the police academy didn't cover scenarios like this. The young officer didn't answer. He continued beaming the flashlight back and forth between Woody and Rhetta.

Rhetta shielded her eyes with her hand and craned her neck to look up at the officer studying her. "Officer, we have reason to believe there's a terrorist attack underway on our power substations. There's a chance that there's one last power station left operating in Sikeston. We just left Perryville and that one's out. Sikeston is the last one in the entire southeast Missouri service area for Inland Electric. We've got to stop the terrorists who are doing this. They'll be heading to Sikeston. I believe we're ahead of them, but not by very much. We need your help to stop them. Call for backup."

The officer shook his head and laughed. "The guys at headquarters told me they'd heard every story in the book, but I'll bet a day's wages they never heard this one." He held out his hand. "Let me have your operator's license and car's registration, please." He kept shaking his head.

Rhetta grappled around the floor of the back seat for her bag. "I know you're aware of the power outages," Rhetta said, determined to make the officer believe her. She snatched the handle on her purse and tugged the bag into her lap. "We know what's causing them." She groped through her bag and came out with her wallet. She located her driver's license. Then she reached over and opened the glove box. After dumping everything from it on to Woody's lap, she fished through the stack and found the laminated registration card. She presented the wallet and the registration card to the officer.

"I know you know what's causing them," he said. "You just told me. Terrorists. Please remove your operator's license from the wallet." His smile disappeared. Rhetta did as he requested.

Clutching her license and registration in his hand, the officer turned toward his car. He stopped and swiveled back to her. "By the way, I love what you've done with the seat coverings." He pointed to the big blue tarp. He chuckled at his own joke.

Rhetta fumed until she realized how she must've looked to the officer—a muddy mess sitting on a blue tarp in a '79 Camaro, ranting about terrorists in Cape Girardeau. Undoubtedly, he must've thought he'd have a tale to tell his grandchildren. She thought that the better story would have resulted from accompanying her and Woody. From the cop's attitude, it didn't seem likely that would happen.

On his way, he shone the flashlight on his booty, reading while he walked.

*He doesn't believe me, either.*

Rhetta removed her foot from the brake, threw Cami into first, and shot back on to the highway.

"Oh, great," Woody said. "Why did you do that?" He twisted around to look out the rear window.

"He blew his chance to help us," Rhetta grumbled, shifting into fourth. The Camaro leapt into the fast lane once more. "We don't have all night." Within seconds, she was doing eighty.

# # #

Cami was the only vehicle on the southbound side of the divided interstate when they screamed past the Cape Girardeau airport exit. After repeated glances in the mirror, she was disappointed to find that the officer wasn't following them. "With any luck, that rookie called ahead to have another cop stop us," Rhetta said. "Maybe we can get them to follow us."

Woody didn't answer.

Rhetta glanced over to the Cape Girardeau Regional Airport, which sat a quarter mile away in a large field. Normally the control tower and airport compound was well lit and readily visible from the exit. Now, the entire vicinity lay in total darkness, just like the rest of the area.

*Strange. They must not have any backup generators.*

Woody had remained silent throughout the traffic stop. After Rhetta had driven down the road a ways, Woody held up the .22 pistol. He'd found the holster on the floor and had stealthily removed the weapon and concealed it on his lap under the unwieldy map.

"What were you planning on doing with that?" Rhetta asked as Woody slid the revolver back into the holster. He opened the glove box and tucked the weapon inside.

"I thought for a minute there I was going to have to persuade that dumb cop to leave us the heck alone and let us get rolling if he wasn't going to help." He shot a look at Rhetta. "I didn't have to. You took care of the situation yourself."

"You were going to do that with an empty .22?"

"He didn't know it was empty."

"Did you want to get us killed? What if he would've drawn his own weapon and fired?"

"He wouldn't have, not with me holding a gun on him."

Woody wasn't acting at all like himself. PTSD? Rhetta began rapid deep breathing. Where was that oxygen when she needed it?

# CHAPTER 44

"Look, there's power here!" Woody shouted as they raced past the Benton exit. The McTruck stop was ablaze in artificial lighting. A quarter mile past the exit, Woody asked, "Shouldn't you have stopped for gas?"

"We're good. Still have a quarter of a tank." Rhetta desperately hoped she wasn't lying to Woody. The gas gauge did read one-quarter, and it had always been accurate. Maybe she should've stopped for gas. She'd debated that long before Woody had spoken. She decided not to. Their window of time was too narrow to risk stopping for gas. There were no time outs left in this game. She'd have to run with the ball.

She'd prayed they'd have enough gas to get them another ten miles.

"Ten more miles, Cami. You can do it," she whispered.

"I heard that. Are you going to run out of gas?"

"No, WE are not going to run out of gas." She hoped she sounded more confident than she felt. "We're coming up to the exit now."

Woody unhooked his safety belt and reached for the rifle. When he didn't refasten his belt, the safety buzzer that Ricky had insisted on installing began its angry notification.

Rhetta knew better than to advise Woody to buckle up. Neither she nor Woody was sure what vehicle to watch for. Her gut told her that they and a vehicle belonging to whoever was behind this were probably closing in together. If anybody started shooting at them, Woody would need to aim and shoot quickly. He couldn't waste time unfastening his seat belt.

Woody checked the rifle. "Ready," he said, his tone all business. He propped the weapon butt-down alongside him, near the door.

He ran his free hand over his head.

A football-sized knot began forming in Rhetta's stomach. With the football came the sour taste of bile. Her gut, along with the rifle, had locked and loaded.

Traffic was moderately congested around the exit. The stores and hotels were open for business as usual. People were moving about, seemingly oblivious to the problems their neighbors were experiencing just a few miles north of them. Rhetta followed a pickup truck off the interstate and down the exit ramp. It turned east. As did she. For an instant, she wondered if that truck carried the terrorists.

"I hope that highway cop sent out an all-points bulletin on me," Rhetta said, pulling out to pass the truck. "We'll need help."

Woody grunted. "What for?"

"It's just you and me and one weapon. Don't you think having the cops with us would be pretty helpful?"

"Don't count on any cops arriving like knights in shining armor to help us. Especially from that dumb rookie who didn't believe a single word you said." Woody jerked his thumb in a backward gesture. "That guy probably thinks he'll look like an idiot if he summons the troops to apprehend you at a remote power substation, and you aren't there."

"But we will be there." She shot past the truck.

"He doesn't believe you. No way."

"Thanks a lot, Woody. You're a real downer, you know that?" She checked her side mirrors. The truck she'd just passed grew smaller and smaller. No other vehicle appeared.

"I don't mean to rain on your parade, but I'm realistic. We're on our own out here, like we've been from the beginning."

"He'll have to report that I ran off from a traffic stop. This car is rather distinctive, in case you've forgotten. He won't want me getting away with driving off."

"All he'll do is hold your license and issue you a ticket. You'll have to go to court and explain to a judge why you drove off. At this point, that cop is irritated at you and could care less."

"Dang it, Woody, it's *couldn't care less*. I wish you'd get that expression right." Rhetta pounded the steering wheel in frustration.

Woody wiped his head. "Whatever."

Then he peered through the windshield and pointed. "There's Highway O, coming up on your left."

By the time he said it, Rhetta had passed the road. She squealed to a stop, did a u-turn in the middle of the road. Through a cloud of dust, she slid a right turn onto O highway. It was an even narrower two-lane road than the one she'd just left.

"You should've told me sooner," Rhetta lamented.

Woody ignored her complaint. "How far is the substation from here?" he said, and reached for the rifle.

"From what I remember, it's about two or three miles down O. We should be able to spot it easily."

She floored the Camaro and rocketed down the dark country road.

# CHAPTER 45

After six or seven minutes without spotting the substation, Rhetta skidded to a stop. "We should've come up on it by now." Throwing the car into neutral, but without turning off the car, she opened the door and stepped out to survey the area. She'd been able to drive at least sixty along the narrow flat road. According to her quick calculations, five minutes of driving should have put them at, or at least near, the substation.

Staring through the darkness, she was barely able to discern trees, pastures, and hayfields. She and Woody were far enough out in the Scott County countryside that there were no houses, no buildings of any kind, and especially no substation. She inhaled the sweet smell of newly mown hay. The blue darkness of the night enveloped them. For a moment, she feared that they had ultimately been too late, that the power was off here, too. When her eyes had adjusted to the darkness, she spotted a soft glow on the horizon.

She leapt behind the wheel just as Woody had hand on the door handle. She shifted Cami into first and stepped on the accelerator.

The momentum knocked Woody back into his seat. "You could warn me before you kill me," he said, groping for the rifle. "Luckily, I didn't have the door open."

"Hang on," she said. They topped a small rise. "We're there."

She heard Woody's sharp intake of breath and saw his body tense.

Upon arriving at the glowing area she'd seen on the horizon, she identified numerous large rectangular masses enclosed by a chain link fence. The bright oasis was an island in a sea of dark fields. The substation.

Rhetta sped past it, barely slowing.

"Why aren't you stopping?" Woody twisted around to look behind as they flew past.

"We made it here ahead of them. Let's find a good place to stash this car. We'll walk to the substation and surprise them when they arrive."

She spotted a turn-off into a field. She slowed and steered carefully across twenty feet of ground with deep tractor ruts into a recently mowed field. The farmer had baled his hay into huge round bales and had stacked them three high along the road. Most cattle farmers preferred the six feet high, seven to eight hundred pound round bales, since they were easier to feed to cattle and could be stored outside all year. They also provided perfect cover.

Rhetta tucked Cami in close behind the bales. She was sure no one could see the car from the road. She turned off the motor, killed the lights. She and Woody sat a moment in the dark, in silence. She heard Woody breathing softly.

"Are you ready?" Rhetta whispered.

"Let's do this," Woody answered. He grabbed the rifle and threw open the passenger door. He sprinted off.

Rhetta yelped from her injured ankle as she hobbled along after Woody across the uneven field. Woody paused to wait for her. A few more steps put them on the solid paved road.

The oversized clown sneakers slapped the pavement as Rhetta hoofed it alongside Woody. Eyeing her footwear, Woody said, "Is that another fashion statement?"

There was enough ambient light glowing from the substation that she was sure that Woody caught her glare this time.

With nearly 200 feet to go before reaching the substation, Woody pointed to an oncoming SUV topping the rise. Rhetta shouted, "It's them! Duck!" and launched herself into the road ditch.

Woody dove in alongside her. A layer of drying mud lined the bottom of the shallow ditch. Rhetta glanced at Woody. He lay on his stomach, chin up, one hand holding his weapon out of the goop. His face was speckled with mud particles. With his other hand, he carefully removed the miraculously unbroken Heineken bottle from under his abdomen. He tossed it aside. Stale beer trickled down his arm.

Rhetta had flopped in on her belly and plowed through mud and stinking McDonald's wrappers and a crushed cigarette package. She spit out the package. Seeing it triggered an urge for a smoke.

Woody grabbed a handful of clay mud and smeared it across his face.

"Camouflage," he said.

When she began to do the same, Woody shook his head. "No need. You're already covered. All I can see are the whites of your eyes."

The SUV slowed when it reached the substation. It pulled in to the gravel drive and turned off its lights, disappearing in the backlight from the substation.

"They're here," Rhetta whispered. Her stomach knotted.

Woody leapt out of the ditch and ran toward the substation. He'd vanished by the time Rhetta had sprung to her feet and began limping after him. She scurried up the drive and skidded to a stop when she heard shouts followed by gunshots, and witnessed bursts of gunfire coming from two or three different directions. There were too many shots to count. The staccato reports reverberated through the night air, sounding to her like they came from the back of the substation. Near the transformer.

Throwing herself to the ground again, Rhetta flung her hands over her head. Her heart hammered with the rapidity of machine gun fire. She couldn't breathe. Her heart thrummed in her chest. Where was Woody? What was happening? Was he okay?

# CHAPTER 46

Ten seconds, then twenty passed, with no more shots. Rhetta dared raising her head. The substation lights were still on. Woody must've stopped them. But where was he?

Rhetta stood and strained her eyes to see into the darkness. She still couldn't find Woody. She crouched low and moved to the east side of the substation. She stared into the glare of the sodium vapor lights mounted on poles at the corners of the chain-link fence that surrounded the substation. The lights pointed toward the front of the substation and bathed the area in an eerie orange glow. Ducking under the light beams allowed her to glimpse the area behind the substation. No lights shone back there. Rhetta stopped, waiting for her eyes to adjust to the dark, praying she'd catch sight of Woody.

The silence was as deep as the night was dark. Not a tree frog belched or whippoorwill called.

A loud crackle of underbrush startled her. She ducked low when she spotted a man in black clothing, inching his way toward the rear of the substation, toward an SUV. She couldn't make out much detail from his dark form. He carried something bulky. Was it Woody? Then the shadowy form passed under the lights. It wasn't a single man carrying something. There were two, and they were carrying something between them. The terrorists. Her pulse raced. Her head began to sweat. Where the hell was Woody?

Frozen in place, praying they wouldn't hear her breathing, she breathed shallowly, afraid that each inhalation would give her away. Since the substation lights were still ablaze, they hadn't succeeded in taking the substation down—yet. Was Woody all right? And where were these two going?

A low moan startled her. It came from the brush. She froze. She peered in the direction the sound came from. The dark yielded nothing. She squinted and gradually was able to discern a shape. The shape she fixed on became Woody. He lay on his back, his rifle by his side.

She scrabbled over to him and whispered, "Woody, are you hurt?" Her heart slammed against her ribs.

Praying the two men hadn't heard her, she scanned the area where the terrorists had just stood. The SUV was still there but the men had disappeared.

"My ankle. I think I broke it when I fell," Woody whispered and pointed to his right leg.

His foot was turned completely backward. She gulped. Woody had to be in serious pain. "Did you shoot them?"

"I got two of them. They're down." He tried to adjust his position.

Two men down? Then how many were there? She'd just counted two walking.

"Are you sure? I just saw two men, Woody. They weren't down."

"Two men started shooting at me and I returned fire. The two I shot are definitely down. Not dead, but down." He pointed. "They were on the west side, over there, when I came up on them.

She felt woozy. She needed to help Woody to stand. There were two more bad guys to catch. "Can you walk if I get you up?"

"No, leave me here. You have to stop the others. Take my rifle." He propped himself up and thrust the Browning at her.

She grabbed it and examined it, weighing its feel in her arms.

"Stay low. They don't know you're here," Woody said. "You can surprise them. I don't have many rounds left, only the four in the chamber. I used up a lot of ammo, wanted them to think there was more than just one of me. If you have to shoot, make every shot count." Woody lay back. He moaned softly. "Don't forget about the recoil," he added.

At first, the weapon felt awkward in her hands. She'd shot plenty of targets with her personal .38 and was a good shot. Mostly what she shot was a cottonmouth snake or two that bothered her while she fished. She'd never shot a rifle before.

Nor had she ever been hunting. This, her first hunt, was a manhunt. As she inched away, leaving Woody in the brush, she tried to remember all the safety warnings she'd heard about carrying loaded guns. Like not pointing them at any of your own body parts.

# CHAPTER 47

The two men she'd spotted earlier were no longer at the rear of the substation. Rhetta feared they must already be inside the chain link fencing. Probably well on their way to disabling the transformer or destroying it, like they'd done to the other substations.

She sucked in a deep breath to free her mind from the fear worming into her brain. Ignoring the little voice that kept telling her to get the hell out of there, she regrouped mentally. The time had come, and she and Woody were the only ones left to stop the attack. Now that Woody was down, it was up to her.

Nearing the front of the substation, she ducked under the orange beam of light and surveyed the fence. It was intact. No sign of the terrorists.

Crouching again, holding the rifle across her arms, she rounded the corner and stiffened. Two men in black pants and hooded sweatshirts were hunkered over, busying themselves at the fence. Their bolt cutters had succeeded in freeing a man-sized hole in the chain link. One man began easing himself through. Rhetta stood and took aim.

"Hold it right there, assholes!" she screamed. Instantly, one man inside sprinted off along the fence. The other turned and fired at her, the bullet zinging close enough to her that she yelped. She raised the weapon, tried to aim, then fired. Missed. She fired again. Missed again. "Crap," she yelled and fired once more. This time the man dropped. Pain ripped through her shoulder. Woody had warned her about the recoil. The vibrating pain shot down her arm and back up to her neck, like the devil was tuning her arm with a hot wire.

*Where's the other one?* He'd run, but where was he?

Then she spotted him. He had stepped away from the fence and was taking aim at her. Her heart thudded. Without dropping the rifle, she threw herself to the ground, her recoil-bruised shoulder absorbing the brunt of her fall.

"Oww, dammit," she cried, rolling on to her back. Something whizzed past her head and slammed into a nearby tree. Bark flew and she heard another *pfft*. Then another. He was shooting at her with a silenced weapon.

Rhetta swung the rifle up and fired. She missed. The dark figure quit shooting. Maybe she knocked the gun out of his hand. *A miracle*. Then she saw him sprinting for the rear of the substation. Rhetta fired again. There was only a click. *Empty. Damn.*

Using the rifle to hoist herself up, she struck out gimping painfully, determined to stop him from reaching his ride. Her foot glanced off the automatic weapon he'd thrown down. She snatched it up, pointed it at him, and fired. Empty. *Of course it was. He'd tossed it. No miracles.*

In spite of limping, she closed in on him. She still had Woody's rifle. She formed a quick plan—threaten to shoot him if he didn't surrender. Before she could shout at him to put his hands up, he stretched out his arm and pointed a device toward his ride. The SUV motor turned over. *Remote start. Damn.* He snatched the door open and turned toward her. In frustration she screamed, "Stop, you son of a bitch!" He didn't.

The man's hoodie had slipped back, baring his head. Illuminated briefly by the SUV's interior light, the clear image of his swarthy face, thin mustache, and black hair seared into her brain.

Placing two fingers at his temple, he paused long enough to salute her before jumping behind the wheel. He barreled straight at her. Pivoting on her injured foot, she managed to hop sideways with barely a millimeter between the wheels and her feet.

Rhetta threw the rifle at the side of the dark green SUV as it passed within inches of her feet. The weapon bounced off the car and clattered to the ground. She limped over and retrieved it.

"Crap, crap, crap," she groused as she hobbled to check the man she'd shot. She stopped at the gaping hole in the fence and peered at her fallen quarry. He hadn't moved. Maybe she'd killed him. Then she heard him moan. He made no attempt to rise, but stayed on the ground, on his side, moaning. Changing direction, she made her way back to Woody, who had not changed positions since she left him earlier.

"I let one get away, Woody. I'm a terrible shot." She set the rifle down. "You said to conserve my rounds, and it took me three to get one guy. I clearly missed the last one. Damn. Damn. Damn." With each "damn" she pummeled her thighs with clenched fists.

Although the summer night air was sultry, Rhetta's teeth began to chatter. She dropped to her knees alongside Woody. In spite of his pain, Woody tried to grin. "Hey, you got one at least, and you're all right. And the substation is still running." He held up his hand in a high five. "We stopped them. No more cascading power failure." Rhetta took a second before she met his palm with her own. Woody lay back. "Now, how we gonna get out of here?"

A high-pitched rising and falling wail pierced the dark silence.

"The police. Thank God," Rhetta came out of her chilled daze and stood. "I'll go meet them. They'll call an ambulance." With her ankle throbbing mightily, she shuffled down the driveway to the road. Her shoulder still vibrated from the recoil.

Two enormous screaming fire trucks followed by a volunteer firefighter driving a pickup with a cab crowned in flashing lights caromed by without slowing down. Rhetta waved her good arm to the parade of trucks and cars behind the emergency vehicles. No one noticed her. Every one of them was heading to the same place, to the flames shooting a hundred feet in the air from a stack of round hay bales about a quarter of a mile away.

*Oh, crap! Cami.*

# CHAPTER 48

No one noticed Rhetta as she shuffled to the edge of the onlookers, mesmerized by the fire gobbling the farmer's entire reserve of winter hay. And her beautiful car.

Two more fire trucks screamed past, slowing just enough to make the sharp turn into the burning field.

"Well, ain't this somethin'," muttered a Lookey Lou as he pulled off a beat up ball cap and ran his gnarled hand through what was left of his thinning white hair. "Guess Ralph'll hafta buy hay fer his cattle after this." He spit a long stream of tobacco. Two men and a woman turned to locate the origin of the foul torrent. In unison, they stepped sideways, giving the old man a wide berth.

"Surely he has insurance," answered a middle-aged woman clad in gray sweat pants and a black T-shirt. The woman stepped over the nasty wad to stand upwind of the projectile spitter.

"Seems someone parked a car by them bales and caught it all afire," said Lou. "Wonder who the damn fool was that done that?"

*That would be me.* Rhetta shifted trying to find a comfortable position. In addition to her ankle pain and her throbbing shoulder, her oversized sneakers were rubbing blisters on her feet.

She wasn't about to let these good folks know the damn fool was inches away. *Do they still lynch people out in the country? They might if they knew I'd just burned up Ralph's hay.*

Another siren powered down as a Scott County Sheriff's patrol car eased past the onlookers. It parked crossways, blocking the road, effectively stopping any advance the crowd might make toward the flames. Two deputies leapt out of the car and began dispersing the crowd.

"All right everyone, time to go home," the taller of the two uniforms said as he wove through the crowd, waving his hands as though shooing away pesky dogs.

"The show's over, folks," the rotund second deputy chimed in. He hooked his thumbs into his belt and marched forward.

"Naw, it's a long way from over," said Lou and contorted his mouth to launch again. The crowd parted.

The wad landed a few feet from the sweatpants-clad woman, who protested loudly and stepped to the other side of the crowd, out of harm's way.

After several minutes of prodding by the officers, the crowd began thinning. Groups of two and three ambled down the road, probably toward their respective homes.

"You suppose them hooligans from up Scott City set the fire?" The old man didn't ask anyone in particular. He looked around as though expecting someone to chime in. No one apparently knew which hooligans in particular the old guy was referring to. The question hung unanswered.

Rhetta remained transfixed, staring at the burned out hulk that was once her beloved Camaro. The adrenaline sustaining her at the substation had drained away. Fatigue and sorrow closed in.

"Ma'am?" asked the rotund lawman who walked up to her. Most of the crowd, including Lookey Lou had melted away. "Ma'am?" he repeated. "You need to leave now. It's all over."

The deputy had exaggerated a bit in saying it was all over. Did he think she couldn't see the flames still licking the sky? Rhetta shook her head, mostly to clear away the images of her burning car. And to revive. "I, uh, don't have a ride, Deputy. Besides, I need to report we shot three people."

Scott County's version of a chubby Barney Fife snapped to attention. "You shot three people?" His eyes grew wide. "Where?"

She pointed to the substation. He snatched her wrist, said, "Come with me," and began tugging her toward the taller officer.

"This woman says she shot three people," said the panting officer as he skidded to a stop in front of his fellow deputy.

"That so?" The stick-thin deputy parked both hands on his narrow hips and tilted his head. He took a hard gander at Rhetta.

She could only imagine what he saw.

*A disheveled crazy woman.*

"Who are you, and who did you shoot?" The tall skinny officer nodded to his partner, who fumbled at a button on his shirt pocket. Finally succeeding in freeing the pocket flap, the stocky deputy withdrew a small spiral notebook from it.

"My name is Rhetta McCarter, and I only shot one. Back there," she said and pointed behind her. "At the substation."

"I thought you said you shot three people," the round deputy said. Rhetta thought he sounded disappointed that there might only be a single casualty.

"No, sir, I said, *we* shot three people. *I* only shot one. Woody shot the other two, after they shot at him. He shot them in self-defense, and to save the substation. Please call an ambulance. My friend is hurt."

The two officers glanced at each other. The tall one slapped his shoulder, activating his radio. "This is Carson. I need back up here at the fire. Code 28."

Rhetta presumed Code 28 meant, "Crazy person standing in front of us."

"Dammit, Carson, you're supposed to give 'em your badge number, not your name." The deputy shook his head.

Rhetta thought how lucky she was to be dealing with Deputy Dawg and Barney Fife.

"I need to see some ID," Carson asked her, ignoring his partner's comment.

Rhetta shook her head. The last time she saw her driver's license it was in the hands of an officer at the traffic stop where she'd driven off. Her purse containing the rest of her identification lay incinerated inside her car.

Choosing not to mention the traffic stop, she said, "I did have ID." She pointed to Cami. "It burned up in that car."

"That was your car?"

She nodded. The shifting wind blew smoldering spirals toward them. The smoke stung her eyes, and the acrid smell of the death of her car seared her nostrils. Using the back of her hand, she wiped her damp cheek.

Carson tilted his head and spoke to his shoulder again. "Carson. I mean Badge 257. I have a suspect in custody for the arson at Ralph Fornfelt's."

Staring at her, he continued, "Mrs. McCarter, you'll have to come with us. You're under arrest for arson." He whipped out a well-worn laminated page the size of a playing card and chanted the Miranda rights.

# CHAPTER 49

R hetta stared at her wrists secured snugly in the handcuffs. After reading her rights and only stumbling over a few of the words, Carson had directed her to hold her hands out in front of her. Fumbling at first, he eventually managed to get the handcuffs untangled and snapped them on her wrists. He led her to the patrol car and invited her to sit in the caged-in back seat. With her securely locked inside the car, both deputies left.

She'd begged them to call an ambulance for Woody. Surely, they would've done that? Although from the cops' expressions, she figured they thought she'd escaped from Crazyville. She couldn't tell how much they believed her. When she started telling them her theory about what had happened to the other power substations, their eyes glazed over.

Carson had called for backup. She remembered that much. Yet Rhetta hadn't seen any other patrol cars arrive. Maybe they went directly to the substation. If Carson had any sense, he'd have directed them there to get Woody and check the three bodies.

One by one, the fire trucks and volunteers left, yet the two deputies still had not returned.

Where had the cops gone? They'd been away at least twenty minutes.

Holding her hands up, Rhetta inspected the heavy steel handcuffs circling her small wrists. Could she get them off? Probably not. Twisting around to locate Carson, whom she'd decided was Deputy Dawg, while his sidekick was Barney Fife, she spotted them galloping toward the car. Definitely moving faster than when they'd left.

Carson leapt behind the wheel and fired up the grey Dodge patrol car as his chubby buddy piled into the passenger seat and slammed the door. Spinning the car around, Carson turned on the siren and burned rubber speeding to the substation.

"Holy moley, lady, you weren't lyin'," said Barney Fife, wheezing. "There's three guys been shot plus a guy down with a broken leg over at the substation." It took less than a minute for them to slide over the small hill and scream into the substation's driveway.

An orange and white ambulance pulled out as they entered. *Thank God. They must be taking Woody to the hospital.*

Rhetta counted at least six vehicles wedged into the short substation driveway. Most were police cars, and one van emblazoned with SCOTT COUNTY AMBULANCE. Once again, Dawg and Fife scrambled out of their patrol car leaving her in back and disappeared into the crowd of law officers.

As she peered into the clutch of cops looking for her captors, one tall highway patrol officer left the others to stride over to her prison on wheels. The two sheriff's deputies scurried to catch up.

Rhetta sighed with relief when she recognized Sergeant Quentin Meade.

Carson opened her door so Meade could speak to her.

"Mrs. McCarter," he said, touching the brim of his hat as he greeted her. "If you'll pardon my saying so, it looks like you're in a shit load of trouble."

# CHAPTER 50

It was nearly midnight when Rhetta laid her head against the padded leather headrest on the passenger seat of the highway patrol car.

"I really appreciate the ride, Sergeant," she said as the Crown Victoria cruised smoothly up the ramp to the northbound interstate toward Cape. The ride to I-55 had taken just five minutes from Benton, the county seat where the sheriff's office was located. And where she spent the last three hours being questioned.

"You've had quite a day, Mrs. McCarter." Meade adjusted the air conditioning controls.

*Massive power failures, shootout with terrorists and losing Cami. Can we say understatement?*

# # #

At one point during her questioning, Rhetta jumped up and boogied when she heard a sheriff's radio bulletin announcing that power was gradually being restored in parts of the city of Cape Girardeau.

"Yes!" She whooped and fist pumped the air. Although her ankle still hurt, she managed victory dancing a circle, her borrowed tennis shoes slapping the linoleum noisily. She plopped back down when two officers hustled toward her.

She held her palms up. "It's all good, officers. Everything's cool." Her stupid grin must have made them doubt her sanity even more than any prior assessment they may have made.

After arguments between the deputies and the highway patrol via radio and telephone, Sergeant Meade had finally taken over questioning her. The Scott County deputies argued for at least a half hour that they had jurisdiction before a phone call from a being of higher rank convinced Dawg and Fife to back off and let the highway patrol investigate.

It took a little over two hours more for Rhetta to tell Meade the whole story. He wrote everything down in longhand in a hardbound black notebook. When Rhetta took a break to stand and stretch her aching muscles, Meade snapped the notebook closed. "Let's get you home, Mrs. McCarter. We'll have a few more questions, and a final statement for you to sign. That's all for now."

Leading the way through the crowded sheriff's office to the side of the brick building, Meade held the door open for Rhetta. The steel door was the kind that could only be opened from the inside. Like anyone outside would want to break into the sheriff's office. Passing by the table where the handcuffs lay, Rhetta glanced at them and rubbed her wrists, remembering how they felt.

The night air felt pleasantly cool following the hot and humid afternoon. Above them, the sky sparkled with celestial jewelry. A star winked at her and Rhetta grinned. *Okay, Mama, I know, I did good.*

### # # #

"I understand that Mr. Zelinski was taken to St. Mark's Hospital," Sergeant Meade said as they sped along I-55 north toward Cape. "Report is that he's doing fine, although his leg is broken, and he's suffering some shock. I'm sure he'll be in the hospital a few days."

Rhetta sat forward. "Instead of taking me home, can you drop me at St. Mark's? I know I look like hell, but I really need to see my husband." She rubbed her still tender shoulder. "And I have to see Woody, too."

"Will you be able to get home? If you'll pardon my saying so, you look like you need to rest."

That may have been what he said, but Rhetta felt sure what he meant was, "You look like crap, and maybe you should go home first and clean up."

"I'll call a friend," Rhetta said. "She'll come and get me, and then take me home."

Since her cell phone was also a victim of the fire, she'd look up *Fast Lane Muscle Cars* in the phone book in Randolph's room. Ricky would come get her. And also give her hell for letting Cami burn up. On second thought, maybe she'd call a cab. On third thought, her purse had also incinerated. She doubted if any cab driver would take an IOU. She sighed. Calling Ricky won out.

She'd let Woody sleep and check on him tomorrow.

# # #

There was no sign of the earlier chaos on William Street. In fact, the main artery was nearly deserted. Even late at night there was always traffic near the interstate. Where was everybody?

"Cape Girardeau has an emergency curfew in place until all the power is restored," Meade said. She knew he hadn't read her mind. Perhaps her head swiveling prompted his comment.

When Meade eased the highway patrol car to a stop at the hospital visitors' entrance, Rhetta pointed to a dark SUV parked at the curb. "That's him," she shouted. Before Meade could answer, Rhetta threw open the passenger door, bolted from the patrol car and trotted as fast as possible on her painful ankle to the hospital revolving door. It didn't revolve. It was locked down in night mode. Pounding on the glass, Rhetta shouted, "Let me in. I have to see my husband." No one manned the volunteer booth inside the dimly lit entry foyer. No one responded to her pounding.

When she turned back to shout at Meade, he and his car were gone.

Rhetta struck out across the lawn instead of following the S-curved sidewalk around to the emergency room entrance located on the opposite side of the building. At the curb sat a green SUV.

Her breath caught and fear clutched her heart in a death grip. Was Randolph lying helpless in his hospital room? She had to get to him.

As she approached the low hedge of monkey grass separating the lawn from the paved driveway under the porte-cochère, the sprinkler system sprang to life. She was drenched by the time she limped the last ten feet to the door.

In vivid contrast to the closed, deserted main lobby, the brightly lit emergency room overflowed with the sick and injured. After making her way across the packed waiting room, Rhetta searched for a doorway to access the stairs. Amidst strange looks and a few pointed fingers, she maneuvered through the crowd and slipped through the doorway marked AUTHORIZED PERSONNEL ONLY. She'd located the stairway. Grasping the rail, she bounded up three floors.

At the fourth floor landing, Rhetta stopped at the sight of two men. She pressed her back against the wall and gulped in a breath. Her heart began thudding so hard she could barely breathe. The men were engaged in a heated conversation. One of them wore a lab coat. He didn't appear to have seen her. He turned to go out the door so quickly that his crimson tie flapped when he pushed open the door.

Something about him was familiar, but he left too quickly. That wasn't important. It was the remaining man who made her gut lurch in fear. He sauntered toward her.

Swallowing the bile that rose from deep in her gut, she stared into the dark eyes of a man clad in black pants and hoodie.

She'd located the owner of the green SUV.

# CHAPTER 51

A lthough the stairwell lights were dim, probably from the hospital conserving electricity, Rhetta managed to see the steel blade quite clearly.

Handling the slim dagger with ease, the man sidled closer to Rhetta, who had scuttled backward until her back was against the wall. He stared at her while grasping the knife, jiggling it, and tossing it from one hand to the other. She fixated on the deadly blade. It seemed as long as a sword.

A smirk crept across his thin lips. Her heart slammed hard against her ribs. She feared she'd die from a heart attack. Is this what it was like to die of fright? Clearly, he was enjoying tormenting her before plunging the blade into her gut. She had no escape, no way around him. Trapped against the wall, there was only one thing to do.

When he heard her scream at the top of her voice, "You son of a bitch," he stopped cold.

Instantly, she took advantage of his pause, reared back, and kicked him squarely in the crotch. The weapon clattered to the floor as the man doubled over, clutching his privates with both hands, cursing loudly in a language she didn't understand. She poised to kick him again. Unfortunately for her, he'd recovered his knife and was straightening. The distraction had bought her some time. Scuttling along the wall, she reached the door and burst through into the hallway, screaming at the top of her voice.

"Help," she whooped. "Over here. Somebody, help!" Two men and a woman rounded the corner. Rhetta pointed to the doorway. "In there, a man with a knife. Call security!" The woman skidded to a stop, gaped at her a second, then turned and retreated down the hall. The two men continued running toward her.

One man holding a walkie-talkie slowed enough to shout into the mouthpiece, "Security Code fifty-six, fourth floor, rear stairwell. Repeat, code fifty-six, fourth floor."

When Rhetta heard the rush of footsteps approaching, probably security, she knew if she stayed, she'd have another zillion questions to answer. She tore off toward Randolph's room instead. Security didn't need to take time to ask her their stupid questions. They needed to be chasing the knife-wielding terrorist. She had to make sure Randolph was all right.

Nearly breathless by the time she reached her husband's room, she stopped outside his closed door to let her heart rate slow, and the adrenalin rush subside. She could barely breathe, and was beginning to feel lightheaded. She found herself suddenly famished. Probably a side effect from the ebbing adrenalin.

She was anxious to see her husband, to know that he was all right.

After a few gulps of air, she slipped into the room.

# CHAPTER 52

I nside, the room was dim. Huddled over the bed, a man in a lab coat was too intent on what he was doing to notice her come in. The only light in the room seeped from a muted night light above the oxygen tank near the head of the bed. Randolph didn't stir. Whatever the man was doing hadn't disturbed her husband's slumber.

The figure straightened, obviously startled at Rhetta's approach, cramming a hand into his coat pocket. There was no tray of vials alongside the bed.

"What's going on?" Rhetta asked. "What are you doing?"

"Rhetta, what are you doing here at this hour?" Dr. Kenneth Reed whirled around at the sound of her voice. His hair was disheveled. His eyes darted from her to the door.

Although shocked at seeing him, she managed to answer, "I might ask you the same thing, Kenneth."

"I needed to check Randolph's vitals and give him some medication," Kenneth said. He attempted to untangle the stethoscope from his necktie. She glimpsed a cylindrical-shaped bulge in the coat pocket from which he had just removed his hand. If he had administered a medication, he would've discarded the syringe and not stuck it in his pocket.

Her eyes shot back to his tie. It was crimson.

"Oh, God, what did you do?" She reached across the bed to grab Kenneth's arm. He jerked it away and ran toward the door.

Grabbing the first thing she found, Rhetta slung the full water pitcher at Kenneth's departing figure and scored a solid hit on the back of his neck. He staggered toward the door. Rhetta raced around the bed and launched herself at him. They crashed to the floor. Throwing her off, he stood and again made for the door. Rhetta leapt to her feet, seized the visitor's chair by its back, and swung it as hard as she could. It caught Kenneth across his shoulders, and he toppled face forward to the floor. The chair skittered away. Panting, Rhetta reached across him for the fallen chair.

Kenneth rolled over and caught her left wrist. Twisting it until she screamed, he used her arm for a handle and slung her off. She slid across the floor and slammed head first into the wall.

Shaking her head from the blow, Rhetta rolled over and pulled herself to her knees. A wedge of light sliced into the room as Kenneth pulled open the door.

Summoning all her strength, Rhetta used the toppled chair to push herself up. She snatched the chair, using only her right hand and hurled it after Kenneth. This time, the blow caught him behind the knees and he stumbled forward, crashing out into the hall. Rhetta was right behind him. She shoved him as hard as she could. He dropped face first and landed with a crunch. Blood spurted from his nose. He didn't move. Probably dazed from meeting the floor with his face. She kicked him squarely in the ribs, then whimpered at the pain that shot from her ankle. She lurched to one side just as Doctor Marinthe appeared.

Behind him were dozens of hospital staff.

A security officer rushed up and snatched her by the arm.

*Here we go again.*

# CHAPTER 53

"Doctor Marinthe, please check on my husband. I think Kenneth gave him something and the empty syringe is still in his right coat pocket." Rhetta shouted to Marinthe while the security officer, a short man with piercing eyes, dragged her away from Kenneth, who was still sprawled on the floor. She struggled against the officer's grip, but he was bigger and stronger than she was.

Even with his awkward gait, Marinthe was able to rush past them and into Randolph's room. Rhetta twisted around to peer over her shoulder and saw the room flood with light when Marinthe switched on the overhead lights.

"Please, you have to get the empty syringe from his pocket," Rhetta implored the security guard who held her fast. The guard gripped her by her right arm. Because her left arm hurt too badly for her to move it, she pointed with her chin toward Kenneth. By now, the second security guard, who had run down the hallway to join in the melee, stood panting. His gaze darted from Kenneth, who lay motionless, to Rhetta held fast by the first guard.

Without loosening his grip, the guard holding Rhetta ordered the second guard, "Use gloves, and get out whatever is in his pocket."

Following instructions, the guard produced a latex glove from his own pocket and slipped it on. Bending over Kenneth, he carefully removed an empty syringe from the doctor's coat pocket. Holding his prize aloft, he stepped away.

Then, addressing the group of gaping onlookers, the guard holding Rhetta said loudly, "Can't someone see about Doctor Reed there?" He pointed to Kenneth. "He's hurt."

The staff snapped out of their apparent collective stupor. A nurse materialized with a tray of supplies and began ministering to Kenneth's bloody face. She shot daggers at Rhetta as Dr. Reed began to revive. Rhetta resisted the urge to stick her tongue out at the nurse. How dare she indicate by her glare, that Rhetta was the bad guy here? The protective nurse pressed a towel to the doctor's face, then helped Kenneth sit up. Blood from his nose quickly turned the white towel a deep red.

Appearing at the doorway to Randolph's room, Marinthe shouted to the security officers, "I must see the syringe from Dr. Reed's pocket." The guard immediately recovered the syringe from Reed, jogged to Marinthe, and offered his gloved hand. Marinthe, also wearing gloves, snatched it and turned it over.

Still gripping it, Marinthe walked to Kenneth Reed. The nurse continued to treat him as he sat. Marinthe thrust the syringe at Kenneth.

"Is this what you used before?" asked Marinthe, shaking the empty syringe in Kenneth's face. Instead of answering, Kenneth turned his head away. Marinthe squatted down so they were face to face, and said something only Kenneth heard. Kenneth's head nodded. Slowly Marinthe stood. Turning to the guard, he said, "Call the police. Hold Dr. Reed." Then glancing at the guard who still held Rhetta, he said, "You must let Mrs. McCarter go. Thank goodness she stopped Dr. Reed."

The guard released Rhetta, then slapped his shoulder radio switch. As she rushed to Randolph's room, she heard the guard calling for help from the Cape Girardeau police. She also heard the answer, "Negative, Johnson. Not enough manpower. He's all yours."

She desperately wanted Johnson and his helper to detain Kenneth; but for the moment, she was too occupied to do anything about that. She needed to know Randolph was safe.

Rhetta burst into the room to find Randolph sitting up and alert. His nose had oxygen tubes inserted, but he appeared fine otherwise. Marinthe followed her into the room.

"I presumed Dr. Reed had used the same drug as before. I started another infusion of naloxone," Dr. Marinthe explained. "It was a good thing you arrived when you did. The anesthetic hasn't been in his system very long. The naloxone has probably already countered the effects. I started oxygen as an additional measure." Marinthe patted her shoulder. "He should be fine."

"Thank you," Rhetta said, her voice catching, barely above a whisper. "I don't understand. Why did Kenneth do this?"

Marinthe shrugged. "I'm sure the police will find that out." He gazed around the room, at the upturned chair, and at all the items scattered across the floor. "Must have been quite a battle," he said, and a tiny smile twitched at the corner of his mouth. "In fact, you rather look like you have been through a war."

*If you only knew.*

Ignoring the pain in her right shoulder and hand, Rhetta threw her arms around her husband's neck. Randolph circled her shoulders and pulled her to him.

"It's all over, Sweets," Rhetta said and nuzzled her husband's warm neck. She kissed his face, and then grasped his hand and kissed it.

Dr. Marinthe slipped out of the room.

After a moment more in Randolph's embrace, Rhetta pulled back and studied the face of the man she loved.

Randolph clasped both her hands. "God, Rhetta, what happened to you? You look like hell."

# CHAPTER 54

O nce more, Rhetta found herself staring out of the window in Randolph's room. Slices of amber light danced across the eastern horizon, signaling the impending arrival of a yellow-orange summer sun.

After the security guards had removed Kenneth, Rhetta filled Randolph in on everything that had happened. The lateness of the hour prevailed, and he eventually dozed off. Rhetta stayed, sitting by his bed and holding his hand. When daybreak approached, she stood, stretched out aching muscles, and limped to the window to savor the morning sunrise. And the peace that accompanied it.

The world below appeared normal. Cars and trucks wound their way in and out of the parking lot. Everywhere she gazed, lights twinkled on as area power was increasingly restored. Things might have looked drastically different had she and Woody not stopped the final attack on the substation. Undoubtedly, the chaos she'd experienced earlier would have been a mere sample of what turmoil could have ensued.

Following the struggle with Kenneth, her left wrist began swelling and the throbbing pain had intensified. Rhetta had asked Dr. Marinthe to look at it. Kenneth had used that arm to launch her across the room, and she feared a broken wrist as the result.

Marinthe came to Randolph's room and examined her arm. He called the night admissions clerk, insisting she come to the room, so that Rhetta could complete the necessary paperwork allowing him to order an X-ray. A half hour after the clerk left, Rhetta was out of Radiology Room 3 with her X-ray completed.

"It isn't broken," Marinthe announced as he came through the door from Radiology into the small waiting room where Rhetta sat. "Soft tissue swelling, however, doesn't show up on the X-ray. I shall refer you to an orthopedic physician who can help. I believe your ligaments and tendons are badly sprained." Gently, Marinthe lifted her arm and examined it again.

"Let's get you in a sling for now to ease the throbbing. You will need to keep your wrist elevated." Marinthe led the way through the physician's entry to the Emergency room. "Stay here a moment," he said, holding up his hand. Rhetta obeyed. Marinthe disappeared behind a curtained partition.

A strong sense of déjà vu washed over Rhetta as she glanced around. How long ago was it that she'd rushed here to see Randolph after hearing news of his accident? Two days? Three? A glance at her watch told her it was four thirty-five. She shook her head. *In the morning?* Panic welled. She honestly couldn't remember what day it was. Was it still Saturday? *No, wait, it's Sunday. Isn't it?* She couldn't remember.

Marinthe returned carrying a sling kit. He motioned for her to follow him. He led her to the elevator.

"What day is it?" Rhetta asked as they rode upward. She pressed against the elevator wall, her head spinning from fatigue.

"It's Sunday morning," Marinthe answered.

She nodded. *Good, I thought it was Sunday.* She wasn't completely crazy, just exhausted.

The soft *ding* of the elevator signaled they had arrived at Randolph's floor.

Marinthe stopped Rhetta outside Randolph's door where he carefully fastened the sling on Rhetta's arm. "You should go home now and get some rest," he said, putting the finishing touches on the knot he tied on her sling.

"I'll call my friend to come and get me, but I don't want to go home just yet. I want to stay here and make sure Randolph is really all right."

"I will be here until eight. Page me if you need me," said Marinthe, and turned to leave.

Rhetta reached out and touched Marinthe's arm. "What will happen to Kenneth?"

"I do not know, Mrs. McCarter." Marinthe turned to face her. "I'm sure however, that it will take a full investigation to determine what he did to your husband."

"Why did he do it?" Rhetta asked. A tear escaped and trickled down her cheek. She found herself deeply saddened by Kenneth's betrayal. Her mind wrestled to comprehend why Kenneth would harm her husband. She needed an answer.

Marinthe merely shook his head, shrugged, and limped away.

# # #

Rhetta pulled the room phone as far away from her sleeping husband as the cord would allow. "Are you up?" Rhetta asked when Ricky Lane answered on the tenth ring.

"I guess I am now. What time is it?" When Rhetta announced it was six in the morning, Ricky said, "Dear God, Rhetta, it's the middle of the night." Stifling a yawn Ricky added, "What's up?"

"I need a ride home from St. Mark's Hospital. Can you come and get me?"

"Of course. Give me twenty minutes. What happened?"

Of everything that had occurred, Rhetta especially dreaded telling her friend about losing Cami. Rhetta sighed. "I'll fill you in on the way home. I'll be at the visitors' entrance."

When she hung up the hospital phone, Randolph woke up. He held his arms out to her and she went to him. He held her close, rubbing her neck and back, picking small pieces of twigs and debris from her hair.

"Babe, I'm fine. Go home and get some sleep." He kissed her cheek.

"I was hoping to check on Woody and Billy Dan before I left."

"You better go and clean up or you'll scare them to death."

Randolph was right. After glimpsing herself in the bathroom mirror, she understood why everyone had been staring at her. Covered in dried mud, twigs, and blood, she resembled a zombie, recently arisen from the grave.

He cupped her face with both of his hands and grinned. "You're my forever hero, Rhetta. But you need a shower."

A smile worked its way across her lips. Then she grinned.

### # # #

Thirty minutes later, Rhetta slid into the passenger seat of Ricky's 1978 Trans Am. As soon as she was buckled in, Ricky gave Rhetta a once over. "I love your outfit. Nice shoes." The Trans Am sped away, all four hundred horses responding powerfully as Ricky shifted easily through its gears. She'd juiced her ride with an LS1 engine like the one she installed in Cami.

"I debated putting the T-tops in before coming to get you." Ricky eyed her friend as they headed up the ramp to I-55. "Glad to know our open air ride won't mess up your hair. What in the devil's recipe happened to you, girlfriend? Have you been through World War III when I wasn't looking?"

*Pretty close to the truth!*

Ricky was a night owl who usually turned wrenches in her garage until after midnight. She yawned. "This had better be good."

"I'll tell you over coffee when we get to the house," Rhetta said, closing her eyes, and melting into the soft leather interior.

She'd have to think of something to explain how she'd let Cami burn up. Randolph had advised her not to tell anyone other than the authorities that there had been an attack on the power grid, and that she and Woody had wounded three of the four terrorists doing the attacking. And that later the fourth terrorist had attacked her in the stairwell of the hospital.

Why cause a panic? And would anybody, including Ricky, believe her?

# CHAPTER 55

"Damn, what's that fool doing?" The Trans Am swerved hard to the right. "Now he's right on me again." This time, Ricky swerved equally hard to the left, her tires squealing in protest.

Rhetta bolted awake, her heart hammering. She twisted around to see which car had provoked Ricky.

Bearing down on them was a familiar-looking, dark green SUV.

"Take this exit, now," Rhetta screamed.

Ricky careened across two lanes, and raced down the off-ramp. The SUV didn't make the exit and flew on past. She pulled over, letting the Trans Am idle at the bottom of the ramp.

"What the hell was that all about?" said Ricky, gripping the steering wheel with both hands.

"Let me have your cell phone," Rhetta said, holding out her hand while checking behind them for any sign of the SUV.

"Where's your phone? In fact, where's your purse? And where's Cami?" asked Ricky as she groped behind her seat and located her cell phone on the floor.

As soon as Ricky dropped the phone into her hand, Rhetta grabbed it and punched 9-1-1.

"9-1-1, what is your emergency?" The police dispatcher answered after two rings.

"I need to speak to Sergeant Quentin Meade, please. It's an emergency," Rhetta said.

"This is the Cape Girardeau police," the operator replied. "I can't connect you to Sergeant Meade. He's with the Missouri Highway Patrol."

Disconnecting without taking time to explain, Rhetta stretched out her leg and dug into her jeans pocket, producing the card that Meade had given her when they got ready to leave Benton on the way to the hospital.

He'd told her to call him if she needed him. She needed him.

"It's a really long story," Rhetta said to Ricky. She focused on dialing the number on the card.

"Please answer, please answer, please answer," Rhetta intoned as she listened to the rings.

"Meade," said a familiar voice.

The phone chirped in her ear. The 9-1-1 operator was calling back. Rhetta pressed IGNORE.

"Sergeant Meade, it's Rhetta McCarter. The terrorist in the green SUV is on I-55 northbound out of Cape. He just tried to run us off the road."

Ricky's hand flew to her mouth. "Terrorist? What have you gotten yourself into?"

Rhetta held up an index finger to Ricky in a signal meaning *just a minute.*

After describing her exact location to Meade, Rhetta disconnected and handed the phone back to Ricky. "It's a long story, and it's a short ride to my house. Let's go. I'll fill you in."

# # #

The same man who had tried to kill Rhetta earlier had nearly run Ricky off the road. Rhetta ignored Randolph's advice not to tell anyone what had happened. Ricky deserved an explanation.

"Does the creep in the SUV have anything to do with your fashion statement, your sling, the highway patrol, and terrorists?" Ricky downshifted, and slowed for Rhetta's driveway.

Mrs. Koblyk popped out from behind a hedge as the black Trans Am eased into the lane. Rhetta waved at her as they sped by, before continuing. "Yes, along with Randolph's accident, Billy Dan Kercheval getting shot, and the power failures." Believing they'd be safer if Ricky's car was out of view, Rhetta added, "We'd better pull into the garage."

Hopping out once the Trans Am rumbled to a stop in front of the garage doors, Rhetta dashed through the walk door and hit the automatic door opener for the side Cami usually occupied. Rhetta's heart turned over. She'd loved that car. Her silver Trailblazer occupied the other space.

Rhetta motioned for Ricky to pull inside, then closed the garage door.

"Where's Cami?" Ricky asked, glancing around as she climbed out.

"Yeah, well, that's part of what I have to tell you."

Rhetta unlocked her house door with a key she retrieved from a hook near the freezer in the garage, and the two women trooped into the kitchen.

"I'll make coffee. You go shower," Ricky called over her shoulder and began opening up the kitchen cabinet doors. "And hurry up! I'm making a double pot. I have a feeling this story's going to be a doozy."

"Coffee is in the refrigerator, and the coffee-maker guts are probably still in the dishwasher," Rhetta shouted, as she limped for the master bedroom.

# # #

After letting water cascade over her for twenty minutes until she depleted the hot water, Rhetta finally stepped out of the shower. After toweling off, she dressed quickly in a pair of Capris and a sleeveless blouse. She left her short hair to air dry, and padded back to the kitchen.

"Cami's really gone? Burned up?" Ricky's face turned to a mask of disbelief.

Rhetta knew that losing Cami would hit Ricky hard. Ricky had been the one to locate the original Camaro that she had transformed into Cami. Additionally, she'd done all the mechanics along with supervising as Rhetta and Randolph restored the interior.

"Randolph is going to be fine. I haven't checked yet on Billy Dan Kercheval or Woody, but not to worry, I was told they're okay too."

"Oh, Rhetta, I didn't mean that I wasn't worried about them. Of course I am." Ricky ran to her friend and hugged her. "And you? What about you? Are you okay?"

# # #

It took over an hour and two pots of coffee for Rhetta to tell Ricky everything that had happened, starting with the bizarre phone message and Al-Serafi's death, up to the shootout with the terrorists at the Scott County substation, and the attack in the hospital.

Everything, that is, except the part where she nearly ran down her own father. She wasn't proud of that. Maybe she should find her father, talk to him. *Did Mama really tell him never to come back? Was he dying now? Will I ever know the whole truth?*

She suddenly felt sick and put down her coffee. Her mother's locket. It had burned in her purse, along with everything else inside the car.

"I guess I'm not enough of a country girl, or I would've known not to park Cami where her exhaust would be close to the hay bales. That was dumb." Rhetta left the kitchen table and carried their empty cups to the sink. She rinsed the cups out. "I'll be okay. I'm just tired. Not even six cups of coffee will keep me from sleeping."

Ricky hugged Rhetta again. "When all this settles down we'll need to find a replacement for Cami," Ricky said, a smile sneaking across her lips. "I may know just the car."

At that moment, the thought of restoring another Camaro didn't bring Rhetta any joy. She was heartbroken over losing her beautiful car and her mother's locket. She forced a smile for Ricky anyway.

Ricky continued, rubbing her hands together in gleeful anticipation. "I know of a 1981 Z28 that's been in a barn in Gordonville for twenty-five years."

Rhetta had to smile. She agreed with Ricky who claimed old muscle cars were the balm to heal the world's pain, and with Bob Seeger, who said rock' n' roll music soothes the soul. Her soul badly needed soothing. As did her wrist, shoulder, and both feet.

# CHAPTER 56

Rhetta burst from sleep into an adrenalin-induced fear. After Ricky left, she laid across the bed to rest her eyes. A scuffling noise from the back deck startled her to her feet.

Heart pounding, she tried to think about what she had nearby for a weapon. She padded soundlessly along the carpeted bedroom floor to her closet and slowly opened the door. Thankfully, the hinges didn't creak as loudly as they usually did. She promised herself to spray them with WD-40 later. Nothing much in the way of weaponry in the closet. Only clothes, shoes—the usual stuff. A glance behind the door revealed her ironing board suspended on a bracket, and next to it, the iron. Wrapping her good hand tightly around the iron's handle, she tiptoed to the back wall of the kitchen where the sliding door opened to the deck. She flattened herself along the wall and inched to the door, her arm raised above her head, ready to strike with her iron.

A shadow moved across the door. She held her breath. A short figure appeared.

Clutching a cat food bag tightly to her chest, Mrs. Koblyk jumped sideways at the sight of Rhetta poised with the iron.

"Mrs. Koblyk, I'm sorry. I didn't mean to scare you," Rhetta said, sliding the door open and stepping outside. "I thought you were an intruder."

"I see the black car leave and I think you must be again away. I come to take care of the little darlings," she said, pointing to the cats who'd begun meowing and entwining themselves around their legs. Mrs. Koblyk looked like someone who'd just seen a ghost. Two bright red circles dotted her cheeks, and she mopped her forehead with her sleeve.

"You're very kind," Rhetta said, setting her weapon down on the deck table.

"Oh, missus, what has happened to your arm?" She pointed to Rhetta's sling.

"Nothing really, just a little sprain. I'll be fine."

"You go on in and let me feed these babies," Mrs. Koblyk said, taking charge and ushering Rhetta to the door. "You must rest." Turning to the cats who were yowling plaintively, Mrs. Koblyk crooned to them in Hungarian.

"Thanks," Rhetta said. She hurried back inside, not wanting to take time out to think of a story to tell Mrs. Koblyk about her arm.

Her ankle pain had eased and after she'd removed the piece of festering splinter that had remained embedded in her other foot, Rhetta was able to walk much easier. It helped that she now had on her own footwear, a pair of leather walking sandals, instead of Billy Dan's oversized tennis shoes.

After five minutes of rustling around the closet, Rhetta found a straw purse trimmed in yellow that matched her Capris. Because she had nothing to put in it besides car keys, she tossed the purse back on the closet shelf. She was sure she'd be able to keep up with a single set of keys. That's what pockets were for.

She wandered around the living room, the bedroom, and finally the kitchen before locating the keys to the Trailblazer. They were hanging on the hook by the back door, where they were supposed to be. She yawned. She was still in fatigue overload.

Once inside the Trailblazer, and after adjusting the mirrors and inserting the key into the ignition, she glanced around, again mourning Cami's empty space. Today, she was grateful for driving an automatic. This, she could manage with her good arm.

It took a few minutes to maneuver past Mrs. Koblyk's car that the neighbor woman had parked diagonally behind both of the garage doors, Rhetta was about to continue backing down the drive when Mrs. Koblyk ran toward her, waving both arms. Rhetta stopped.

"I'm sorry I block the driveway. I can move." The old woman panted.

"No, no, I'm fine, no problem."

God love her.

Rhetta arrowed down the county road, but eased up on the accelerator, not wanting to get stopped yet again. Especially with no driver's license.

She'd have to ask Sergeant Meade exactly how she should go about getting it back. She'd probably get it returned with an invitation to court stapled to it.

Out of habit, she reached for her phone, then remembered where it was. Then her heart cracked like an icicle in the sun as she remembered the lost locket.

# # #

The entire city of Cape Girardeau was up and running like nothing had happened. All of the signal lights worked on her way into Cape. She'd chosen Kingshighway instead of using I-55. She knew all the signals worked because she caught every one that turned red. Fast-food signs blazed, reminding her that it had been years since she'd eaten. Her stomach rumbled.

Regretting now that she hadn't fixed herself a PBJ at home before taking off for the hospital, she groaned. She had no money. She also had no keys, so she couldn't get into the office to raid the petty cash drawer. Oh, well, maybe starving was good for her diet. Maybe she could snatch something off Randolph's tray at the hospital.

Singing along with the Beach Boys, she pulled into the hospital parking lot. Rhetta continued singing about driving like an ace as she locked the car. She imagined the young Beach Boys zipping to the California beaches in first generation Camaros and Firebirds while belting out their songs.

As she got out of her car, a malevolent whisper scorched her neck. "Your friend, she drives like an ace, like you say. This time, you don't get away."

The heavily accented voice launched a cascade of ice in her blood.

# CHAPTER 57

T hat's when everything erupted.

Although her blood had just run cold, now Rhetta boiled over in rage. She whipped around with the ignition key in her hand and lashed it across the swarthy face standing inches behind her. The man's cheek spurted blood. He cursed loudly and grabbed Rhetta's hand, spinning her around hard, slamming her against the front fender of her car.

With a vivid memory of the deadly blade this maniac had wielded the last time they met, Rhetta twisted around hoping to bring her knees up to his groin.

Anticipating her move, the man shoved her hard, sending her to her knees. He held the knife in front of her, inches from her throat. He took a step toward her.

"Who are you?" Rhetta asked, her voice cracking in fear. She wanted to get him talking. Maybe she could figure a way out of this.

"It's nothing to you, so do not ask," he answered. He snatched the front of her shirt and began to drag her to her feet.

"You will walk ahead of me, toward that green SUV," he ordered.

She thought of Randolph lying in a hospital bed, undoubtedly put there by this creep and his thug friends, and her anger surged.

Before she could formulate an escape plan, a different man's voice shouted, "That's all Razeen, drop the knife." Her assailant shoved her aside and began running. She fell to one knee, but gazed up in amazement as two men tackled the would-be assassin, shoving him to the ground. Without further pause, one man jerked Razeen's arms behind him, clamped handcuffs around his wrists, and began reciting his rights.

*Do terrorists have rights?* The crazy thought bounced around Rhetta's head as she stared at the yellow block letters that spelled *FBI* across the backs of the navy shirts of her rescuers.

# # #

A dozen more agents materialized from behind cars, pillars, doors, and everywhere else. Police radios crackled. Where did they come from? How did they know that this Razeen was going to be waiting for her when she pulled into the parking space?

"Mrs. McCarter, my name is Harold Wexler, Agent in Charge," said a tall, blue-shirted officer wearing a bulletproof vest, and a black ball cap emblazoned with the letters that matched his shirt. The freakin' G-men!

Rhetta's hand trembled as she extended it to Wexler. He grasped hers firmly. Then the agent pulled off his cap and ran a hand through his curly brown hair. She was too astonished to speak. She was lucky she remembered her manners enough to accept his handshake.

"How did you know he was here?" she finally managed.

"When you called Sergeant Meade, he notified us. We've been searching for Razeen ever since he escaped from the shootout at the Scott County substation. We located him on the interstate and followed him. We knew he had more up his sleeve." Wexler tilted his head. "By the way, Mrs. McCarter, that incident in Scott County? That was the bravest and dumbest thing I've ever known a civilian to do."

*Dumbest? Crap.*

Before she could launch into a defense, Wexler took her good arm and began guiding her to the door. "Let's go tell your husband you're all right."

She acquiesced. Who was she to argue with her knight in blue-shirted armor? *But still, dumbest?*

# # #

Wexler accompanied Rhetta into the hospital. "Can we stop and see Woody? I'm worried about him."

Wexler agreed. They stopped at the orthopedic wing. After getting directions to Woody's room from the station nurse and walking the length of the hallway to his room, Woody was gone. His bed was made. A nurse's aide followed them into the room.

"Can I help you?"

"Where's Mr. Zelinski?" Rhetta said, searching the room for Woody.

Wearing a hospital bathrobe and hopping on his good leg, Woody pushed open the patient's bathroom door and lumbered back into the room.

"I thought you were gone," Rhetta said, stepping sideways so Woody could pass.

"Yeah? Well, I wish I was gone, but the doc says he won't release me for awhile." He pointed to the temporary cast on his leg. "My ankle's broken. Doc says they're going to operate on it tomorrow. Put some pins in it, I guess."

"Mr. Zelinski, you aren't supposed to be walking without help," scolded the perky blonde aide.

"I had to go to the bathroom," Woody answered, as though that was explanation enough. The aide made clucking sounds as she pulled back the sheets on the freshly made bed and helped Woody climb in.

"Agent Wexler," Woody said and nodded to the agent. "I see you found her."

"What?" Rhetta swiveled from Woody to Agent Wexler. "How do you two know each other?"

"I came by here earlier and got Mr. Zelinski's statement concerning the shootout, Mrs. McCarter. We were looking for you, too. We'll also need a statement from you."

"I see." *More statements. Crap.*

Woody lay back and closed his eyes. The aide rolled hers. "He's not a very obedient patient. He shouldn't be walking without help."

With his eyes shut, Woody said, "Don't scold me. My wife is the only one allowed to do that. She's on her way here now, probably to give me a blistering lecture."

"I can scold you, too," Rhetta piped in. "You better behave yourself and follow instructions."

His eyes popped open. "Right. I always follow orders. And look where it got me." Woody waved around the room, then closed his eyes. "I need to rest up for the Jenn barrage."

"I think we need to go now, and let Mr. Zelinski wallow in peace," Rhetta said, marching out of the room. He lay back against the pillows. She stopped at the doorway, then went over to Woody's bed. She leaned forward and kissed his cheek. His eyes flew open.

"Thanks, Woody."

"That's sexual harassment," Woody said, rubbing his face. A slow grin split his grey beard.

# # #

When they reached Randolph's floor, sounds of laughter and loud conversation floated down the hallway. Rhetta discovered the reason inside Randolph's room.

Billy Dan sat on the side of Randolph's bed, and the two men seemed to be sharing something humorous, if their laughter was any indication.

As Rhetta came in followed by Wexler, Billy Dan stood. Agent Wexler introduced himself and shook hands all around. "We'll need a statement from all of you." Everyone groaned in chorus. Wexler raised both his hands, palms up. "I know, I know, it sucks. But we gotta have 'em." Billy Dan returned to his spot on the side of Randolph's bed. Remnants of a recent meal lay on the nearby tray table, and Rhetta eyed it hungrily. Rhetta kissed her husband and then glanced around. The machines were gone. Grinning, she snatched a small Styrofoam bowl of fruit and a spoon.

Wexler pulled out a chair for Rhetta. She sat alongside the bed and dug in. Answering her husband's raised eyebrows, she mumbled around a mouthful of fruit, "I'm hungry."

"I can tell," Randolph said.

"Mrs. McCarter, Judge," Wexler said, "I'd like to let you know some of what happened. It's classified, but you should know some of this." Wexler removed a folded sheet from his back pocket and unfurled it. He handed it to Rhetta. She stared at the picture of the man who'd tried to kill her.

Wexler tapped the picture. "This is Razeen Bin-Hajji, the leader of the terrorist cell that was operating here."

Rhetta sucked in a breath. She'd been right, but hearing it from the FBI made it real enough for her stomach to flip over. The flipping, however, didn't deter her munching the fruit.

"The cell consisted of a radical Muslim group that planned on taking down the electrical grid. This was a trial run, to see how it would go." Billy Dan, Randolph, and Rhetta all nodded. "The cell came close to succeeding. Dr. Kenneth Reed was a key man in the operation."

Rhetta gasped. Randolph said nothing. His expression was sober.

"We questioned Dr. Reed extensively today, before he lawyered up. He insists he didn't commit treason and that he didn't know about the plan to shut down the grid." Wexler removed his cap and again ran his fingers through his hair. He replaced the cap and smoothed the brim. "Reed claims he was paid handsomely to bring in certain Muslim doctors to work in the hospital, and in the affiliated practices in the area. In his position as Medical Outreach Coordinator for the hospital, it was Reed's job to find good foreign doctors to come to Cape Girardeau. It was easy for him to place Muslim doctors who were part of the cell, along with the valid placements. Not all the foreign doctors are terrorists." Rhetta was thankful. Several of those doctors, like Marinthe, had been invaluable to Randolph's recovery.

Wexler continued, "Reed received huge sums of money for placing the terrorist operatives."

"Why would Kenneth ever agree to do that in the first place, even if he didn't realize they were terrorists? Didn't he find that request suspicious?" asked Rhetta.

"He owes hundreds of thousands of dollars in gambling debts. Apparently, he sure loves that new casino here in Cape."

Sergeant Meade appeared at the doorway just as Wexler finished. Rhetta leapt to her feet, set aside the fruit cup, and hugged him. He looked abashed at her enthusiasm. He stopped at the bed and shook hands with Randolph.

"Judge McCarter, good to see you, sir. Hope you're doing well."

"Doing great, now, thanks, Sergeant," Randolph said reaching for his wife's hand.

Rhetta introduced Meade to Billy Dan. After shaking hands, Meade found a chair out in the hallway and dragged it in to the room. Once settled he said, "We've arrested Doctor Reed on state charges."

He nodded to the FBI agent. "For the attempted murder of Judge McCarter. Looks like Dr. Reed is the one now in a crap load of trouble."

"Why did Kenneth try to kill Randolph?" Rhetta asked, gazing at everyone in the room.

Wexler answered. "When Razeen found out Judge McCarter survived the car accident, he gave Doctor Reed orders to finish the job. Reed broke down when he told us that, and that's when his lawyer showed up. He didn't get to tell us more. We'll eventually get the whole story. By the way, Agent Cooper in St. Louis was one of Razeen's first victims, since Cooper was the one to initiate an investigation into Al-Serafi." Wexler had everyone's attention. The nightmare of events raced through Rhetta's head.

"Razeen ordered everyone who'd seen the schematic killed," Wexler continued. "Hakim Al-Serafi was a victim of his own stupidity, for leaving that message on Mr. Zelinski's phone. Razeen believed that particular blunder would raise suspicion." Turning to Rhetta, he added, "As it did with you and Mr. Zelinski, when you reported it to the FBI."

Rhetta turned to her husband. "That was Razeen, then, at the impound lot when Woody and I went to look at Al-Serafi's car. And I bet that's who tried to run us off the bridge when we left the lot."

Wexler nodded and answered, "You had the misfortune of being spotted by Razeen when you went to the lot to examine Al-Serafi's car. It was easy enough to find you after that, especially with that car you drive."

"Used to drive," Rhetta said. "What about Billy Dan?"

"He was a threat because he knew exactly what generators would and could be affected."

Billy Dan joined the conversation. He angled his head toward Rhetta. "Judge, your wife here saved my life." He held up his bandaged arm. "For a minute there, I thought she was going to kill me first."

Everyone laughed. Then Rhetta sobered quickly, remembering Peter LaRose. "And Doctor LaRose? Is that why they killed him too, because he'd seen the schematic?"

Sergeant Meade shook his head. "We received the preliminary report from the Cape Girardeau police on Doctor LaRose. It seems he was suffering from leukemia. That's what killed him."

A tear trickled down Rhetta's cheek.

The room was still somber when Ricky Lane burst through the doorway, waving a slip of paper.

"Hey, everybody, I just bought that '81 Z28 for Rhetta. We need to go load her up. Let the fun begin!" Whooping in glee, she danced around the room.

Rhetta introduced her ebullient friend to everyone present. Billy Dan scooted over and made a place for her beside him on Randolph's bed. Her red hair swung loose and for once Ricky wore a skirt, a short purple one that showed off tanned legs. Rhetta watched as Billy Dan eyed her. Ricky eyed back.

Doctor Marinthe arrived to check Randolph. Everyone took that as a cue to leave and hugs were passed freely. Rhetta even hugged Agent Wexler.

As everyone trooped out, Rhetta noticed Ricky helping Billy Dan as he walked down the hall, an arm around his waist to support him. They were talking animatedly.

Marinthe checked Randolph's vital signs, then said, "You are doing well, Judge McCarter. You should be going home in a day or two." Then Marinthe took a turn sitting on the bed. "Do you know an attorney named Albert Claymore?"

"I do. Why?"

"Apparently Mr. Claymore was paying some of the staff phlebotomists to find clients for him."

"Clients?" Rhetta said, as she and Randolph exchanged puzzled glances.

"It seems when certain accident cases appeared to be caused by drunk drivers, some of Claymore's paid technicians mishandled the blood tests in the emergency room. The results always showed an elevated blood alcohol, and *voilà*, Mr. Claymore stepped in to become the drunk driver's lawyer." Marinthe patted Randolph's arm. "Like he tried with you. Luckily, your wife observed how your test was done. That is what put me on the trail."

Randolph shook his head. Rhetta fist pumped. "Yes!" She circled in a small victory dance. The DUI would be dismissed.

Marinthe rose slowly and went to the doorway. "Mrs. McCarter, perhaps you should become a detective, *non*?" Grinning, he pulled the door closed as he left.

Randolph pulled Rhetta to him. "The answer to that is a great big *non*," Randolph said, imitating Marinthe's accent. "Don't you ever go detecting again, hear? You nearly got yourself killed."

# CHAPTER 58

O n Saturday, a week after Randolph was discharged from the hospital, an off-duty Sergeant Meade had shown up at the McCarter's home to hand deliver Rhetta's driver's license and car registration. She examined her license front and back.

"Is something wrong with it?" Meade asked.

"I'm looking for my invitation to court," Rhetta answered, turning it over again.

"The Cape county prosecutor wasn't too happy, but I talked him out of issuing you a ticket for running off from an officer. In fact, it took a great deal of persuading to convince the Scott County prosecutor not to file any charges either. I convinced him you and Mr. Zelinski were acting in self-defense."

"Hey, they were shooting at us first," Rhetta insisted.

Randolph cleared his throat.

Meade raised his hands in mock surrender. "If I may repeat myself, Mrs. McCarter, what you did was incredibly foolhardy." Then a small smile wrinkled the corner of his mouth. "But I don't know anyone who's ever done anything as brave as what you and Mr. Zelinski did." He tipped his ball cap at her, and started to leave. Then he added, "But that won't stop you from getting a speeding ticket when you get that replacement Camaro running over the speed limit."

They all laughed.

Rhetta had another question. "Sergeant Meade, I never did find out something. What the heck is 'enhanced 9-1-1'?"

"When an area has enhanced 9-1-1, the emergency operations center has an immediate computer coordinated map of the location that's tied to the phone number of the caller. In areas without it, like Bollinger County, all the operator has is the caller ID. The 9-1-1 system is expensive to purchase and maintain. Counties with a small population have a tough time getting it, and usually rely on grants from the phone companies to acquire one."

"Enhanced 9-1-1 should be available for everyone," Rhetta said. "It's a safety issue."

Randolph put his arm around Rhetta's shoulder. "Now you have a new cause to pursue, and can quit chasing terrorists." She thought she just might work on that.

# # #

Three weeks later, Woody showed up for work with metal crutches.

When she spotted him, their secretary, LuEllen, jumped from her swivel chair at the front desk and ran to the door. She held it for him as he wobbled in, balancing his briefcase under one arm.

"For heaven's sake, Woody, are you supposed to be back to work already?" Then she relieved him of the briefcase and followed him to his desk, scolding him all the way.

Woody carefully set the crutches in the corner before lowering himself into his oversized chair. He gazed around his desktop, and arranged the pens, the phone, the blotter. He swiveled around to LuEllen and to Rhetta, who'd sidled up.

Rhetta grinned. "Couldn't stay away, could you?"

"It's time to get back to work. Just your claims alone would keep me busy."

Rhetta had already filed the insurance claim on Cami. She'd accompanied Ricky to inspect the replacement, a dirt-encrusted 1981 Z28 which Ricky gleefully called a "barn find." The car spent the last twenty-five years forgotten and abandoned in a farmer's barn. The old man who owned the property and to whom Ricky had paid for the car, had died of a heart attack the day before Rhetta and Ricky had originally planned to pick it up. It took a while to get the title transferred. Two days ago, the title finally came in the mail. Rhetta had ridden along to help Ricky load the car on to the car hauler and take it to Ricky's shop.

Rhetta pondered what she'd call her new ride. They'd already compiled a long list of parts to order.

### # # #

Once settled in behind his desk, Woody booted up his computer. As was his newsaholic habit, he opened the local affiliate television station's streaming news.

LuEllen returned to her desk and was out of earshot. While waiting for his computer to load, Woody said to Rhetta, "Wexler said there wouldn't be anything about what happened on the news."

Agent Wexler had sworn everyone involved to secrecy for the sake of national security. Rhetta hadn't yet told LuEllen about what had happened to Woody's leg, nor exactly what had caused Cami to burn up.

Woody had suffered a bout of depression combined with his PTSD after the shootout. Rhetta called him daily. Jenn reported Woody was recuperating, and nearly back to his old self. Rhetta understood why he'd returned to work as soon as he could. He needed to get busy and get his mind off what happened. Rhetta had taken him to lunch a few times while he was out on sick leave. His leg was healing nicely, and now, she was relieved that his spirit was healing too.

"Wexler told me the terrorist cell was cleaned out," Rhetta said, patting Woody's arm. "It's all over. There won't be an attack."

Woody shrugged and gazed at the newscast.

Rhetta said, "He also assured me the book was closed, the terrorists were rounded up, and there would be no charges filed against us, since our shooting them was in self-defense. The entire thing has to be kept ultra-secret and nothing would appear in any news media. In fact, according to the news, Cami setting the hay bales on fire was the biggest thing that happened in Scott County that night."

"I didn't want it to be on the news," Woody said. "It'd scare customers off." He couldn't conceal his smile behind the whiskers. "What about the power failures? How did they cover that?"

"Inland Electric called it a 'perfect storm,' and said it all started with lightning striking the substations in Marble Hill, which caused an overload in Cape County. In Perry County, they said a bird's nest caught fire in that substation, causing it to crash."

"Must've been a bird the size of Delaware."

Rhetta smiled. Woody's sense of humor was also returning.

"I also found out from Billy Dan that there are tripping stations on the nationwide power grid that would prevent a complete cascading power failure that would take out the entire grid at one time."

She continued after adjusting her chair, sitting, and turning to face Woody. "Wexler also said that the cell here was taking out our power stations as part of a national plot to see what would happen. He confirmed that every transformer had holes shot at points that matched the markings on the schematic. Wexler also admitted that, although the FBI knew who the members of the cell were, they hadn't discovered their plan. There had been absolutely no chatter."

"Did Wexler ever find out where the money from Al-Serafi's refi went?"

"When I asked him if Mahata escaped with it, he only shrugged. He implied that the FBI had been unable to track down Al-Serafi's wife to question her. She and the money are probably holed up in a country friendly to terrorists."

"Guess she never did get to sunbathe at Lake of the Ozarks," Woody said. Swiveling around to Rhetta, he asked, "How's Randolph?"

"He's back to painting up a storm and planning his one-man show coming up at the gallery. He's locked himself in his studio in a painting frenzy. He wants plenty ready for the show." Grabbing a brochure off her desk, she waved it at Woody. "In fact, he's doing so well he ordered a brand-new, three-quarter-ton Artmobile. Otherwise known as a Ford."

Woody chuckled, then turned serious. "Not much left of the first Artmobile, was there?"

Rhetta added quietly, "He's quit drinking altogether." Woody nodded without speaking.

Rhetta hadn't managed to quit smoking yet, but was working on it. She was also trying to locate her father. It was impossible to find any of his records. The only thing she could find was his birth record. So far, she was unable to find anything else. Even the military records, so far, were a dead end.

The buzzing intercom interrupted Rhetta's thoughts. "Miss Ricky Lane is on line two for you," LuEllen said.

Rhetta punched the blinking light "Hey, what's up girlfriend? Do we need more parts?" Rhetta had already written Ricky a substantial check for the first batch of aftermarket parts to restore the

Z28. The new LS1 engine was already on a truck making its way from Ohio.

She pulled open the drawer in search of her checkbook. "How much do I owe you?" She didn't want Ricky to shoulder a large parts bill.

"No, no, that's not it. We're good on the parts." Ricky, lowering her voice as though not wanting anyone to overhear, asked, "Do you remember Malcom Griffith?"

"Sure. He was the real estate developer who scammed his business partner several years back, then took off with millions in escrow funds."

"Did you know that the business partner Griffith scammed was Jeremy's father?"

"Jeremy, as in your new love interest?"

"Yes."

"Why are you telling me this?"

"I just found Malcom Griffith's wallet wedged into the frame of your Z28."

The End

**SHARON WOODS HOPKINS**

Sharon's mystery series featuring mortgage banker Rhetta McCarter and her '79 Camaro hits close to home. Sharon is a branch manager for a mortgage office of a Missouri bank. She also owns the original Cami, a restored '79 Camaro like Rhetta's.

Sharon's hobbies include painting, photography, flower gardening, and restoring muscle cars with her son, Jeff.

She is a member of the Mystery Writers of America, Sisters in Crime, the Southeast Missouri Writers' Guild, and the Missouri Writers' Guild.

Sharon also spent 30 years as an Appaloosa Horse Club judge, where she was privileged to judge all over the US, Canada, Mexico and Europe.

She lives on the family compound near Marble Hill, Missouri with her husband, Bill, next door to her son, Jeff, his wife, Wendy, and her grandson, Dylan, plus two dogs, one cat, and assorted second generation Camaros.

Watch for Rhetta McCarter and the second book in the series, *KILLERFIND*, coming soon.

Made in the USA
Charleston, SC
03 October 2011